NEMESIS II

The FOLD

NEMESIS II

The FOLD

By

Tehuti Atum-Ra

Published by

Midnight Express Books
POBox 69
Berryville AR 72616
http://midnightexpressbooks.com

NEMESIS II
The FOLD

Copyright 2012© Tehuti Atum-Ra

ISBN-10: 0985768622
ISBN-13: 978-0-9857686-2-1

Published by:

Midnight Express Books
POBox 69
Berryville AR 72616
http://midnightexpressbooks.com

NEMESIS II

The FOLD

By

Tehuti Atum-Ra

ACKNOWLEDGMENTS

I would like to take the time to thank the Source for allowing me to access this gift to write and the wisdom to understand it is a gift. Much love goes out to my wonderful mother, Mae Christine Williams who, after all I have put her through, has never forsaken me. Her love for me has been just as strong as it was the day I came into this world. It was her love and belief in me that kept me focused and strong. And my respect and love for her was, is and will never cease to be. May she rest in eternal peace.

Mad love to my stepfather, Delaney Simmons for all you have done and continue to do. Thank you for making my mother so happy. She couldn't have chosen a better man. Nor could I have asked for a better man to come into her life.

To my daughter, Zamia Iman Carter, her husband, and my three grand-children; my love for the five of you goes without saying. I have lived my life and it has been an experience I have no wish to repeat. Now, I live for you.

Endless respect to my Baby-mama, Sherena Boyd for blessing me with a beautiful daughter who turned out to be an exceptional woman. You've done a wonderful job in raising her, all by yourself, to be the exceptional woman, wife, mother and daughter she is today.

To my big sister, Diane Williams-Pate, You said something to me that woke me up. For that, I thank you. My love and respect for you has never ceased. Nor will it ever.

To my two nieces and nephew and their families, I hope I can be someone you all could be proud of.

To my aunt Ella, thank you for your love and support and being there for my mother during her last days on earth when her own sons wouldn't, or couldn't. You are truly a woman of substance.

To Linda Williams for all you have done for me in more ways than you could possibly imagine. You are an exceptional woman and I love you for your friendship, your belief in me, and your support.

To all my nydugus on lock-down, love is love. To my lil 'bruh', Bobby White, Bomani and his wife, Maria - I rise, you rise. To my fellow writers; John 'Yah-Yah' Springs III, Michael 'Starchild' Stanton, Andre (Fish) Alston, Gary Samsadeen Davis and so many others I have neglected to mention.

To Londell D, Joey L, Michael H, Leonard 'Balaal' D, Reggy F, Johnny W, Keith 'KiKi' Whimberley rest in peace, Jersey City's notorious 'Shorty', Noney Tole, Jahi Shakur, Carlton Franklin, Frank & 'Bizz' D, Willie 'Yasin' Williams, Humphrey C, Gregory 'Damani' W, Heru H. Atum-Ra, Jene 'The Fool' J, Omari Atiba, Sly 'Saeed' W, D. Rawls, Ronald Africa L, N. Shabazz rest in peace, Crag 'Mustafa' Loyal, Black-Sun, Carl 'Self' Williams

And last but not least, I would like to thank Victor and Linda Huddleston, founders of MIDNIGHT EXPRESS BOOKS. For all the hard work they've done helping me realize my five year plan in getting my books ready for publication. Without them, I probably would be still pounding the pavement and dodging sharks.

For those of you on lock down trying to get published, I strongly recommend MIDNIGHT EXPRESS BOOKS. They do great work, are inexpensive and most importantly they're honest, hard working people. Yeah!

PROLOGUE

When the cheap clock radio abruptly woke Joey from a peaceful sleep, he jumped out of bed as if the small apartment he shared with his sister, nieces and nephew was being raided by the police. It took a minute for him to realize he had set the timer on the clock prior to going to bed last night. And a few more minutes before realizing why. He had exactly one half hour to be ready by the time SunRise arrived to pick him up.

Ms. Parks, an elderly woman had been watering her plants in the window of her small row-house apartment when she noticed the well dressed youth who took his time walking across the courtyard. She smiled and whispered, "Pride-walker." It was a name she had given the man-child who always seemed to carry himself with the up-most respect. As he passed by her, she wanted to tap on the window just to say hello but decided against it. She didn't know him personally and knew of no one who did. As Ms. Parks continued to watch her pride-walker until he disappeared into the next building. She remained in the window holding the tea-pot she had been using to water her plants while thinking about all the other young adults now-a-days. Secretly wishing they were more like her pride- walker. Someone a mother could be proud to call her son. Instead, they were loud, unruly and cared nothing about their appearance. She called them nocturnals mainly because the only time they made their presence known, had been during the night. She thought back to a time when she was about their age and realized she would have been home fast asleep.

Ms. Parks had been one of the few senior citizens still living in the C.C.P. Built in 1960 she had seen it change from predominantly white, to all black over the decades. With the exception of one or two white and Latino families still living there, blacks dominated just as they have in every other urban city with a high concentration of low-income housing project.

Ms. Parks could remember a time when there were truant officers patrolling neighborhood making sure children were in school. To housing cops strolling through each building making sure everything was okay. Now-a-days, the children quite school in the third grade to sell drugs and tote guns. While the housing cops look the other way, or extort them for not paying for protection. Shaking her head in shame from the mere thought of it, she closed her curtain and walked away from the window.

The third floor was pitch-dark when the man-child Ms. Parks referred to as pride-walker entered the hallway. This did not bother or surprise him in the least. The C.C.P. was filled with the worse hoods society had to offer. Even its youth aspired to become a king-pin or stone cold killers.

When he reached the apartment door of his friend, he knocked three times and heard a female's voice shout from inside, "Who is it?"

"Rise!" he replied loudly.

The door opened abruptly and SunRise found himself staring into the face of a thin, dark-skinned woman with beautiful brown eyes. "Hi, baby," she greeted him with a fake smile. "You got a twenty I can hold until my check comes? If you want, maybe we can work something out?"

He glanced at the dirty house-robe she did not bother to fasten and quickly asked to see her brother, Joey.

The woman licked her full chapped lips seductively and eased up close to him. "Hold up, baby," she whispered, "I'll wake him in a minute. What about that twenty?" She intentionally allowed her robe to open even more, exposing her breast.

SunRise quickly backed away and frowned not just because he found her offer repulsive; it was her breath that repelled him. Seeing her like this sadden him. What was once a vibrant, sophisticated, career woman and the mother of three was now a section-eight recipient with a huge monkey on her back. And even though she had managed to maintain her glow, it wasn't hard to tell she was 'out there'.

Before she had a chance to ask what was wrong, Joey grabbed her by the back of her collar and yanked her back into the apartment.

"BOY!" she shouted. "What the hell wrong with you grabbing me by my collar like that!"

"What's wrong with you? Disrespecting my company like you ain't got no sense. You should be ashamed of yourself," Joey said while looking at his sister with utter disgust. "Look at you? You haven't even washed your face," Joey pointed out as SunRise stepped into the apartment and stood by the door.

"Oh go to hell!" she shouted before storming off into her bedroom.

Joey looked at SunRise and apologized for his sister's behavior.

"No apologies necessary, Joey," he replied as the two men silently left the apartment.

SunRise parked on the upper part of Gram street and was about to get out of the car, but turned to Joey and asked, "Is there anything else I should know before paying them a visit?"

"There's a lot more you should know, especially about her. But the important thing is, they owe FOLD a favor." Joey took a deep breath and slowly exhaled. "You don't mind if I wait for you in the car, do you?"

"No. In fact, it would probably be best you do." He glanced at his watch and said, "I won't be long," before getting out of the car.

As SunRise casually strolled up the street and disappeared into a three story apartment building, Joey watched. It was a far cry from the shabby tenement Londell use to live in. And as much as he would have liked to have gone with SunRise, he knew what they were about to discuss, was not meant for his ears.

Joey looked around nervously. It was not a safe area to be at any time of the day. A drug infested playground for thugs, stick-up kids and desperate addicts. Most people went out of their way to avoid having to cross the upper section of Gram Ave.

As Joey continued watching his back, he noticed three young women sitting on the front steps of an old run-down house. Each of them were slumbered over with their heads bent between their legs nodding-out in an opium dream. The only time any of them ever bothered to lift their heads was when someone walked passed on their way out, or into the house. Because of their behavior Joey immediately concluded they were heroin addicts. He also deduced the house in which they sat in front of, was more than likely a dope-house – a place where drug users went to buy, or get high. "Damn shame," he thought, noticing the expressions on their young faces as they briefly came out of their nods to scratch, which gave him a much better look at them. And even though they were all attractive young women, they each had that droopy, drowsy look addicts usually acquire during long periods of using. Making them appear much older than they actually were.

After a forth female came out of the house the three females stood and the four of them proceeded down the street.

Unable to pull himself away, he begin feeling sorry for them. Mainly because he knew, like his sister Wendi, somewhere along the line they got lost. Hopefully, he thought, they would eventually find their way back before it was too late? Hope was all he had to work with. At the moment, he considered it better than having nothing at all.

Immediately after SunRise left, Londell quickly climbed back in bed next to Vicki. He had been expecting the visit from the young nationalist. He just wasn't expecting it so early in the morning. And although both men were well aware of each other's reputation from a mutual friend, it was the first time the two of them had actually met.

He looked over at his wife. Still sleeping soundly, he snuggled up close to her under the covers. She smelt good and felt even better. She had come a long way since teaching her his trade. He thought about the very first time she had put in work at Butterfly's house over a year ago and wished he could have witnessed it that night. But the bullet that put him down would not allow him the privilege. The papers called it a massacre. He called it, divine retribution.

He thought about Big Moon and regretted killing him and his crew so soon. Mainly because he never got the chance to find out why Big Moon tried to push him? He looked at his wife and smiled. He often wondered why she never made the trip to Camden that day. And because she never volunteered the information, he never asked. He was just thankful she returned when she had. Because if she hadn't, he knew he would have been history.

Since, the two of them have put in a lot of work in and out of town. Londell never introduced Vicki by her government name. He presented her as, Nemesis. Initially it was for safety purposes. Later, he began to see her as such. He couldn't quite explain it, but it was almost as if she was protected by some unseen force.

Vicki opened her eyes and found Londell fast asleep next to her. She smiled while staring at his huge, red lips and with her index finger, gently touched them. Soft to the touch, she leaned in and kissed them. It was then when she noticed the permanent scar he received. It happened over a year ago by an assassin's bullet that grazed him just above his temple. She hated seeing that scar. It was a reminder of just how close she came to losing him which brought her thoughts to the massacre on Bunker Hill. She often wondered why they had tried to kill him. But the thing that really bothered her was why they used two dirty cops to do it. She turned on her back and stared up at the ceiling. She never told him about her encounter with the two dirty cops. The weird little nerd who tried to rape her or the man she encountered coming out of the garage that night. The man she thought for sure the blow she delivered to his head killed him until hearing otherwise from Joey Lemon. Who, in a conversation she manage to overhear, told Londell about Big Moon and his boys finding their friend outside the garage leaking from a head wound. Once they realized he was still alive. They immediately rushed him to the hospital.

Because of the head wound no one actually thought he'd ever wake from the coma. Not even Vicki. And when he did, she tried to finish what she had started, but was unable to get to him. A week later, he just seemed to have disappeared. The hospital said he had been discharged and she had no reason not to believe them. She felt guilty about not telling Londell. She wanted to, but saw no reason to open old wounds. As far as she was concerned, Moon and his boys were all dead.

It had been more than a year now. Still, she just couldn't stop wondering when and where this man would show up to revenge his crew.

When Londell woke, Vicki was sitting up in bed. From the worried look on her face, he suspected something was bothering her. "You a'ight?" he asked. She looked at him and smiled as he yawned and stretched before sitting up. "Guess who finally paid us a visit?"

"Who?" she asked without moving.

"SunRise."

She looked at him and asked, "Why?" She too had never met SunRise, but heard a lot about him through Joey Lemon.

When Londell got out of bed, Vicki's eyes dropped straight to his crotch. He noticed and smile, "Work related," he said before going off into the bathroom. Vicki rapped her arms around her knees and waited for him to return before asking anymore questions. "It was early as hell and you were still sleep when he came by," he shouted from the bathroom. Vicki heard the toilet flush, then water running in the sink. Londell was drying his hands when he got back into bed. "He didn't say who the target was gonna' be. When I asked, he just said he had to check a few things out before making a decision." When she snuggled up close to him, he smiled.

"What you smiling about," she asked, looking at him suspiciously. Still smiling, he cut an eye at her but said nothing. "I wonder what made him come to us?" she thought aloud with hopes of him filling in the blanks.

"You forgot we owe them a favor? The first thing he said was Joey recommended us to him."

Vicki inconspicuously glanced at him and asked, "You remember Joey telling you about some guy that's been in a comma for over a year? The one Big Moon and his boys found just before we pushed them. Remember?'

"Yeah, Kenny-Sam. I remember, why?"

"I heard he finally came out of the comma'?"

"He did more than that. Aside from him not being able to remember shit, I heard he made a full recovery and left the hospital," Londell said before looking at her to ask, "Why?"

"No reason. So you have no idea when he wants it done?" she changed the subject.

"He said something about the third week of this month."

Vicki thought for a moment. "We have two extra weeks before then. Can we go some place? Just the two of us for a few weeks? We never go anywhere. I'm not talking about leaving the country. Just someplace nice and warm so we can relax and enjoy ourselves?" She got on top of him. "Please-e-e-e?" she asked between kisses.

Because he already knew where her mind was heading, he smiled. She smiled back and closed her eyes. What started as a soft and tender kiss, turned into the both of them trying to devour each other's lips. Without so much as a brief pause, he found his way into her. A low moan of pleasure escaped her throat as she grinded her hips on top of him. As his manhood grew in length Vicki squirmed with a combination of pain and pleasure. Flipping her onto her back, she spread her legs wide into the air, giving him full access of her shiny, wet, pink.

Immediately he climbed between her legs and rammed his manhood into her in one powerful stroke. Vicki screamed as he drilled deep inside of her. Never have she ever had anyone who could match the pleasure he had been able to provide. His manhood was so thick, so long, so hard. Each time she closed her eyes, she actually thought she was being mounted by a baby bull. He was the most exciting lover she had ever had; the kind of man whose roughness excited her with every thrust. He made her a slave to the pleasure he was able to provide. With each thrust, came another pre-orgasmic moan from deep within. It was all she could stand when he grabbed her around the waist and, without dislodging himself, flipped her over on her stomach. Vicki moaned as he shifted her thighs, spreading her legs further apart while driving his manhood so far into her. She squirmed under him in a fit of lust while tilting her ass back so he could dog her that much harder.

With her apple bottom tilted in the air. She gasped, and cried out his name while rocking her head from side to side.

With one great inward thrust, he jammed his manhood deep inside and let out a deep howl while the muscles of her walls excitedly clenched the length of his man-hood.

Moments later, the two of them collapse with him on top of her back, exhausted. Vicki's body twitched from the previous excitement. "So... can we go... someplace... nice?" she asked between breaths with a hoarseness in her voice.

"I don't care. I just have to let Ma' and SunRise know where we'll be just in case." Vicki waited until he fell asleep before showering, dressing and sneaking out.

Baby-Sams had been chilling in the courtyard of the Alabama Housing complex with a few of his buddies when Asmar West came rolling through. Baby-Sams didn't know Asmar personally, but definitely knew who Asmar was. As Asmar approached, Baby-Sams had expected him to keep walking. Instead, Asmar stopped and greeted him. "What's good, yo'?" said Asmar. Baby-Sams was caught completely off guard.

"Ain't nothin'. How you?" Baby-Sams said awkwardly. He tried his best to look hard, but couldn't help feeling Asmar saw right through it.

"I heard your brutha' finally woke the fuck up? How's he doing?" He waited for Baby-Sams to either deny, or confirm.

"Yeah, yeah. My mom was happy about that, son. For a few, she thought she was gonna have to pull the plug on that nigga, know-I-mean. He's still in that hospital, but he doing a whole lot better. Still can't remember shit, though."

"He remembers you, right?"

"Yeah, yeah," Baby-Sams said. "He just can't remember what happen that night, know-I-mean."

"Yeah, yeah. I feel you, yo'. Damn! I wonder what's that like? waking up a year later? That's got to be fucked up. Nigga crack me up side my head, he betta' kill me. You feel me?"

Baby-Sams smiled, but did not comment. "Yo'! Why the fuck you ain't get with those niggaz yet, yo?"

"Oh don't worry. I will," Baby-Sams said, trying to appear hard.

"When?" Asmar continued to pry.

"As soon as I find out who it was that did that to him."

"He ain't tell you?"

"Naw'. Naw'. Nigga got amnesia. He can't remember shit. Otherwise, it'll be curtains for them niggaz'. Know-I-mean, son?"

My mom wants him to come home, but the doctors said that was out of the question. Nigga gotta' go through some serious physical therapy, know-I-mean."

Asmar thought about it. "That shit has got to cost, yo'?"

"It ain't nothin'. Shit already paid for, son.

"Who the fuck paying for it, your mom? Shit gotta' be expensive, yo'?"

Baby-Sam thought for a moment and said, "I heard it was Michael Henderson, but I'm not sure?"

"Damn! I ain't know your brutha' knew Mike like that? Big Moon, yeah, but Mike?" Asmar said while thinking. "Shit, that nigga up to something, yo'. Ain't no way in hell he gonna' just pay Kenny-Sam medical bills and don't want nothin' for it, you feel me? I just can't see it?"

"Why you say that?"

Asmar looked at him strangely. "Wasn't Mike responsible for waxing Big Moon when he found out Moon sent them niggaz' to murk' Butterfly?" Asmar waited for Baby-Sams to reply. He knew Michael Henderson wasn't responsible for his driver's murder. He just enjoyed throwing a line out to see if he could get a bit. When Baby-Sams didn't comment, Asmar knew he wasn't going to get anything else out of him. "Next time you go see your brutha'? Tell him Mr. Bang sends the peace. Later." Asmar glanced at Baby-Sams two young buddies and gave them a complementary nod before stepping off.

Baby-Sams knew he had made a mistake using Michael Henderson name. But it was the only person he could think of with that kind of money. He couldn't believe Asmar, of all people, still believed Michael Henderson had something to do with the murders on Bunker Hill last year.

"Yo', son. I thought you said your brutha' was in Wildwood doing his thing?" one of Baby-Sams friends asked.

"Yeah, nigga. Why the fuck you tell Asmar Kenny was still in the hospital?" the other one asked.

"Because it wasn't none of his business. I don't know that nigga like that."

"Damn, son. He sure asked a lot of questions. Why you ain't just tell the nigga to mind his fuckin' business?"

"Yeah, yo'. I woulda' told that nigga to kick rocks. You feel me." The two men laughed, but Baby-Sams had something else on his mind. It was the fine honey he spotted coming their way. As soon as his two buddies noticed her, they both shouted, "DAMNNN!!!" "Who the fuck is that, son?" one of them asked while all three teens eyed her as she casually approached.

"Ain't you Kenny-Sam lil' brutha?" she stopped and asked Baby-Sams while ignoring his two friends.

"Yeah, yeah. That be me. What's your name, sweetness?" he tried to be cool and was sure he had succeeded when she smiled and eased up close to him. When his two buddies giggled. He shot them a warning, not to fuck this up for him, look.

"They call me, Nemesis. You look just like your brutha. How old are you?"

"Old enough. Know what-I-mean." he said.

"She smiled. "Is that so," she said briefly glancing at his crotch. When she was sure he noticed, she continued. "I'm surprised Kenny never mentioned me. We have a long history together. I heard he got hurt?"

"Yeah, yeah, but he good now," Baby-Sams said while sizing her up. "So how come I never seen you around before?" he asked, trying to keep the conversation focused on the two of them.

She smiled. "I moved away years ago. Just came back to see a few friends and family. I was hoping to see Kenny before leaving?"

"He in south Jersey!" one of Baby-Sams fiends yelled.

She looked at the teen and smiled before returning her attention to Baby-Sams again and asking, "Is that true?"

"Yeah, yeah, he's been gone 'bout a week now. Doctors couldn't believe how fast that nigga recovered, son. They tried to keep him up in there, but Kenny wasn't having none of that, know-I-mean?"

"Yeah. That sounds just like him," she said with a smile. "Well, I live in Lakewood now. How far down is he?"

Dumb-struck by her beauty Baby-Sams blurted out without thinking, "Wildwood. West side."

She smiled. "Maybe I'll look him up sometime. What did you say your name was?" she asked.

"They call me, Baby-Sams," he blushed with hopes that she was interested in him. She smiled again and lightly brushed his cheek with her hand before walking off.

11

When she heard one of his friends say "Yo' man! You see her eyes?" She glanced over her shoulder.

"Man! That bitch was fine!" said the other one while patting Baby-Sams on the back for handling himself so well in the presence of what they considered, a fine ass bitch.

CHAPTER 1

Driving for more than three hours, Robin was relieved when she spotted the over-pass sign that read, "Welcome To Atlantic City". The tiring drive from New York bored her to no end while the aching pain in her back, neck and shoulders did nothing to ease the weariness she was beginning to experience.

Heading up-town towards the shopping district in the midst of rush hour she considered herself lucky when she found an empty parking space a few shops from her destination. Just before getting out of the car she glanced at herself in the rear-view mirror, then peeked at her watch. It was already after five, but the 'OPEN' sign hanging in the small antique shop's window she spotted while driving by, assured her that she was not too late.

Upon entering the small shop, an array of small chimes hanging above the door alerted the presence of a small, neatly groomed old man who quickly stepped from behind a glass showcase counter to greet her. "Robin!" he excitedly acknowledged with a heavy Italian accent. "I was beginning to think you were not going to make it?" he smiled while gently placing a hand on her shoulder.

"I was beginning to wonder whether, or not you'd be here once I did?" she replied.

"I stayed open a little late just for you. Now, let me get a good look at you," he said, holding her slender shoulders at arm's length. "You get more and more beautiful each time I see you."

She blushed. "You always did know what to say to make a girl feel good even if it meant exaggerating a lil'," she teased.

"But it is true," he said, stepping over by the door to lock it. "You are growing into a lovely young woman, Robin."

At a loss for words, she smiled while watching as he flipped the 'OPEN' sign over so it would read 'CLOSED' from the outside. Then continued to move about the shop, turning off all the lights while rambling on about what a beautiful woman she was becoming. Robin followed the old man behind the counter to his office in back. "Please... have a seat," he gestured with a wave of his hand while sitting on the edge of his desk in front of her. "Did you have any trouble getting in?" he quickly asked.

"Not in the home. The safe was another story. I don't know what he was so careful about protecting. Aside from the stones, there wasn't much else worth taking."

"Did you get everything in the safe as I instructed?" he asked with obvious concern.

"Yeah, but...."

"Good! May I see what you have?" he anxiously asked with an extended open palm.

Robin reached into her shoulder bag and pulled out several items. One of which were legal documents which he carelessly tossed to the side. When she handed him a manila envelope, she couldn't help noticing how his eyes lit up as if he had just hit the jack-pot. When he opened the envelope and peeked inside, she immediately asked him about it. But instead of an answer, he quickly placed the manila envelope inside his desk drawer and locked it.

The last item was a small suede pouch. As he opened the pouch and looked inside, Robin leaned back in her chair and watched as he rushed to a chair behind his desk and emptied the contents of the pouch onto a silk handkerchief that had been carefully spread out over his desk-top. Robin slid her chair closer as a cluster of small sparkling diamonds spilled out on to the handkerchief. She couldn't really tell if he was pleased, or disappointed. She hated not being able to read his expression. Still, it was one quality about him she had become accustom to. He once told her, in his line of work it was a business strategy.

When he strapped a jeweler's loupe to his forehead she sat back in her chair and waited as he began to carefully examine each stone, one by one. Having gone through the same procedure many times in the past, she sat patiently while he counted and graded each stone. She knew it was going to take a while.

Twenty minutes later, the old man began carefully placing the diamonds back into the brown suede pouch. As soon as she realized he was done, she asked about her money. "As you know, Robin," he began while pocketing the pouch and placing the legal documents she previously gave him, in his desk. "I do not keep that kind of money here with me at the shop. You will have to...."

"Wait a minute," she quietly, but angrily interrupted. "You were supposed to have my money, remember? Payment upon delivery. I didn't come all the way down here just to go back empty handed. This is business, Rossi. We had a deal!"

"I am not trying to alter our agreement, Robin. You would understand that, if you would have allowed me to complete my sentence. You will get your money, just as we have agreed. That is, if you do not mind accompanying me to my home?"

A weak smile framed her small, oval shaped face. She was embarrassed, mostly from jumping to the wrong conclusion. She hated opening a window of opportunity for one of his many lectures - especially after being lectured by him so many times in the past. "What was in that envelope you locked inside your desk?" she tried to change the subject but it didn't work.

The old man eased out of his chair and began preaching about the fine points of knowing when, and when not to speak. "Why?" he went on to explain. "Because that is how others judge us. Each time we speak, in a sense, we reveal ourselves. What we know, how much we know, or if in fact we know anything at all. Silence, Robin, is the thing that makes us interesting to others. A wise man once said..."

"Here we go," she silently thought.

"...it is better to be thought of as a fool, than having opened your mouth, removing all doubt". I suggest you try to remember that." When he grabbed his coat from the hook of a polished brass coat-rack behind his chair she came over to give him a hand putting it on.

Then the two of them went into the front, where she waited by the door as he set the alarm-system. He was about to leave when he thought of something. Rushing back into his office, he returned a few minutes later. "You know, Robin. You are going to make some nice, young fellow a very good wife one day."

She laughed a little before correcting him. "You mean some cute guy with a little class, and a lot of cash is gonna' make a good husband for me, don't you?" They both laughed.

"Yes," he proudly agreed before unlocking the door so they could leave. "I suppose you are right. Of course, in my eyes no one will ever be good enough for my little Robin."

"Oh, stop."

"But it is true. I have always held you near and dear to my heart."

Insulted by his last remark, she frowned and left the shop to wait for him in her car.

After locking the front door to the shop, he proceeded to pull a huge metal gate down that concealed the face of his store before stepping over to her car. "I will meet you there," he said before walking up the street to his car.

Eighteen minutes later when the old man pulled onto his small estate in Egg Harbor Township. He spotted Robin's car parked in front of his home.

As the two of them casually approached the front door, he began making conversation about all the nice, young men he wanted to introduce her to.

She, however, ignored him. Anxious to get paid, she impatiently waited as he took his time punching in the code that deactivated his elaborate alarm system.

Inside, she waited for him in a lavishly decorated front-room while he vanished up a flight of white carpeted steps, only to return moments later with a white, business-size envelope.

He handed her the envelope and said, "Spend it wisely, my dear."

Without haste or shame, Robin quickly tore it open and pulled out a stack of brand new one-hundred dollar bills. Using an index and middle finger she skillfully flipped through the stack, making sure the count was correct. It was something the old man had often encouraged her to do. Once she was satisfied everything was in order. She placed the bills back inside the envelope and placed it into her coat pocket. "Well," she began, glancing at her watch. "I really wish I had more time to spend with you. Unfortunately I have to be getting back. I'm running late as it is."

The moment she turned to leave, he stopped her with an insulting comment. "Still home-sick for the gutter?" he asked.

Robin was just short of reaching the door when she stopped, turned, and smiled, but said nothing. From past experience, she knew he was trying to force her into an argument. One she so desperately wanted to avoid. Instead of encouraging him, she just stood there listening.

"I do not understand why you will not at least think about coming back here to live? A big city such as New York is no place for a single, young woman of your means."

"Please, Rossi, don't start with that shit again. Besides, I like living in New York. And I like living alone. You, of all people, should know how much I value my privacy."

"Then I will buy you a cottage. A very good friend of mine has one not more than a mile from here. You will be much safer living here than in some big city."

"Why do we always have to go through the same shit?" she angrily asked. "Every time I come down here it's the same damn thing all over again."

"I care about you, Robin even if you do not care about yourself."

"And just what the hell is that suppose to mean!" she angrily snapped.

17

Grasping his hands behind his back, he went over his thoughts before answering. "Look, Robin," his tone was calmer now. "I am well aware of your obsessive need to be in the company of uncultured, belligerent people; people who care nothing about you."

"Number one, I don't have a need to be around anyone! Whoever I choose to associate myself with is none of your damn business!" She had never taken such a tone with him before and was beginning to regret she had let her anger get the best of her.

Shocked and surprised at her behavior. He stood there staring at her in disbelief. His face was red with anger, eyes watery with hurt. "My god, Robin; will you listen to yourself? I do not know you anymore. Living in the city has changed you."

It was the way he looked at her that made her realize he was right. She had changed, but living in the city had nothing to do with it. She was becoming her own person. She just wasn't sure if she liked the person she was becoming.

"I didn't mean to yell. I just get so angry when you try to run my life," her tone was calm and caring. "You have to understand, Rossi. I'm a grown woman now quite capable of taking care of myself."

"I know, Robin. But I cannot help feeling...."

"Please don't worry about me living alone in New York," she interrupted him. "I can handle New York and any other big city just like it. Living down here in this small-ass town was driving me crazy." She noticed a sudden change in his expression after her last comment. "I'm not like you. I have to be around people. In case you haven't noticed, there are no blacks in this town. The few, who just happen to live in neighboring counties, either think they're white, or are ashamed of being black. Either way, this place isn't for me. I hope you understand." She turned and began walking, but Rossi followed.

"I understand, Robin. However, your desire to be out on your own will not stop me from worrying about you," he said, trailing close behind her. "New York is a very bad place. Let me get you a nice little town-house in Atlantic City? At least we will be close. Besides, I am going to need someone I can trust to help run the business."

"I don't have time for this shit!" she said just before stepping out of the house.

"Fine!" he roared behind her. "But do not call me once you get yourself into something you cannot get out of. If you would rather be around those people, then call them to help you."

Robin was about to get into her car when his words hit her. "What the hell you have against black people?" she yelled back.

Rossi's eyes widen with surprise as he approached. "If you are implying that I am a bigot? How dare you, young lady! I have never said anything against the Negroes! Not to you! Not to anyone! Do not try to lay that on me! I am not a racist!" he yelled with a glare in his eyes she had never seen before.

"You're no different than the rest of these phony-ass people around here. You never come straight out and say anything, at least not around me. But believe me. Your feelings couldn't be more obvious."

"And just how do I feel, young lady? Perhaps you can tell me?"

She stared at him angrily while wondering why he refused to acknowledge his shortcomings. The mere fact that he, like so many other self-righteous whites, still referred to blacks as Negroes, was not only an insult, but an indication of how he and those like him, truly felt. "For some twisted reason," she proceeded to read him, "you feel black people are subhuman! As if they're not good enough for me! I hate to be the bearer of your desperately needed wake-up call, but I'm black!" she spat with a venom that made his brows rise. "So how the hell do you think it makes me feel each time you put black people down? That's something you need to think about." She then turned, but the old man would not allow her to leave so easily. Not without first having his say.

"Just you wait one minute, young lady!" he violently grabbed her by the arm and spun her around to face him. "Do not try to make me out to be the bad guy! I am not the one who, at any given time, would not hesitate to openly disrespect you! Yesss! You think I do not know how disrespectful the coloreds are to one another? More importantly, how disrespectful they treat young women. Young colored women." Robin was about to speak, but he was not through having his say. "How can anyone respect those who do not respect their own women?"

"Look! I'm a strong woman who demands respect. I don't know about anyone else, but Robin gets hers."

"Yes... and I suppose being referred to as a bitch, or ho' is respectful." He paused, shaking his head slowly from side to side. "But that does not bother you. Why, because you have become so use to being treated in such a way. It has become as common to you as the air you breathe." He paused once more to catch his breath. "I do not understand you anymore, Robin," his tone was softer and caring now. "The Robin I know would never allow herself to become subjected to such abuse."

"Look... I know you mean well, but you really don't have to worry about me. I can take care of myself. Besides, I would never associate myself with the kind of people you've just described. Contrary to popular belief, all black men aren't disrespectful to women just as all white men aren't respectful; the blade cuts both ways."

"I guess it depends upon where the observer is standing?"

Unsure of what he meant, she stared at him somewhat confused. Instead of asking for an explanation, she got into her car. But before she could close the door, he leaned in and said, "It is not about blacks, or whites, Robin. It is about the company you keep. You are viewed as a mirror image of the company you keep even if that image proves to be false. It is just a matter of time before you become like those with whom you associate yourself with." She looked at him, but didn't comment.

He was about to speak again, but she slammed the car door shut and pulled off.

Heading down the drive-way, she began to give serious thought to some of the things he had said about her life-style.

She knew he meant well, after all, some of the things he said were true. But sometimes he made her so angry, she felt like screaming. She thought about the manila envelope he locked inside his desk back at the shop and couldn't stop wondering what was in it. She remembered asking, but he wouldn't say. She had a good mind to check for herself, but knew that would be unprofessional.

CHAPTER 2

Too tired to make the long drive back up north as she had originally planned, Robin decided to drive back to Atlantic City and check into a hotel for the night. But not before stopping at a club for a drink or two.

A master jewel thief at the tender age of twenty, Robin had managed to survive the mean streets of New Jersey in spite of the odds that had been stacked against her. The product of a "jungle-fever" fling she had been often asked, "What are you?" which was a question she had no trouble answering. Robin Hoods was a black woman, and that was a fact. A fact some blacks, and many whites, never allowed her to forget. Not that she wanted to. She was extremely proud of who and what she was. It was others who had trouble accepting her as is; others who often went out of their way to make her feel out of place. As if she didn't belong anywhere, or to any race.

She never knew her father, who was suppose to have been white and vaguely remembered her mother, who died when she was just a little girl. She did, however, remember the day the state came to take her away after her mother became too ill to take care of her which was a time in Robin's life she will never forget primarily because, two weeks after being taken into the custody of the state, she received news that her mother had passed away. At such a tender age, she wasn't quite sure what that meant. Until an insensitive social-worker informed her that she would never see her mother again.

The next four years would be spent in Foster Care before the state finally found a couple who was willing to take a ten year old bi-racial girl.

The couple was young, rich, white, and unable to have any children of their own. For the first couple of weeks, everything went well until the wife began showing signs of jealousy - jealousy of her husband's fatherly affection towards their newly adopted daughter.

When a social-worker stopped by to see how Robin was adjusting to her new environment, the wife accused Robin of trying to seduce her husband; a charge the husband clearly denied. But at the wife's insistence, Robin was subsequently removed from their home.

Instead of being placed back into 'Foster Care'. She was placed into an institution for troubled young girls where she was beaten on a regular basis.

Three years later Robin would manage to escape, and had been on her own since.

Standing at five-feet, five-inches tall, she was a perfect size four with an exotic appearance that was sure to hold the attention of any man.

Back in Atlantic City, Robin found herself sitting at the bar of a small, predominantly black club called, Linda's Lounge.

Linda's Lounge was a small local club located up-town. There was a bar, and several tables that seated two couples, a small stage for live entertainment, and a large dance floor.

Sipping on a white wine at the bar, Robin couldn't get over how packed the club was, especially for a Monday night. "This place must take in a fortune on the weekends," she muttered while watching as young men and women shouted at one another over the loud Hip Hop music.

Linda's Lounge wasn't a bad club, she concluded. But with no admittance fee at the door, there was no discretion on who its patrons were. As far as she could tell, it appeared anyone was allowed in. And those without the proper identification were no exception; which told her a lot about the owner.

As a young woman who always prided herself for wearing the proper attire, she was shocked at the sight of so many women who proudly sported dirty tennis shoes on the dance floor.

Robin knew she was out of place. But it wasn't until several men began annoying her before realizing it was definitely time to leave.

Quickly finishing her drink, she paid the bartender and glanced at her watch. "Leaving so soon?" asked a brown-skinned man who seemed to have appeared out of nowhere. Startled, she quickly turned and looked at him then rolled her eyes away annoyingly. "Do I know you?" she asked without looking at him.

"No, but I have a feeling that's about to change," he said while sitting on a stool next to her.

"Dream on," she replied while standing to leave. The moment she went to grab her shoulder-bag from the counter, he gently placed his hand over hers. Startled, she looked at his hand appallingly and snatched hers away. But not before noticing the huge, three carat, blue-white diamond ring he was flossing on his index finger. "You have a problem with your hands!" she yelled over the loud music.

"I apologize if I offended you. I was just trying to get your attention, that's all," he warmly replied.

"You didn't have to touch me."

"To get your attention... yes... I did."

"And what's so important that you found it necessary to put your hands on me to get my attention?"

"Well... I asked you a question several times. When you didn't answer, I assumed you didn't hear me." He ran his fingers down the length of his mustache to his square shaped goatee in a grooming fashion. He was of average height and looks, but there was something about him that Robin found very attractive. Maybe it was his deep voice? A plus quality she found in a man. Or perhaps it was the twelve thousand dollar gold watch he made sure she noticed. Whatever it was, she had already made up her mind she wasn't going anywhere. Not just yet, anyway.

He had unwittingly managed to attract her full attention the moment she spotted the diamond on his index.

"Oh I heard you. I didn't respond because I wasn't interested."

Pleased with the fact that she hadn't left yet, he smiled.

"Well maybe if you allow me to buy you a drink. It'll give me an opportunity to start again. Who knows, maybe you'll change your mind?"

Robin studied him indecisively. Though she had every intention of taking him up on his offer, she did not want to give the impression that she was easy.

"Don't worry," he said with a warm smile. "I don't bite."

"We'll see."

His smile turned into a wide grin. "By the way," he turned to her and spoke. "I'm Johnny Williamson, the proud owner of this club. I've been checking you out from the moment you walked up in here. I also saw some of these fake-ass thugs sweating you. Which was why I came out here," he said while trying his best to appear smooth.

"Yes, well, maybe now you can understand why I came off the way I did," she said with a more composed tone while sitting down again. "I'll have another white wine, thank you."

He quickly raised his hand to flag the bartender's attention. After the bartender immediately rushed over, he instructed him to get Robin another white wine.

While the bartender ran off to get their drinks. Robin thought about something he had said earlier; something about eyeing her when she first came in. What she couldn't figure out was why she never noticed him watching her?

After placing their drinks in front of them the bartender gave Johnny the thumbs-up before walking off.

"What did you say your name was?"

Robin took a sip of her drink, and for the first time, got a really good look at him. He was old, she thought; old enough to have been her father and definitely not her type at all. Not that she would have anything to do with someone like him in the first place. The way she saw it, he was a man-whore. "Diane. And you're Johnny, right?"

"Yeah, I also own this club," he reminded her.

"So you've told me. You know... it's a shame we can't go some place a little more private to continue this conversation. It's a little hard hearing you over all this noise," she hinted, hoping he would take the bait, but he didn't. Either he wasn't biting, or he was too dense to take a hint. "So..." she proceeded to try another approach, "Did you enjoy the view?"

"What view?"

"Earlier you said something about eyeing me when I first came in. I was just wondering did you enjoy the view."

He grinned with recollection. "Oh yeah... right," he said, feeling a bit embarrassed. "Let me put it this way," he went on. "If I hadn't, I wouldn't be sitting here with you now. Besides, a fine honey like you don't come up in here too often."

"I wonder why," she sarcastically muttered under her breath.

"You say something?"

"Oh... I was just noting the fact that I'm getting a little high," she lied.

He grinned then whispered in her ear, "Would you like to continue this conversation in my office? It's fully equipped with a mini-bar and my very own private stash. Coke, smoke, whatever floats your boat."

"Sounds good to me." Somehow she knew once she had mentioned the fact that she was high, he would make his move, a move that had nothing to do with conversation. Any self-respecting woman would clearly see through a guy like Johnny Williamson.

As they stood, she grabbed her bag and followed him to the back of the club where they entered his office through a large metal, sound-proof door.

Inside the office, two huge men were sitting on a sofa talking. A few feet from the sofa was the mini bar. The moment the two men saw Johnny, they stood and proceeded to leave, but not before eyeing Robin extensively.

"Make yourself comfortable," he said, sitting at his desk on the other side of the huge room.

She looked around and proceeded to take off her coat while heading towards the sofa by the lounge area on the far side of the room.

"This is his office?" she muttered under her breath while looking around the huge room that was large enough to easily be converted into a studio apartment. She laid her coat across the arm of the sofa and sat while looking around. Aside from the well stocked mini bar. There was a small refrigerator leaning up against the wall next to it. "How convenient," she thought suspecting he brought females into his office each time he felt like getting his freak on. She glanced across the room at him and smiled to herself. His game was so weak; she found it very difficult to believe any woman in her right mind would be taken in by such a pedestrian approach. On the other hand, it told her a little something about the women to whom he associated himself with. "Can I fix you something to drink?" she yelled.

Without looking up from whatever he had been doing at his desk. He shouted, "I'll have what you're having."

Robin removed a small capsule form her bag, lodged it under the band of her wrist watch. Then grabbed her bag and strolled over to the mini bar. There was a bottle of rum that would go nicely for what she had planned. She grabbed the bottle of rum and filled two glasses half way while glancing to see if he was watching. Satisfied he wasn't, she retrieved the small capsule and emptied the contents into one of the glasses, then swallowed the empty shell. "Do you have any cola, or would you prefer your rum straight up?"

Looking up briefly from what he was doing, he yelled, "I'll take cola with mine. It should be some in the frig; throw a couple of rocks in it for me."

When she was done with the drink, she grabbed her bag along with the drinks and sat them on top of an old wooden coffee table that was stationed in front of the sofa. Then, she took his drink to him at the desk. "Sorry I took so long," she said, placing one of the glasses on top of the desk in front of him.

"I should be the one apologizing for keeping you waiting, but I have to have these papers in the mail by morning."

"Of course it'll give me time to freshen up a bit. By the way," she added while scanning the front of the office. "Is there a bathroom in here?"

He looked up long enough to direct her attention to a door directly behind his seat.

"I'll just be a moment," she said. With her drink in hand she walked towards the bathroom door and inadvertently noticed a tall file-cabinet posted in an obscure corner on the opposite side of his desk. On top sat a small combination safe. She smiled mischievously before closing the door behind her.

Inside the bathroom, she set her drink on top of the sink and looked around. Though the bathroom was sanitized, it wasn't the sort of place a lady would feel comfortable using. She ran the water in the sink, then slowly moved over to the door. Stooping at the large skeleton key-hole, she began peeking through. With a clear view of Johnny's back, she couldn't quite see what he was doing. She did, however, notice every now and then, he would glance up over the office door at a nine-inch security monitor. The monitor would periodically display various sections of the club giving the viewer visual access to the customers, as well as the staff. Which not only explained how he knew she was about to leave, but also, why she hadn't noticed him checking her out. He had been watching her the entire time, right from his office.

"What a dog," she found herself muttering under her breath. He was a predator who saw her as prey. Someone he thought would be an easy lay. And for that reason alone, she was going to make him pay.

Still at the key-hole, she watched as he finished with the paperwork and took a big gulp of his drink. He then pulled a large plastic zip-lock filled with a white powdery substance, from his bottom desk drawer. She assumed it was cocaine.

After all, he did say something about having some earlier. When she took her eyes from the key-hole to glance at her watch, he abruptly slid his chair back and stood. Startled, she scuffled back over to the sink, and stood there for a while with a hand over her heart to calm her nerves. Content with what she had seen thus far, she began patting her face with water. Then dried off and poured her drink down the sink before turning off the faucet which was an indication that she was on her way out.

Robin stepped out of the bathroom just in time to catch him sitting down at his desk again. Inconspicuously, she scanned the top of his desk. There were no signs of the plastic zip-lock; however, she did notice he had managed to finish his drink.

"I'm going to have another drink. Can I get you a refill?" she enticingly whispered into his ear.

"Why not," he said looking up at her. She smiled at him before strolling off to the bar with the two empty glasses.

She knew he was watching. She could feel his hungry stare on her derriere.

As she stood in front of the bar mixing drinks, she heard his chair slide back. She turned and smiled at him just as he was sitting on the couch. Once she finished with the drinks, she joined him.

There were several nicely rolled blunts lying in an ash-tray on the coffee-table that was not there earlier. There was also a hand-held mirror on the table that was not there before. She grabbed her drink and took a bogus sip while gazing at him.

Johnny was pleased with his newly acquired catch. The smile on his face told her he was full of himself. She watched as he reached into the inside pocket of his cheap suit jacket and pulled out a small plastic bag filled with what appeared to be cocaine.

"Is that coke?" she asked.

He put the bag on the coffee table and pulled out a twenty dollar bill. Without saying a word, he began rolling the bill lengthwise before emptying some of the contents of the bag onto the hand-held mirror. Spreading the powder into four thin lines, he looked at her and said, "This is more than just coke. It's the top of the line shit. My man up north gets his shit straight off the boat. Help yourself." He handed her the bill that had been rolled into a slender tube, but Robin quickly declined.

"But I will have one of these," she said taking a blunt from the ash-tray instead. As she held it to her lips to indicate she needed a light. He saw this as the perfect opportunity to ease closer to her. She knew he was on the verge of making his move. She also knew, if the drug she slipped into his drink didn't work soon he was going to be all over her. She took a few hits off of the blunt and casually struck up a conversation with hopes of buy herself some time. As the conversation progressed, she made sure he did most of the talking. A little trick she had picked up from her good friend, Rossi. Johnny was a big bragger. She knew it would be just a matter of time before he told her everything she needed to know. All she had to do was pose the right questions and sit back and listen.

It didn't take Johnny long to finish his second glass of rum, providing her with the perfect excuse to get him another re-fill. While she was gone, he filled his nostrils with the powdery poison that provided a momentary escape from reality.

After handing him his third drink, she sat down again. "Who were those two men that left the office when we first came in?"

Before answering, he took a big swallow of his drink, sat the half filled glass down and slid even closer to her. "Those two fools work for me," he whispered. He was sitting so close she could feel the warmth of his breath bouncing off of her lips.

"You sure you don't wanna do any of this coke?" he asked, changing the subject.

She couldn't help noticing how much trouble he was having keeping his eyes open. Even his words had begun to slur.

31

"I'm sure." She was about to ask another question. When, without warning, he kissed her. When he saw she gave no resistance. He kissed her again. Only this time, it was all tongue.

As disgusting as she found it she had to admit, he sure knew how to twirl a tongue. But when his hands began taking liberties all over her body she pushed him off of her with very little effort. "What's wrong?" he asked with a drunken slur.

"I don't appreciate you trying to manhandle me. I thought you said you don't bite?"

He stared at her with a strange look in his eyes. A look she had seen many times before; mostly in the eyes of dirty old men. She knew he was anxiously anticipating the possibility of conquest. She also knew he wasn't about to take no for an answer. But instead of taking the aggressive approach as she had anticipated, he did something that threw her completely off guard. He apologized with a sincere smile.

"No harm done. I guess we both got a little beyond ourselves. Not that it's a bad thing. It's just... we have all night to get fully acquainted. Let's just take our time and do this right. Okay? The last thing I want this to be is a one-night-stand. I like your style and I want this to last."

"LAST? Bitch, um' married."

"WHAT?"

"You hookers kill me. Always wanna be treated like a lady when you know damn well you been fucking out of both drawers. Fuck I look like? A sucker? I already know how you bitches get down."

His words caught her completely by surprise and before she had a chance to set him straight, he grabbed her firm breasts and began lightly squeezing both nipples with his index and thumb. She gasped in a combination of shock and surprise. Her first reaction was to slap him. But as luck would have it, he had managed to find the one spot on her body where she loved to be touched by a man. She wanted to say something. Anything, except what was really on her mind which was how badly she needed to be had by a man. Not just any man. Someone who knows what a woman need, and how she needed it. The two pulls she took from the blunt made her horny.

As he continued teasing and manipulating her nipples which were responding nicely to his skillful touch. She felt herself getting weak. With what little will-power she had left, she quickly jumped up from the sofa.

"I don't know who the fuck you think you are, but you better think again. 'Cause you ain't him."

Wearing a smug smile, Johnny said nothing. He just sat there staring up at her as if she was an edible delicacy. She glanced down at her own breast and noticed her nipples protruding through the white cotton fabric of her sweater. They were still tingling from his touch.

"Don't be mad, bitch. It is what it is. Now sit your ass back down and polish this knob."

She frowned, then glanced down at the massive bulge in his crotch. Unconsciously she gasped, and looked up at him. He was staring at her with an arrogant smile. In a perverse sort of way, she was beginning to find him somewhat attractive. "You want another drink while I'm up?" she asked, feeling a little embarrassed for getting caught staring.

"Umm good; sit back down and do like I told you."

The very moment she sat down, he grabbed her and proceeded to stick his tongue down her throat while fondling her body. He had verbally disrespected her and was now physically violating her but she didn't care. Robin suddenly found herself immensely enjoying the assault on her body. Allowed his hands to have their way in places she was even self-conscious about touching. Every fiber of her being was itching with anticipation to be kissed, fondled, and caressed.

As he continued, there was a part of her that wanted to yell, "Nigga! Take your greasy-ass hands off of me!" But the other part, the part that was in desperate need of a man, was enjoying it too much to stop him now.

Unconsciously, she found herself rubbing his crotch.

"Suck it," he whispered in her ear before she actually realized what she had been doing. When she snatched her hand away, he stood up in front of her with one hand gripping his bulge. "You know you want to." As he slowly began to unzip his fly she sat there staring in a hypnotic trance of lust gleaming in her eyes, waiting. Her heart began to pound with growing anticipation until he finally managed to pull it out.

Horrified by the mere sight of it she unconsciously muttered, "Oh my god!" Dripping rock-hard, it was frighteningly huge, grotesque in shape and repulsively ugly. She had never seen anything like it and could hardly believe any human could possess such a monstrosity. "I know you can't take the whole thing. Few bitches can. Just wrap those lips around the head," he instructed.

Robin was still in shock from the sight of it. She tried to speak, but nothing came out.

"Yeahhh, bitch!" he began while his massive, pulsating member stood inches from her face as he slowly stroked on it. "I peeped your ho' card the moment you stepped yo' fine, yellow ass up in here. I know a freak when I see one. Here; suck it! You know you want to," he said, swaying drunkenly from side to side as if he was having a difficult time standing. In fear of him falling, Robin quickly jumped to her feet to help him sit down.

The moment he was seated on the sofa, he passed out cold with his massive penis still hanging out. Robin carefully stretched him out on the sofa then glanced at her watch before running across the room to lock the office door. The last thing she wanted was for his men to walk in on her. Not that there was a chance of anything like that happening. Still, Rossi had taught her to always take every action to protect against possible failure. She rushed over to the desk without stopping to think twice, and began going through the drawers. Totally focused, she knew she had to move fast before the adrenaline stopped pumping and fear set in.

Finding only a half ounce of refer, she ignored it and stepped over to the file-cabinet to size up the small safe that sat on top. First, she tried the latch. It was open. "Stupid muthafucka' was so anxious to get his dick wet. He forgot to lock his safe," she found herself saying while going through it. Every now and then she glanced across the room at him. He was still lying in the very same position, out cold. Robin went through the safe with the intent of taking everything of value.

The first thing she saw was the zip-lock bag of cocaine he had been fidgeting with at his desk earlier. Assessing she could get a nice price for it, she immediately grabbed the zip-lock and tossed it on top of the desk. She then spotted a stack of cash sitting on the bottom shelf. She quickly scooped up all the bills, then closed and locked the safe.

With everything on top of the desk she rushed over to the sofa for her coat and bag. Johnny was now snoring quietly. She took one last look at him and smiled. "Next time maybe you'll remember every female ain't a ho' and all woman ain't slow." She was about to walk back over to the desk for her bounty when she noticed his watch and index ring. "I'm not that cold," she whispered grabbing a fresh blunt from the ash-tray instead.

While placing the money and cocaine inside her bag, she noticed her hands were shaking. Fear was beginning to set in. She looked up at the security monitor. The club was still in full swing, making her getaway easier than she had anticipated.

But first, there were a few things that needed to be taken care of. She quickly sat her bag down and messed up her hair a little.

After leaving the office, she made sure to close the door behind her. The club was even more packed than when she had left.

As she headed towards the exit she began to experience an overwhelming fear that everyone was watching her. She convinced herself it was just her nerves and tried not to panic. That is until she passed by a table occupied by the two men who were sitting in Johnny's office earlier. They weren't just watching her, they were snickering and whispering to one another.

Robin knew their source of humor probably had something to do with the way she was walking, which was the idea. After all, Johnny Williamson was hung like a horse on steroids. There was no way any woman could survive undamaged after being mounted by him.

Just before she reached the exit she glanced back at them. They had stood up and were heading in the direction of Johnny's office. As soon as she was out of the club, she ran to her car as if she had just robbed a liquor store.

CHAPTER 3

After the stunt she had just pulled. Robin knew it was much too dangerous to stay in the city. Instead of checking into one of Atlantic City's many luxurious casino hotels as she had originally planned. She checked into a small motel in a small town called, Pleasantville just outside of Atlantic City.

The room was of average size. There was a king size bed, dresser, and an old nineteen-inch color television that had been bolted on top of the dresser. A small hallway led to a small bathroom with a small window over the toilet. In order for Robin to check and see if the window was locked. She had to stand on the toilet-seat to reach it.

Next, she searched the entire room thoroughly before proceeding to take off her coat and boots. The last thing she wanted was to find someone in the room after letting her guard down.

Still fully dressed, she turned on the television to catch the 11: p.m. news. Then laid across the bed, and lit the blunt she took from the ashtray just before leaving Johnny's office.

When she woke the next morning, the television was still on. She must have drifted off to sleep shortly after smoking the blunt. After checking to see if any of her personal effects were missing. She quickly washed before checking out. Even though she was anxious to get back up north. She just couldn't leave without first clearing the air between her and her old friend Rossi. She had said some horrible things to him yesterday. Things she had no right to say. Especially after all he had done for her.

She checked the time and realized Rossi would be opening his shop in fifteen minutes or so. She would have preferred to apologize to him at his home, but knew if she took a chance by trying to catch him before he left. She would more than likely miss him. She also knew it was dangerous showing her face back in Atlantic City so soon. However, it was a risk she was willing to take. Besides, it was early. The thought of

Johnny Williamson combing the streets looking for her this time of morning, was highly unlikely.

She drove past the antique shop, but Rossi had not arrived yet. Instead of waiting, she kept driving until she spotted a Seven-Eleven and stopped for the Morning Addition, coffee, and something to nibble on. She had never been crazy about caffeine, or sweets, but at the moment, she was in desperate need of something to clear her head and fill the pit in her empty stomach.

Parking a few stores down from Rossi's shop Robin made sure she had a reasonably good view while sitting in her car sipping coffee, reading the newspaper and nibbling on a doughnut.

It wasn't long before she spotted her old friend unlocking the front gate of his shop. Before getting out of the car she took a quick peek in the rear-view to make sure her appearances were up to par. Next, she folded the newspaper and laid it over the box of doughnuts. Almost as if she was trying to conceal it. With her coffee in hand, she got out of the car and casually strolled up the block towards the shop. As soon as the old man saw her, his face lit up. "Robin! I thought you would be long gone by now?"

"Yeah... I thought so, too, but as it turned out, I ended up staying overnight. I didn't realize how tired I was until I got back on the road," she explained while looking around nervously.

"Well," he said, "I am pleased you thought enough of me to stop by before heading back. It saves me the trouble of having to catch you by phone," he replied while holding the door open for her to come in.

Robin took one more sip of her coffee before dumping what was left in an outside waste basket. "You found some work for me already?" she asked, stepping past the old man on her way into the shop.

"Perhaps; nothing is certain at the moment. Either way, I will give you a call in a few days." He deactivated the alarm system, turned on all the lights and flipped the 'CLOSED' sign on the door over to read 'OPEN' from the outside. "Are you still angry with me?" he asked.

"No. But I have to admit, you sure know how to make me crazy." They both laughed a little, and then she stared at him before suggesting, "You're the one who should be angry with me. I said some nasty things to you yesterday. None of which I meant, though. I guess I was just a little tired. You know how cranky I get." She looked in the glass showcase at a Native American fertility necklace.

"I could never get angry with you; disappointed perhaps, but never angry." She looked at him and noticed the large wooden crate he was trying to pry open. After realizing the trouble he was having with it. She immediately rushed over to give him a hand.

With the crate now open, Robin reached in and pulled out a beautiful hand-carved wooden mask. Holding it up to the light, she could easily tell from its structural features it was African in origin. Intrigued, she couldn't resist inquiring as to its tribal background.

"I take it this particular piece interests you?"

"It's nice! Whoever carved it sure put a lot of work and detail into it." she said while carefully holding it with both hands. "How much would a piece like this go for?"

Without answering, he took the mask from her and placed it back into the crate. "If you have to ask, then truly, you are not interested." Feeling somewhat insulted, she glared at him. The old man, however, hadn't noticed one way or the other.

"You know... all this time we've known each other. I never realized how valuable all this stuff really was."

"Stuff?" He smiled and changed the subject while going over the inventory of several other items. "Promise me one thing, Robin," he said without looking at her. "You are a young, beautiful, and intelligent woman. You have plenty of money to go and do as you please. Take my advice and find a good young man and have some bambinos."

"Please, Rossi. Don't spoil it!"

"No, I am not trying to tell you how to run your life. I am just saying... you should seriously consider settling down. Raise a family. You know I am going to need someone to run the business some day."

"Which one?" she playfully teased with a light laugh.

The old man did not find her humor amusing. Once she realized he was being serious, she immediately asked, "Is everything a'ight?"

He stared at her searchingly and slowly approached standing directly in front of her. He gently placed both hands on her shoulders, demanding her full attention. "Listen to me, Robin, I love you."

"I love you, too. But...."

"Please!" he interrupted her. "Just listen." She noted the seriousness in his voice even though he had always been serious when it came to her life-style. This time, it was different. There was something in his tone that made her feel uneasy. Without saying a word, she watched as he reached for his wallet and pulled out a small business-card.

She took the card and examined it closely before asking, "What's this?"

"Me looking out for you," he said before continuing. "If anything should ever happen to me I want you to contact the individual on the card. He will know what steps to take."

"Nothing is going to happen to you."

"Just remember what I said!"

Robin stared at him intensely while pocketing the card.

He was beginning to frighten her. "Are you sure everything is a'ight?" she asked once more. Concern was clearly displayed all over her face.

"You better get going now," he said, reassuring her with a warm smile.

Robin held his hand as he led her to the door. She was about to speak when he kissed her lightly on the cheek and made her promise to seriously consider settling down. She promised, and then left.

On her way to her car she couldn't stop thinking about what he had said. Once she finally reached her car. She noticed a man standing across the street, watching her. His face looked familiar, but she was unable to place where she had seen him before.

Without giving it a second thought. She quickly jumped into her car and sat there for a moment thinking about her conversation with Rossi. She pulled out the business card he had just given her and studied it once more. 'Steven B. Barry, Attorney At Law', the card read. Unsure what to make of it, she stuck it between the blinders and pulled off.

On the fourth platform of a parking lot in Paterson, New Jersey a conservatively dressed Caucasian man of middle aged stood outside his black Mercedes, waiting. With one hand tucked in his full length top-coat pocket, he adjusted his gold, circular frame glasses on his nose with the other while cautiously looking around. The moment he saw the black limousine screech around the corner and head in his direction, he removed his hand from his pocket and took a few steps forward as the limousine came to a complete stop in front of him.

He watched while a huge, casually dressed driver got out to open the door for his employer, Michael Henderson. Also casually dressed with his hair twisted into plates, Mike got out of the limo' wearing his trademark dark shades he rarely was ever seen without. "Spurlock." he said as if he was expecting to meet with someone else. "Hope I ain't keep you waitin'? I got my knob polished."

"That's Mr. Spurlock to you. You're late!" Spurlock angrily yelled.

"Whatever. And you can take that bass out your voice before you fuck around and get beat the fuck down up in the mutha'. The important thing is, I'm here." Spurlock stared at Mike and his huge new driver with such intensity. He didn't like being talked down to and hated even more being threatened. "Well what the fuck! You just gonna' stand there looking stupid, or tell me what the fuck Crain found so important that got me here?"

"That's Mr. Crain to you."

"Whatever, man! What the fuck you got to tell me, delivery boy?"

Spurlock eyed him angrily before getting to the point. "He wants you to know the shipment is on its way. You can pick it up at the address in three weeks." He handed Mike a slip of paper with an address on it. "He also wants to know what you intend to do about this, Spivey Wise character who manage to move in on our profits?"

"You tell Crain I said, Spivey ain't no treat. Once I get the shipment, he'll be working for us. I already got two of his so-called trusted lieutenants in my pocket," Mike said with a hard laugh while looking the address over.

Spurlock was about to get in his car when he stopped, "Oh, one more thing."

"Yeah, what's that?" asked Mike.

Spurlock smiled maliciously before saying, "Besides Mr. Crain, you're the only other person who have that address."

He gave Mike a wicked smile before getting into his car and pulled off.

As his car passed, Mike shouted, "You just tell Crain, I got this!"

CHAPTER 4

Still a little groggy from last night, Johnny sat at his desk totally confused. For the life of him, he just couldn't remember anything passed tonguing some fine young woman he met last night at his club. He did recall her telling him her name was, Diane, but because of what happened, he seriously doubted she had been telling him the truth.

Standing on the other side of the desk were, Smitty and Wells, the two men who worked for him. "The bitch got that off, Johnny. I know you ain't gonna' let that ho' get away with it?" said Smitty.

"Word-up, Johnny. She played you like a fine tuned violin," added Wells.

For the first time, Johnny lifted himself from the slump in his chair and sat up straight. "If anything," he began, "She slipped something in my drink. She had to. 'Cause I can't remember shit!" he said. Trying to convince himself, under normal circumstances, she would have never played him like that. He looked up at the two men and shouted, "That bitch coulda' murdered me and got away with it! You two sorry ass fools let her walk right up out of here with all of my shit. What the fuck you think I pay you for? To stand around looking stupid! That dirty bitch is probably out there right now laughing her ass off!"

The two men looked at each other dumfounded. "You want us to try and find her?" asked Wells.

Johnny stared at him with an anger gleam in his eyes. "You think? Of course I want you to find her, stupid! Ain't that what the fuck I pay you for?"

"That's easier said than done," Smitty quickly pointed out. "How the hell we suppose to find her when you ain't gave us shit to go on. At best, we know her name is, Diane. At least that's what she told you. Chances are, she was lying. Hell...she could be in Philly by now. It's kind of silly trying to find some bitch in a big-ass city like Philly especially when we don't have a clue who the hell we looking for."

"Yeah, Johnny," said Wells, totally in agreement with his partner.

Johnny thought about it. He knew Smitty was right, but he didn't care. Being played by a female was a terrible thing for a man in his position. His pride was hurt and reputation at stake. "Look, Smitty. I don't give a damn how you find her, just do it! And take that idiot with you!" Both men left the office mumbling under their breath. Even with their limited intelligence, they knew the woman Johnny was sending them to find, was long gone by now.

Fifteen minutes after the two men had left. Johnny got a call from his bartender, Rob who informed him that he had just seen the very same girl Johnny had been looking for.

"Where? When?" Johnny shouted into the receiver.

"I spotted her inside that old antique shop on Atlantic Avenue."

"She still there?" he immediately asked.

"No. She left about ten minutes ago. I followed her until she got into this '93 Altima, and pulled off."

"Did you get the plates? And don't tell me no. I can't take another disappointment."

"Sorry, Johnny man. I was too far away," he lied. "But I can tell you this. Those plates were from New York. Maybe that's where she's from?"

"Are you sure she had New York plates?"

"I'm sure. Why don't you get Smitty and Wells to squeeze the old man? He should know something."

"What old man?"

"The old man who runs the shop I saw her come out of."

"And how the hell is he supposed to know anything? You think each time he gets a customer, he take their name and address? Come on, Rob. Don't be stupid! I expect that from those other two idiots, but not you?"

"No, Johnny man she wasn't in there buying anything. She went there to see him! Hell, he wasn't even open when she stepped her fine, yellow ass up in there. I even saw that old bastard kiss her before she left."

"They kissed?"

"Yeah...but not like you think. He just kissed her on the cheek, that's all. Still, a kiss has got to be more than just a casual friendship, you know?"

"Are you sure, Rob?" Johnny asked. This was the best news he'd had all morning, but he had to be certain Rob had his facts straight.

"Positive."

"Okay. That's all I wanted to hear. Give me the address of this shop one more time."

"It's on Atlantic Avenue. About a block before you get to that new Seven-Eleven that just opened. You can't miss it."

"Good work, Rob. I owe you one."

After hanging up, Johnny beeped his two men, Smitty and Wells. While waiting for them to phone in, he went over the conversation he'd just had with Rob. Whose suggestion about sending Smitty and Wells to question the old man wasn't a bad idea, even though he knew they would find a way to screw it up.

Shortly after the two men returned Johnny quickly filled them in on everything the bartender had just told him. Instead of trusting them to check the old man out on their own he thought it would be best if he went along with them.

❖ ❖ ❖

As instructed, Wells parked a block from the antique shop.

Johnny, who sat in the back seat of Smitty and Well's old two door Ford, tried to figure out the best way to handle the situation. Smitty, however, was quick to suggest he and his partner, Wells, go in and beat the information out of the old man. Johnny, on the other hand, was totally against it. "Here's what I want you to do, Smitty. Go find out what time he closes. We'll deal with the rest when the time comes." While Johnny sat in the car watching with Wells, Smitty made his way up the street only to return moments later. "That was quick!" Johnny noted. "Did you find out what time he closes?"

"Five O'clock."

"You sure!" Johnny yelled.

Smitty turned in his seat and looked at him with pure hate.

"Yeah!" he yelled back. "He's got a big-ass sign hanging up in the window. Now what? We gonna' just sit here and wait?"

Uncertain of his next move, Johnny sat quietly in back, thinking.

Instead of giving Smitty an answer, he gave Wells the signal to drive.

On the way back to the club Johnny came up with an idea. "This is what I want you two knuckle-heads to do," he calmly began to lay out his plan. "I want you to go back to that shop at a quarter to five and wait for the old man to leave. When he does, follow him wherever he goes. I want to know where he lives, and who lives with him. That bitch drives a shiny black '93 Altima. Check to see if her car is in the area. She has New York plates." Johnny stared out the window with an angry gaze and begin mumbling under his breath, "Umma' find that dirty bitch if it's the last thing I do!"

Both men peeped at him inconspicuously. "Don't worry, Johnny. Me and Smitty gonna' find her for you," Wells tried to reassure his boss while grinning stupidly.

"So after we follow him, then what?" asked Smitty.

46

"Then... you report back to me. You two knuckle-heads think you can handle that?" Before either of them could answer, he yelled, "Don't fuck it up!"

After Johnny got out of the car in front of his club, he watched as the two men pulled off. He didn't want to doubt their capability to handle such a simple task. But deep down, he knew better.

At approximately 5:15 p.m., Smitty and Wells watched from their car as Rossi closed his shop for the day. When he got into his car and pulled off, Wells was literally right behind him.

"Yo', man! Don't follow so close. You gonna' fuck around and tip him off," Smitty warned. Wells glanced at his partner briefly and allowed two cars to pass between them.

Not more than twenty minutes later, their pursuit led them to Egg Harbor Township where they followed until Rossi turned off on to what looked like, private property. Careful not to arouse suspicion Smitty instructed Wells to park down the main road. As dusk turned into night the two men remained in the car with no view of Rossi's home.

"Damn, man!" Smitty complained. "This ain't working at all."

"You ready to head back?" asked Wells. "We got the address."

"Head back where?" Smitty frowned while staring into the night.

"Back to the club. Johnny said…"

"To hell with Johnny! What he don't know won't hurt him."

Wells glanced at him. From past experience, he knew Smitty was up to something; something that would eventually get them into trouble. The kind of trouble they may not be able to get out of. "Check it out, partner," Smitty offered. "This old muthafucka' lives all the way out here in 'no man's land'. We can roll up in there. Beat the info' out of him and whoever else is in that house. By the time Johnny finds out what happened, we'll be moving our own product. The half of 'bird' that bitch burnt him for? Should be a nice little come-up. You feel me?"

Wells smiled; he was all for it. After all, Johnny Williamson was the very same person who put him and his partner down every chance he got. As far as he was concerned, there was no love lost between them. "Word up, Smitty!" Wells shouted. "You already know um' down!"

"Keep your voice down, ass-hole," Smitty whispered while pulling out a .380 before laying out his plan. "Dig, we gonna' roll up in on him like Patti Johnson did back in the day. Everybody gets pushed! Feel me?"

Wells looked at him confused. "Who the fuck is, Patti Johnson?" he asked.

Without looking at him, Smitty whispered, "A muthafuckin' legend. Now let's roll."

With growing anticipation, Wells anxiously whispered, "Word up, Smitty. Let's do this."

The moment both men got out of the car, Rossi's car pulled out on to the main road and drove right past them. In a state of panic, Smitty and Wells quickly jumped back into the car and proceeded to follow him all the way back to Atlantic City where they watched, as he parked on the boulevard and picked up a well known prostitute by the name of, 'BigButt' Lee.

"Damn!" Smitty murmured in disbelief. "That old cock-sucker must be hard up fucking with that!"

"Word up, Smitty. He ain't got no taste. He must be a cold freak?" Wells was quick to imply while turning up his nose as if he smelt something foul. Smitty cut an eye at him. He knew Wells better than Wells thought. And disgust was the last thing Wells felt for, BigButt Lee. And anyone who knew Wells knew it.

When Rossi pulled off with his date for the night, they followed him in the parking-lot of a small motel just outside of the city.

Parked under a burnt out lamp-light several cars from where Rossi had parked, Smitty and Wells watched as Rossi got out of his car and rushed into the motel office leaving BigButt standing outside waiting.

"That dirty old bastard left Lee standing in the cold," Wells whispered under his breath.

Smitty looked at him and said, "Shit... so would I! That trifling-ass-bitch might steal something."

As soon as BigButt saw the old man returning with the key to their room, she ran up to him as if they were newlyweds.

Right after the old man and his date disappeared into one of the rooms, Smitty and Wells got out of their car. Neither one of them were quite sure of their next move. So when Smitty made his way to the back of the motel, Wells followed and waited to be filled in on the plan.

With the element of surprise in mind, Smitty was hoping to find a back door. Instead, he found a small bathroom window about eight feet overhead. Once he figured out which window lead to the old man's room. Smitty tried to pry the window open, but found it too difficult with Wells holding him up. When Wells found a large garbage-can for Smitty to stand on, Smitty told him, "When I'm in, go to the front and wait for me to let you in." Without waiting until Smitty was through the window. Wells ran around to the front of the building leaving no one to watch his partner's back.

Unable to call out to Wells without being heard by others. Smitty angrily, but quietly mumbled several choice words before easing through the small window.

Richard Smith, also known as Smitty, was a thirty-nine year old two-time loser with a jail-house GED he had acquired while doing time at New Jersey's notorious Trenton State Prison.

At six-foot-four, two-hundred and sixty-five pounds, he had been nine time champ of the New Jersey State Prison's power-lifting team. With a bench press of over four-hundred and seventy pounds, he was nothing short of solid muscle. In combination with his rugged dark features, clean shaven head, and deep voice. He often intimidated those who did not know him. But those who did knew he was no threat to anyone but himself.

His partner and long time friend, Benney Sylvester Wells was a short, stubby man. At five foot eight, he had a beer-gut, and half-fro which made him appear fifteen years older than his actual forty-years of age. Wells had a third grade education and no problem-solving skills. Also a two time loser, he more than often depended upon the sole advice of his partner, Smitty.

Both men had spent the better part of their childhood, and most of their adult lives in one jail or another. The only reason they were hired by Johnny Williamson was because of Smitty's imposing look. Wells, on the other hand, was along for the ride.

Easing the window down, Smitty found himself standing on top of the toilet-seat in a small, dark bathroom. With the door ajar, BigButt's voice could be clearly heard coming from the front room.

As Smitty slowly moved towards the door he pulled out his .380 while peering out, but was unable to see anyone. On tip-toes, he quietly eased out of the bathroom and slowly moved down a short, dark hallway that led to the front room. As he stood in the shadows watching the old man and his date, Smitty was repulsed by what he saw.

While the old man laid in bed, totally nude. BigButt, who was also nude, squatted over the old man's face. Just as he was about to make his presence known, he noticed BigButt binding the old man's hands and legs to the bed-post. Things could not have gotten any easier, he thought while waiting until she was done.

Once BigButt had him tied down, Smitty appeared from out of the shadows. The first to spot him was BigButt Lee. "Nigga!" she shouted, startled by the unexpected presence of the intruder.

"Where the' hell you come from!"

"Shut the fuck up, bitch! Don't either one of you cock-suckers move!" he shouted while holding both at gun point.

Without taking his eyes off of either of them. He slowly eased over to the door and opened it. Wells quickly rushed in.

"Damn, man! What took you so long?" he complained, rubbing his hands together in an effort to warm them. Smitty moved over to the bed and ordered BigButt to sit down while placing the barrel of his gun up against her head.

"Look, nigga!" she said with bass, "I ain't got no money, he ain't paid me yet. So if y'all gonna' rob him, let me the fuck up outta' here! Y'all fools ain't getting me caught up in this shit!"

"I told you to shut the fuck up, bitch!" He pressed the barrel of his gun up against her temple and nudged it.

"Ouch, nigga! That hurt!" she whined.

"Dig, Smitty man," said Wells, staring at BigButt's huge breasts while unconsciously rubbing the bulge in the front of his pants. "Let Lee go. She's one of us."

Smitty indecisively glanced at his partner. He then looked coldly at BigButt. Finally, he told her to get dress and get out. "And hurry up, hooker before I change my mind!"

"Yeah, Lee," said Wells. "You ain't seen nothin'; you ain't heard nothin'. You got that?" he yelled, trying to be the good guy with hopes of copping a freebie from her later.

"What y'all do, is y'all business," she said, squeezing into a pair of dirty white pants that were clearly too small for her huge thighs. After she managed to get them on, she began taking her time moving about the room while gathering up the rest of her things.

Smitty suspected she was up to something which was why he felt it necessary to watch her closely. "Will you hurry the fuck up, bitch!" he yelled at her again.

Still taking her time, she angrily glanced at him before grumbling, "Um' going as fast as I can. Damn!" while going through the old man's pants. When she found his wallet and car-keys, she headed straight for the door. But not before Smitty snatched the wallet and car-keys out of her hands. "Wait a minute!" she cried. "How the hell umma' get back 'cross the bridge?"

"Hitch-hike, hooker!" He grabbed her by the arm and pushed her out of the room. With her bottom lip poked out, she rolled her eyes at him just before he slammed the door in her face.

"Dig, Smitty. You want me to make sure she heads for the bridge and not for the motel office to call the cops?"

"Man...fuck that bitch! We got work to do," he replied while standing over the helpless old man. "Don't be afraid," Smitty whispered. "We ain't gonna' hurt you."

"Yeah! We just wanna know where that bitch is," said Wells. Smitty stared at Wells with anger, indicating that he himself would handle the interrogation. Once he was sure Wells got the message, he continued. "Look, old man. Some female visited your shop this morning. Just before, or after you opened. We just wanna know where she can be found?" Paralyzed with fear, Rossi just laid there staring up at the two men. "If I have to ask you one more time, umma' take this here barrel and stick it up your ass before pulling this trigga'. Now... tell us what the fuck we wanna know, or...."

"Several young women patronized my business this morning, Sir," Rossi heard himself blurt out.

Smitty glanced at Wells and smiled. "Now did I say anything 'bout her being young?"

"Word up, Smitty! How he know she was young!"

Smitty sat on the edge of the bed and stared coldly at the old man. "I don't remember saying a damn thing 'bout her being young." Wells began to grin. He was pleased to see how well Smitty was handling the interrogation.

"At my age, Sir," Rossi began. "All women are considered young." His eyes shifted nervously from Smitty to Wells and back again.

Not quite the answer Smitty had expected to hear. His face twisted with anger and frustration. "Um trying to be patient with you," he said, rising from the edge of the bed. With his back now to the old man, he began whispering in Wells' ear.

Rossi watched wide eyed as sweat began to roll profusely down the side of his brows. As Wells approached the bed, laughing wickedly, Rossi began pleading. "Please, Sir. I have no idea to whom you are referring, I swear!" But his pleas went un-heard.

With a snap of the finger, Smitty gave Wells the signal, and watched as Wells pulled out a seven inch switch-blade. Waving it in Rossi's face, he waited impatiently for Smitty to give him the okay to start cutting.

"Umma' ask you one more time," said Smitty, "Who the fuck was that bitch!"

"I-I-I am not sure!" he stuttered while shaking his head nervously from side to side, but Smitty wasn't buying it.

"He lying, Smitty!" yelled Wells. "Let me stick 'em? I'll make his ass talk."

"No! Wait!" Rossi cried. "Perhaps you are referring to Robin."

"Robin who?"

"Robin Hoods. She was the only visitor at my shop during the time you specified."

Smitty began to laugh. He couldn't believe the old man would even consider lying to them. Not in the position he was in. Nevertheless, Smitty wasn't about to take any chances.

"Trick!" he shouted in the old man's face. "Do we look stupid to you, or was that the only name you could come up with on such short notice?"

"Word up, Smitty, this trick thinks we stupid. I told you, man. Let me stick 'em?"

"I am not lying. I am telling you the truth. Robin was the only female who came to see me during that time. I have known her for years."

"Why the hell should we believe you? You've been lying to us from jump-street?"

With his eyes still trained on the seven inch blade Wells had been waving in his face. Rossi turned to Smitty and said, "You have the keys to my car. My rolodex is in the glove-compartment. Her name is programmed on it. I drive a...."

"We know what kind of car you drive, pussy!" yelled Wells.

Smitty peered angrily at the old man. "Go check it out, Benny," he ordered, tossing Wells the keys to the old man's car. Wells hesitated, as if reluctant to leave. "What's wrong?" Smitty quickly asked.

Wells frowned irritably. "What the hell he talking about, Smitty? What the hell is a, rolodex?"

"Just bring back anything that looks like one of those battery calculators. Like the one I had when we was in Trenton. Remember?"

Wells' face lit up in recollection as he rushed out of the room.

As Rossi found himself alone in the room with Smitty. He tried to find out why they were so interested in finding Robin.

After Smitty told him why, Rossi quickly offered to pay five times the value of their loss. Smitty just laughed in his face. Not because he doubted his sincerity, but because he didn't believe the old man had that kind of money. The way he saw it, the old man was just speaking out of desperation. Smitty knew he had no idea what the going price for a kilogram of cocaine went for.

"From the looks of that raggedy ass shop you run, you probably couldn't afford to make car payments on that new ride you drive."

"My car is fully paid for, Sir."

"Yeah... I'll bet!" Right at that moment, Wells rushed into the room.

"Did you find it?" Smitty quickly asked.

Wells held up a small, electronic gadget and asked, "Is this it?" Smitty quickly snatched it from him and showed it to Rossi.

"Is this it?"

"Yes! That is exactly what I was talking about. If you will just untie me I will be happy to show you how it works."

"Just give me the code to unlock access!" Smitty angrily demanded.

After gaining access, Smitty punched in the name Robin Hoods on the small LCD display and waited. When a P.O. Box and phone number appeared directly under the name Smitty shouted, "I got it! We got that bitch now!"

CHAPTER 5

The phone ranged twice before the answering-machine picked up the call. "Hello," Rossi's recorded voice began. "As you may have surmised I am not in at the moment; however, if you would like to leave a message. I will get back with you momentarily."

Robin waited for the beep before speaking. "Hi, Rossi. It's me again; Robin. Please give me a call when you get in. Bye-bye."

After hanging up, she sat on her bed thinking about what he had said to her the last time they talked. Overwhelmed with concern, she knew she wouldn't rest easy until she at least talked with him. If for nothing else than the reassurance that everything was all right.

Robin stood and headed straight for the shower. She had a long day ahead of her and trying to get rid of the package she stole from Johnny Williamson was an important part of it.

Robin lived in a small, furnished, single-bedroom apartment in an integrated neighborhood in Brooklyn. The fact that she had been able to find such a nice apartment her first day in New York, was nothing short of luck. The apartment was convenient for her limited needs; most of the time she was out of town on business. It was after returning that made her appreciate it most. Having never had a place to truly call home, she was pleased with the mere fact she finally had a place to call her own.

After showering she sat on the edge of her bed while drying her hair before making another phone-call. "J's Corner." A female with a heavy smoker's voice answered.

"Is Tyrone Sharp there?"

"One minute, I'll check."

While waiting with the receiver to her ear. Several people could be heard talking in the back-ground. She glanced at her watch that sat on the end table next to her bed and began to wonder what type of people spent all morning hanging out in a bar. And the man she was trying to find was by no means an exception.

"Yeah... whaz' up?" she heard a man's voice ask through the receiver.

"Tye?" she anxiously asked, making sure she had the right party on the line.

"Yeah. Who's this?"

"Robin. Robin Hoods, remember?"

"Little Red Robin Hoods. Now how can I forget a name like that," he teased. "So how you been, baby girl? I haven't seen you in a minute. Whaz' up?"

"I been around. Just not around town. Listen... I came across something I'd rather not discuss over the phone. I was hoping you knew someone who could probably use it?"

"I would first have to know what it is. But because the matter is too delicate to speak about over the phone, I take it you wanna meet?"

"Just tell me when and where?"

"As usual, you can find me here, at the 'Corner'. I'll be here until noon. After that?"

"I'll be there! See you soon." After hanging up, she walked over to the dresser to retrieve her shoulder-bag. She deposited the fee she received from Rossi in her statement account as soon as she returned and then did a lot of running around. By the time she got home, she was too tired to thoroughly examine the bounty she stole from Johnny Williamson which was something she could no longer put off. After all, in ninety minutes or so she was about to meet someone who had the connections to help her move it all in one shot.

Robin curled up on her bed with the bag and pulled out the zip-lock of cocaine. Holding it up to get a better look, she tossed it to the side. Then retrieved the money she took from Johnny's safe and began counting it.

"Almost three grand," she mumbled disappointingly. Oh well, she thought, tossing the bills on top of the end table while sliding off the bed to get dress. She tried to convince herself that twenty-eight hundred dollars wasn't bad for a few hours work. But the truth was, she had made five times as much in less than half the time.

Robin stepped out of her apartment in a white and black cotton pin-stripe pant suit and matching bag. She deliberately placed her full-length, lambskin trench comfortably over her shoulders while taking her time strolling to her car. She knew she was running late. But as an addict to attention, her ego told her someone, somewhere, was admiring her magnificence. And she had never been one to disappoint her fans.

Robin was a stylish woman who had a thing for looking sleek, and tastefully tailored. With the exception of a dark eye-liner and shadow to give her light brown eyes that evening look. She usually never wore make-up. She didn't have to. She was, in every sense of the word, a natural beauty.

Robin parked right across the street from the seedy bar, and sat there staring at a group of young men standing on the side of the bar sharing a bottle of cheap wine. Normally she would never be caught anywhere near a place like J's Corner.

Judging from the outside, it appeared to be a scruffy place, located in the worse section of Redhook.

She looked around but did not see Tyrone's car until she actually got out of hers. The white BMW was parked about four cars up the street from the bar.

Careful not to scuff her new black leather Moschino booties she took even steps, one foot in front of the other while hurrying to get where she was going. She tried to understand what attracted a man like, Tyrone Sharp to such a place. A place that was so sleazy, the worst society had to offer, gravitated to 'J's Corner'.

Inside, she spotted Tyrone sitting on a stool at the bar.

A half dressed older woman leaned close up against him. As soon as he saw Robin approaching he quickly dismissed the half dressed woman who, before leaving, rolled her eyes hatefully at Robin.

"Baby girl!" he greeted with a warm smile. "You almost missed me." he said, briefly glancing at his watch.

Robin smiled and looked down at the empty stool next to him. Before she sat, she produced a white, cotton handkerchief from her black, leather handbag and shook it free from its FOLD. After placing it over the worn, wooden stool, she sat.

"I need your help to get rid of something I came across. If you can move it I'll put you down for twenty percent."

"I still have to know what it is."

She looked around cautiously before moving closer to speak.

"About half of ki of coke," she whispered. "I'm not sure how many times you can step on it, or if it has been stepped on already?" She waited for a reaction, but received a cold stare instead. A reaction she did not expect. "You think you can help me move it?" she asked.

"Look, baby girl," he began. "Normally I would just say no. I'm not into using, selling, or helping others sell drugs. However, seeing how much of the stuff you have. I think I might know someone who might be interested." he said, looking frighteningly stern.

She wasn't quite sure what to say. Once again his response had caught her completely off guard. The idea of having to do business with a total stranger wasn't what she had in mind.

She had been hoping he would act as the 'middle-man' for her.

Which was what the twenty-percent she promised to pay him was for.

"I don't know." After giving it serious thought, she made a decision. "Well... I was kinda' hoping you'd be the go-between. I don't feel too comfortable meeting with some strange drug-dealer. Those people are crazy!"

He smiled. "This particular brutha' is different. In fact, I think you'll find him interesting."

"And what makes him so different than all the rest? Drug dealers only care about one thing - getting paid."

"If that were true, the two of you should have quite a bit in common."

Her eyes widened. "What the hell is that suppose to mean?"

"Look, baby girl," he said, glancing at his watch again.

"I don't have time to sit here debating the issue of morality with you. If you trust me then trust my judgment. If you want to meet him, be here tonight around nine."

When he stood to leave she eased off of her stool and followed him. As they headed towards the exit she quickly asked, "You think I should bring the package?"

"Only if you want to get rid of it," he said before adding, "The people you'll be meeting tonight are from Jersey. Don't disappoint us by not showing up."

"I'll be here," she assured.

As she maneuvered through the morning traffic she felt good about being able to rid herself of the package. Once again, she thought, Tyrone had come through for her. She had always viewed him as a hustler with a talent for selling anything with a substantial monetary value. Instinctively she knew he could be trusted not to cross her. Having met him through a jewel-fence who was unable to handle some merchandise she had been trying to get rid of, Tyrone Sharp came highly recommended. Despite the fact she virtually knew nothing about him, she had come to consider him a reliable friend. Each time they met, it was strictly business which was probably why their relationship had never had the chance to develop on a social level. Still, that did not stop her from entertaining the thought of a possible booty-call with him. Being a workaholic, she couldn't remember the last time she had been with a man. She was lonely, and often found herself lying in bed at night wondering what it would be like to have such a man lying next to her. And why not? He was tall, dark, intelligent, and handsome which were all qualities every woman looked for in a man. But deep down, she knew they would never be together on an intimate level. Not because he wasn't the type of man she had envisioned herself settling down with. It was because, her fantasies of being with him were that of a one-night-stand; someone who might ease the pain of loneliness. Because of the risk of him reading something more into what she would consider a 'fling', she left well enough alone. The business relationship she had managed to build with him meant everything. She wasn't about to destroy it just because she was horny.

Robin arrived home late that afternoon. After doing some shopping, she was exhausted; too exhausted to put her things away. Dropping her bags and coat the moment she stepped into the apartment. She had just enough strength to kick off her boots before curling up on the sofa to scan through some mail she picked up from the post-office.

After reading the mail, she started her bath water and began to undress. Once her bath was ready, she wasted no time getting in. She must have soaked for more than an hour before finally emerging only to take a desperately needed nice, long nap.

Robin was well rested when she finally woke. With plenty of time before her appointment she lounged around the apartment listening to soft music in an effort to relax. But nothing seemed to work. The thought of having to meet with some ruthless drug-dealer in a bar she felt absolutely uncomfortable being in, terrified her.

It was almost show-time when she stepped out of her apartment donning a dark gray, heavy wool pants suit. Clinching tightly at the collar of her onyx, gabardine trench she rushed to her car to escape the chill of the night air. Before pulling off, she sat there for a moment wondering what was she about to get herself into.

Outside the bar was packed with all sorts of characters.

For those who favored the night, J's Corner was the place to be. There were thugs, dealers and addicts standing around. While others looking to have a good time negotiated deals. Petrified, Robin hurried across the street towards the bar, zooming pass a few hookers who turned out to be men in heavy drag.

Inside, she found herself squeezing through a crowd of sweaty bodies when all of a sudden, someone squeezed her ass.

When she turned to confront the person who had outright disrespected her, she saw two hard-looking, thug-out females wearing men's clothing. She wanted to say something, but knew it would probably be in her best interest to let it go.

The bar was hot, smelly, and filled with stale cigarette smoke that was so thick she found it very difficult to focus on a single object. She was becoming frustrated as she desperately searched for Tyrone, but was unable to fine him.

Just as she was about to give up her search, she heard a familiar voice from a dark booth in the corner, call out to her. Squinting towards the booth, she saw two men. One of which was Tyrone Sharp. She smiled with an overwhelming feeling of relief while rushing towards his both.

Tyrone was sitting with an impeccably dressed young, black male who appeared to be younger than she was.

"Have a seat, Robin," said Tyrone as he slid out of the booth to make room for her.

Smiling nervously at the impeccably dressed young, black male Robin looked around and realized they were being watched by two tough looking, dark-skinned females who were sitting in another booth not far from where they sat. "This is SunRise, the brutha' I was telling you about," said Tyrone. "SunRise, this is Robin."

The young, handsome, light-skinned male smiled. "How you doing, sista'?" he politely asked with a medium heavy voice.

Unable to get over how young he appeared to be Robin just stared at the well-groomed youth.

"Well now that I've brought you two lovely people together. I'll leave you to handle your business," said Tyrone. Just as he was about to walk off, Robin grabbed him by the arm. Startled, he looked down at her with a reassuring smile. "It's a'ight, baby girl," he said. "You couldn't be in more capable hands."

Robin smiled nervously while easing her grip from his arm. She glanced at the youth and found a certain warmth in his eyes that suddenly put her fears at rest. She then looked up at Tyrone and said, "I thought you were gonna' hang around?"

"I've already done my job, baby girl. What you two have to discuss is none of my business. You know the rules, sweet-heart." Robin didn't say anything because she knew he was right.

If he wasn't a part of the transaction, the less he knew, the better off everyone else would be.

After Tyrone left Robin found herself sitting in the dark booth with someone who did not look old enough to be in the bar, more less conducting a business transaction. "He's right, you know," said SunRise.

Robin looked at him strangely and asked, "About what?"

"You couldn't be in more capable hands."

"Let's hope so," she arrogantly replied before coming straight to the point. "I understand I have something you might be interested in?" she said, trying to make a strong impression.

He noticed and smiled, displaying a set of well kept teeth.

"Judging from what I've seen so far, I'd say so," he flirtatiously replied.

She blushed a little before looking around nervously.

"Is something wrong?" he asked when he noticed her discomfort.

"I just don't feel comfortable in here. I keep getting the feeling we're being watched."

He casually looked around before telling her to relax.

"Did you bring the product with you?" She reached in the black, leather handbag and pulled the zip-lock out. Still feeling a little apprehensive she was very careful not to draw attention to their booth while slipping it to him under the table.

While he examined it, she proceeded to look around again. The same two women she saw watching her when she first sat down, was still watching. "Those two women keep watching us!" she whispered to him in confidence. He looked up briefly and without saying a word, resumed examining the package.

"You interested?" she quickly asked while looking around for Tyrone, but he was nowhere in sight.

SunRise laid the bag on top of the table in front of him and folded his hands over it. "I'd like to meet the people you copped from?" he said.

"What?" she yelled, "I was under the impression you were interested in what I have? Not who the hell I got it from!"

"Calm down, sista'. I never said I wasn't interested."

"And you never answered my question? I'm not here to make introductions. I came to get rid of something. If you're interested, the asking price is ten which I think is very reasonable considering the going rate."

Without displaying any emotions he thought about her offer while staring at the package. He then looked up at her, but didn't say a word.

"What's it gonna' be? You want it, or what?" she impatiently asked while glancing at her watch.

Instead of giving her an answer he raised his hand and twirled two fingers without once taking his eyes off of her. Before Robin knew what was going on. The two women who had been previously watching from a nearby booth, quickly came over and stood by his side.

Mesmerized by the women's presence, Robin found herself staring up at the two women, speechless. Aside from their lack of emotions both women were tall, dark and rugged looking in an attractive sort of way. Each sported long, thick dreadlocks, and full length, black leather coats. Neither of them spoke, or smiled, giving Robin the impression she was being robbed.

Her first thoughts were, she had been set-up. She looked at the youth and watched as he handed her package to one of the women.

While the other woman stood off to the side watching their backs.

Robin nervously looked around for Tyrone, but he was nowhere to be found. She glanced at the youth, who watched as the women opened the zip-lock and dug a well manicured pinkie-nail inside. Scooping up a small gap, she placed it to her lips and dabbed at it with her tongue.

"Is it worth the trouble?" SunRise asked her.

The tall woman nodded once, affirming the quality before closing the package. After the tall woman had placed the package back on the table in front of SunRise, he looked at Robin while dismissing the two women with an obscure tilt of his head. As both women returned to their booth, Robin smiled with a sense of relief.

For a minute, she thought she had been set-up to get robbed.

She couldn't have been more pleased to know everything was going according to plan. "I'll pay the asking price," he finally spoke.

Taken by complete surprise, she couldn't resist asking, "You mean, you're not going to try to haggle?"

Folding his hands over the package once again, he looked her straight in the eyes. "I'll pay the asking price on one condition."

"Which is?" she asked with evidence of nervousness in her voice.

"I need to know the names of the people you got this from. And how I can get in touch with them?"

"That's two conditions," she reminded him.

He smiled. "So it is. Do we have a deal?"

She studied him closely before coming to an understanding. "Only if you promise to give me your word that you'll keep my name out of it; it's bad for business, you understand."

He smiled again. This time his well kept teeth were clearly displayed. "Deal."

After shaking on it, Robin quickly asked, "Did you bring the money?"

"Of course," he said. "We can finish up in my ride if you don't mind?"

"Fine by me," she told him. "In the mean time, I'll hold on to this." She grabbed the zip-lock and slipped it back into her handbag.

"I understand," he said standing. "Just give me a minute to let Tye know we're leaving."

"Okay," Robin said. "I'll wait for you in my car." After she gave SunRise the description and location of her car she quickly made her way out of the hot, crowded bar.

As Robin hurried across the street to her car she began fumbling in her coat pocket for the keys until she found them.

In a hurry to get out of the cold, she was about to unlock the door when someone came up from behind her.

"Yo', bitch! Remember me?" a heavy voice snarled. Robin angrily turned around and found one of Johnny Williamson's thugs standing behind her. Still managing to maintain her composure, she tried not to show any fear. She had been confronted with situations many times in the past that she had to act her way out of. But never once had her life been on the line. That is, not until now.

"I know damn well you didn't just call me a bitch!" She yelled in an effort to attract as much attention as possible.

"Just wait 'til my husband get out here. We gonna' see who the bitch is! You guys just think you can talk to a sista' any type of way you want. Muthafucka, you don't know me!" she spat.

Smitty nervously looked around, then pulled his gun out and stuck it up against her ribs. "Oh... I know you, bitch! We followed your stupid-ass from the post-office. Now get the fuck in the car; we going for a little ride. And you betta' have my shit!" he angrily whispered, nudging her in the ribs with the barrel of his gun. Robin was terrified as she nervously opened the door. She wanted to say something to stall him, but somehow knew there was nothing she could say that would make a difference.

Still cautiously looking around, he yelled at her when he realized she was moving too slow. "Hurry up, bitch!" Just as Robin was about to slide in on the driver's side someone in front of the bar called out to her. Both she and her captor stopped, turned, and looked. It was SunRise. He had just stepped out of the bar in time to notice something was wrong.

"SunRise!" she called out in desperation. Hoping her captor was smart enough not to shoot her without first getting the package back.

"Is everything a'ight, Robin?" he asked while he slowly approached.

Robin was about to speak when Smitty nudged her with the gun.

"Everything's fine, lil' nigga. Mind your fucking business while you still can." Smitty answered for her.

Still approaching, SunRise calmly replied, "The sista' and I have business to conclude."

Robin looked at Smitty. She just knew he was going to shoot SunRise. She also thought SunRise was totally insane for getting involved, but happy he did.

Smitty nervously scanned the area for other hostiles. Though there were a number of people hanging in front and around the bar, no one seemed to be paying them any attention. Convinced SunRise was alone. He smiled wickedly and yelled at Robin to get into the car without taking his eyes off of SunRise.

As SunRise neared the two of them, he looked at Robin and asked, "You know this clown, Robin?" Standing by the open car door with fear displayed in her eyes she immediately shook her head from side to side, indicating that she didn't. It was at that moment that SunRise noticed the large gun being held at her side which was when he realized he had a serious problem.

SunRise stopped in the middle of the street and spread his arms out to show he was not holding.

Smitty grinned with a closed mouth. "That's right, pussy! Beat-it for I pop your lil' young ass!"

As SunRise stood there trying to keep Smitty from entering the car. Smitty never saw the two, tall women heavily armed with Russian assault rifles approaching from opposite directions until both women stood by SunRise's side.

Smitty's arrogant grin suddenly turned into a nervous stare, "Who they 'pose to be, back-up?" he sarcastically asked before yelling at Robin, "Don't make me tell you to get the fuck in the car again, bitch!" When he glanced at SunRise again, the two women had spread out in opposite directions. "Okay, muthafucka'! You think um' playing games!" he shouted, snatching Robin out of the car before she had a chance to fully get in.

With his arm wrapped tightly around her neck to shield himself from possible incoming, he yelled at SunRise, "I ain't gonna' tell you again, lil' nigga. Take your young ass back where the fuck you came from. And don't forget those two amazon bitches you brought with you!"

"You got that, big bruh'." SunRise turned and slowly began walking towards the bar, but both women remained stationed.

Smitty looked at the two women, then yelled out to SunRise, "Yo! You forgot your two bitches!" But SunRise ignored him and vanished into the crowd now forming in front of the bar.

When Smitty was no longer able to see SunRise he brutally flung Robin into her car and was about to join her when he heard automatic weapons being cocked. He turned and saw both women closing in on him from opposite directions. "OH SHIT!" he sighed in a state of panic before dragging Robin back out of the car.

Still using her as a shield, he yelled at both women. "Yo, man! What the fuck you two bitches want?" but neither one answered. With his back now up against Robin's car. He tightened his grip around her neck and yelled towards the bar. "Yo', little nigga! You betta' come get these two bitches of yours for I blow your woman's brains out!" As the two women slowly proceeded to advance, he placed his gun to Robin's head and began threatening her life. When SunRise failed to answer he yelled in Robin's ear, "Yo' bitch! Call your boyfriend, or umma' blow your fucking brains out. YOU HEAR!"

Robin hesitated. But when he pressed the gun to her head and cocked it in her ear, she quickly complied. "SUNRISE? PLEASE! HE GONNA' SHOOT ME!" she shouted in a state of shock.

Instead of a reply from SunRise, someone from the crowd yelled, "Smoke that ass, 'Bop!"

Smitty took his eyes from the two women long enough to glance towards the crowd. The moment he noticed everyone hiding behind parked cars he quickly returned his attention back at the two women. Who, with their weapons trained on him, just stared without so much as a blink.

"What the fuck y'all want? I ain't got no beef wit' y'all!" he yelled, but neither one responded which only frustrated him more. Taking his gun from Robin's head, he opened fire on the two women. But instead of returning fire the two women dove behind nearby parked cars. This lead Smitty to believe he held the upper hand. With Robin as his shield, he dragged her into the middle of the street while yelling like a madman, "You think um' playing! You stupid bitches think this is a game! Y'all don't know who the fuck y'all fucking wit'!" while letting off a round, or two for effects. Robin screamed and struggled to break free from his grip. But as his life-line, there was no way he was letting her go.

Moments later, an old Ford pulled up alongside of them.

The moment Smitty tried to go for the car door. Both women suddenly reappeared and opened fire. In a state of panic, he lost his grip on Robin who fell to the ground screaming and crying. In Smitty's attempt to drag her to the Ford, he caught several bullets in the left side of his upper chest from the barrel of one of the woman's assault rifle. "SMITTY!" cried the driver of the old Ford. When Smitty didn't move the driver jumped out of the car to help his friend, but the onslaught of lead quickly chased him back inside of his car.

Realizing there was nothing he could do for his partner. He screeched off down the street in an effort to get away. The crowd in front of the bar stood and roared with applause as the two women rushed into the middle of the street spraying a host of bullets at the fleeting car. The sound of hail the size of golf-balls crashing to earth was nothing more than an assault of lead ripping through the exterior of the old metal Ford. As the driver lost control, the car crashed into another parked car and exploded on impact.

Robin was still on the grown next to Smitty's blood-drenched body, screaming in horror when one of the armed women grabbed her by the arm, and dragged her to her feet. A silver-gray, 1969 Jaguar pulled up alongside of them. The tall woman opened the passenger-door, pushed Robin in, and slammed the door shut behind her. Robin tried to get out, but the car immediately sped off. Leaving tire marks in its trail.

Still crying and screaming, "Let me the fuck up out of here!" Robin banged on the window while trying to get out of the car.

It wasn't until a soft, familiar voice said, "Calm down. You're safe now," before she realized SunRise was the driver.

"You?" she said with total surprise. "You son-of-a-bitch!" she screamed between sobs. "You left me back there, you bastard!"

"Look, sista'," he began without taking his eyes from the road. "I wasn't holding. There wasn't anything I could do, except get myself killed. I left you in good hands. Otherwise you wouldn't be here with me now."

"If you talking 'bout those two crazy-ass bitches who almost killed me, you..."

He immediately interrupted her, "Those two crazy ass bitches, as you so tastefully put it, saved your life."

She looked at the speedometer and noticed he was doing eighty across the Brooklyn Bridge. "Um' sorry," she said, wiping her tear stained face.

"It's okay. You're up-set. I understand."

She peeked at herself in the rearview. "I must look a mess."

When he glanced at her, she held her head down. Almost as if she didn't want him to see her in such a state. He smiled at her vanity. Here was a woman who just escaped death by a thin margin and the only thing she was concern with was her appearances.

"You didn't get hit back there, did you?" he asked. Instead of answering him, she just stared out the window in a zombie like state. He wanted to ask her about the man who tried to abduct her, but it was obviously a bad time. Because he knew she was an emotional wreck, he thought it was best to allow her time to collect herself. A few minutes later when he glanced over at her, she was fast asleep. If she was experiencing shock, rest would be the best thing for her, he decided. No one could go through what she just did without somehow being damaged.

At least she wasn't physically hurt he thought while wondering would she be strong enough to deal with what just happened once she woke.

CHAPTER 6

Robin woke to find SunRise parking in the lot of a housing project. Still very much in fear for her safety, she looked around apprehensively. "Where the hell are we?"

"Somewhere you'll be safe."

"Safe! You call this place safe?" she said while searching the car floor.

"Lose something?" he asked before getting out of the car.

"My bag! I can't find my hand-bag! Where the hell is it?" she yelled in frustration as she continued to search the car floor.

SunRise walked around to the passenger side of the car and opened the door for her. "If it's not in the car you didn't have it when you got in. Which means...."

"I must have left it back there?" she finished the sentence for him. "If the cops find it, they gonna' think I had something to do with killing those two men?"

"Not necessarily. You could have easily lost it during all the confusion. You know how folks get when somebody starts shooting. It gets kinda' chaotic especially when your life is on the line. I wouldn't worry too much about it. If it's there, my people will find it," he concluded.

Robin got out of the car yelling, "What the hell you mean, don't worry about it? That damn coke was in my bag. Not to mention my driving license. I could be in serious trouble and you telling me not to worry about it! Are you fucking crazy?"

"Keep your voice down!" he whispered. Robin could tell he was angry, but was very good at concealing it. "Look," he calmly continued as the two walked towards one of the tall buildings. "Whatever you have to say concerning what happened tonight can wait until we're in my apartment."

"Your apartment?" she asked. The thought of anyone claiming to have an apartment in the dilapidated, low-income housing projects would have been laughable if she didn't find it so sad.

"You'll be safe here."

She looked at him and frowned. "Safe? Are you serious?"

When he didn't answer she was about to say something else, but before she had the chance to. He forcefully grabbed her by the arm and led her towards one of the fifteen story buildings.

"HEYYY!" she complained, glancing back briefly at the 1969 XKE-type they just pulled up in.

As the two of them approached the entrance, there was a crowd of hustlers hanging outside the building congregating.

Robin clung tightly to SunRise's arm. Aside from the broken glass and trash scattered throughout the entire courtyard. The bottom portion of the building had been vandalized with gang graffiti and ghetto art.

While waiting for the elevator, a young, tomboyish female dressed in Timberland Boots, baggy male jeans and a tan Bubble-Goose coat argued with an elderly man. Who, by the tone of the dispute, obviously owed her money. When the young female caught Robin staring, her face twisted into an angry frowned.

Robin quickly looked away, but made the mistake of getting caught looking again. This time, the female pulled out a large semi automatic hand gun and cocked it. Terrified, Robin quickly looked away again. But this did not steady the young girl's anger.

Wearing a screw-face any young thug would be proud to own. She was about to approach, but when she realized Robin was with SunRise. She abruptly stopped and said, "Oh, damn. My bad."

Her expression softened as she spoke. "I ain't see you standing there, 'Rise!" SunRise looked at her and then at the gun she was tucking back into the waist of her pant. He gave her a courtesy nodded, then looked at Robin. The young female briefly glanced at Robin before resuming her conversation with the old-head she had been previously arguing with. "Get my shit, nigga!! I ain't trying to hear that shit you talking, yo!"

"I got you, Punchie. Just..."

"WELL GIMME'! Before you fuck around and get got!" she yelled while following the old-head out of the building. Words couldn't describe how relieved Robin was after the young female and old-head left the building. She could still hear the laughter and loud conversation from the people they had passed on their way in, followed by a few gunshots which was something she was clearly not use to. Jumping each time she heard a gun go off, she clung tightly to SunRise's arm. SunRise looked at her and asked was she all right? It wasn't hard to tell she was terrified. He just assumed she was in shock from her previous ordeal at J's Corner. But it was the young boyish-girl with the automatic that had her shook. She expected the young, thugged-out female to burst into the building with her crew and guns blazing any minute now, but it never happened. She looked at SunRise. He seemed oblivious to her concerns.

"Nice ride," she tried to engage him in conversation, but he did not respond. "Where the hell are we anyway?"

"In Paterson. You have to stay here until my people and I can find out what happened back there," he finally spoke.

"Look! No offense, but I don't know you? Besides, what the hell do you care? That guy was after me, not you and your female crew. Anyway, he's...." she paused when she saw the look he was giving her. Not only did it make her think twice before continuing, it turned her on as well. She had always been the type of woman that appreciated a man who knew how to assume the dominate role. Not to the point of being physically, or emotionally abusive, but someone who knew how to put a woman in check with a single glance especially when she needed to be checked.

Once he was convinced she had gotten the message, he folded both hands in front of him and waited patiently for the elevator.

Feeling a little more secure, she eased closer to him. He smelt good to her. "You never answered my question," her tone was passive now. When he ignored her, she began to focus on her surroundings.

The lights in the lobby where dim and the floor was sticky from long periods of neglect. Graffiti of profanities and gang signs covered the walls. Robin felt herself getting nauseous.

There was a strong aroma of something foul brewing that emanated from one of the E-floor apartments. "Is the elevator working?" she impatiently asked, but her question fell on deaf ears. She looked around again and noticed a flashy dressed man watching her. She quickly looked away. A few moments later when she looked again, two more men were standing with him. "Those guys keep watching us," she fearfully whispered. SunRise turned and looked at the three men. Two of which were major stick-up artist from across the bridge. SunRise didn't know any of them personally.

But the reputation of Ghost, and Bomani Africa had been well known to most P-town residents. The third man, Asmar West was another story. While Ghost and Asmar left the building, Bomani remained behind, coldly staring at SunRise as if he was trying to detect the slightest bit of fear. As SunRise stared back, Robin looked at the two men fearing the worst. Finally, SunRise nodded. Bomani smiled and gave SunRise a closed fist 'power sign' before joining his two friends outside the building. The unruly racket from the young hustlers outside of the building suddenly ceased. SunRise assumed once everyone learned of the three men's presence, they all left in a hurry. Robin looked at SunRise with relief. She was glad the three men were gone and suspected SunRise was, too. "Friends of yours?" she asked, trying to get him to open up. Instead of a reply, he gave her a vague smile. She wasn't sure what it meant, but it was a start.

When the elevator finally arrived Robin was hesitant at first about getting on. It was an obvious death-trap. But once SunRise got on, she quickly followed. SunRise pressed for the ninth floor, and waited. As the door closed, the elevator jerked a few times before going up while making squeaky noises on the way.

Not having said two words to her since they entered the building. He finally turned to her and said, "Look. I know you don't trust me. True indeed, you shouldn't. After all, we just met. But if you have any respect for your friend, Tyrone. Then all I ask is that you trust his judgment."

"I don't know him like that. As far as I know, the two of you could have staged that whole thing back there at that horrible place you called a bar." She stared at him with skeptical eyes. As if she was trying to detect a hint of deception.

He smiled and was about to speak when the elevator suddenly jerked, and then slowed down before coming to a complete halt. After getting off, she followed him down a clean, well lit hallway that smelt of detergent. She couldn't believe the difference between the E-floor and the ninth. It was like they were in two different buildings. The black and white tile floor had been cleaned and waxed to a glassy shine. And there was no graffiti on the freshly painted walls.

He stopped in front of an apartment door and produced a key. "Whose apartment are you taking me to - your mom or girlfriend's?"

"The lease is in a bogus name." he said, holding the door open for her. The apartment was pitch dark when she stepped in. There was a faint aroma of his presence throughout, as if a part of him lingered long after he had left. When he turned on a dim lamp-light, she found herself standing in a tiny, but neat contemporary styled living area. "Nice lil' crib," she complimented while looking around. "You don't live here alone, do you?"

"Normally, I do. Sometimes I have guests," he said while taking her coat. Before putting it away, he held it up to the light.

"What's wrong?" she quickly asked him.

"I'll have this dry-cleaned for you in the morning," he said.

Because she wasn't sure of what he meant. She immediately rushed over and snatched the coat from him. "Damn!" she yelled, holding the coat to the light. The back of it was smeared with what appeared to be, car-grease.

"It probably happened when you fell," he concluded before taking the coat from her. "Make yourself at home. I'll be with you in a few." Robin sat down on a large leather sofa and watched as he took off his coat, and hung it up in the closet along with hers.

"Do you mind if I fix myself a drink?" she asked when she saw the bar next to an entertainment center. "I need something to calm my nerves." He briefly glanced at her before walking over to the bar to fix her a drink. As soon as he handed it to her she scanned the burnt, brown substance in the bowl-like glass and asked, "What's this?" before tasting it.

"Cognac. It'll warm you up," he told her.

She took a sip, then another. "It's good!" she said.

He smiled before excusing himself. While he was in back, Robin sat her drink down and looked around while slipping off her booties. She curled up on the soft, white leather sofa and grabbed her drink. When she saw the collection of CDs, she set the drink on a glass-top coffee table and walked over to the entertainment center. Running her fingers through the large collection of CDs until finally finding something she wanted to hear. As she removed the CD from its protective casing, she carefully slipped it into the player, adjusted the volume and waited until Sade's, 'No Ordinary Love' echoed throughout the front room. She didn't actually know if it was the few sips she took from her drink, or the music itself, but she felt much more relaxed now. Singing along with the music while continuing to look around, she walked into a small kitchen with an even smaller connecting dining-room and looked around. There was a door in the dinning room that seemed somewhat out of place. Upon further investigation, she learned the door led to an extremely small patio overlooking the courtyard and another apartment building. She was extremely impressed with his sense of style. The three front rooms were painted white with a skinny black trim that set off the clean, horizontal black and white wall-to-wall which was something different altogether. Under any other circumstances, the carpet might have been considered, 'bad taste' But somehow he made it work. She had suspected the white leather sofa she had been lounging on made a big difference. There were also two leather matching recliners facing the sofa. The two recliners were also strategically placed to separate the dinning-room from the living-room.

Over the sofa, she noticed for the first time a large oil painting. The painting was that of an Egyptian queen. At least that's what she had assumed. An assumption stemming from, not so much the ancient Egyptian garb and gold jewelry the woman was wearing in the painting. Her assumptions stemmed mainly from the large white crown the woman wore. In the center of the crown, there was a gold cobra emblem coiled in the form of an ankh.

She took a few more sips of her drink and tried to recall the conversation she had with Tyrone concerning SunRise. Who was he? And why was he risking his life for someone he don't even know? He had to realize, if someone was after her, they'll surely be after him?" She didn't know what to make of the situation. But one thing she was sure of; his behavior was not typical of your everyday drug-dealer. There was something about him. Something she couldn't quite put her finger on.

A few minutes later, SunRise returned apologizing for keeping her waiting. Before taking a seat in one of the recliners he sat two spliffs in an ash-tray on top of the coffee table. As Robin assured him no apologies were necessary, she eyed the two spliffs in front of her and asked with a coy smile, "Are you trying to get me high, or something?"

"I'm trying to help you feel at ease," he quickly answered. "Whether you realize it or not," he continued while standing, "you've just been through a traumatic experience. It ain't hard to tell you probably need something to calm your nerves."

He grabbed her empty brandy glass and walked over to the bar.

"Did you have to bring that up? I was trying to forget it ever happened!"

"Yes... I did," he said, setting the refill in front of her. "You can't just forget about something like that. You have to confront it so you can get passed it. To do that, it would be helpful if you talk about it."

She rolled her eyes at him. When she reached for her drink she noticed her hands were shaking. She looked up at him hoping he hadn't noticed, but he had. She tried to play it off with a nervous smile while mumbling something about being cold.

"Try this?" he said, grabbing a spliff from the ash-tray.

After lighting it, he handed it to her. "It'll relax you."

Robin took the spliff and looked at it before taking a small hit.

"If you rather not talk about it, fine. I understand, but as a favor to your friend and mine, I have to keep you here where you'll be safe. At least until I can find out why those men were so adamant about taking you with them.

"What difference does it make? They're dead."

"True. But someone else could be out there looking for you? Whether you realize it or not Tyrone cares about you."

"Tyrone hardly knows me," she replied before looking at him strangely. "So what's your excuse?" she flat out asked.

He stared at her but didn't reply. It was then when she noticed something about him she hadn't noticed earlier. Aside from his boyish features, he was very handsome with the prettiest dark brown eyes which went nicely with his flawless yellow skin. One would probable get the impression he was a pretty-boy, but she didn't see him as such. His handsome, clean-shaved face cast a favorable masculinity. She looked at his freshly cut hair that was a few inches away from bold and wanted to run her fingers over it. She tried not to stare at his imposing physique which showed no evidence of excess pounds anywhere on his five-foot-eight-inch frame before pressing for an answer.

"Well?" she insisted upon hearing his reply.

He reclined in the white leather chair and said, "We were in the process of closing a deal, remember? When I saw that clown dragging you to your car it was obvious something was wrong. Which was why I asked, were you a'ight?"

"But I never answered?"

"Which was an indication that something was wrong." He stood to change the CD. "You don't mind if I change this, do you?"

When she didn't answer, he looked at her. Still sitting on the sofa with her legs folded to the side while nursing the Brandy glass with both hands, she just looked at him. "I asked you earlier did you live here alone and you never answered me." she changed the subject.

Before replying, he sat without changing the CD. "I remember the question. If I'm not mistaken, my answer was, yes." He glanced at his watch. "I noticed you fell asleep in my car. If you're tired, you can rest in my room."

"That's very generous of you," she said with a hint of suspicion. "But where you suppose to sleep, if you don't mind me asking?"

He looked at her oddly. Obviously she was still somewhat fearful of his intentions. And why shouldn't she be? After all, he was a complete stranger who had taken her to his apartment. After giving her something to relax her nerves, he was now offering her his bed. "I have a guest-room."

"Then why don't I take the guest-room and you can sleep in your own bed? I would hate to wake in the middle of the night and find you sleep-walking."

"I'm not a hard sleeper. I offered you my room because it's better equipped for your needs. The guest-room isn't."

She smiled at his quick-wit. He not only had a sensible answer for every question she posed, he also spoke with the prudence, and command of a natural born leader.

"How old are you?" she curiously asked.

"You ask a lot of questions, don't you?"

"I'm just curious," she said with a smile.

"How old do you think I am?"

"I don't know. Seventeen, eighteen maybe?" she said, sipping her Cognac while entertaining the idea of a booty-call with him. It was obvious he had his shit together. But still, she knew she could never allow herself to fall for someone who dealt with drugs.

"Very good," he simply said.

"So how long you been dealing drugs?" she boldly asked.

He leaned back in the recliner, crossed his legs, and just stared at her. There was something in his eyes that told her she had asked the wrong question. Too late to retract, she waited patiently for him to answer.

"I don't," he finally said without changing expressions, or elaborating.

Robin sat up straight and sat her glass down on the coffee table. She was confused. "If you're not a drug-dealer why the hell were you at that bar trying to cop?"

"It's a long story."

"Looks to me like we have all night?" He laughed lightly.

It was the first time she had ever heard him laugh. As much as she enjoyed seeing him with his guard down. She did not appreciate the fact that his humor was at her expense. "What's so damn funny?" she angrily asked.

"Sorry. It's just... somehow I knew you wouldn't leave it at that," he paused before continuing. "I'm not a drug dealer. I don't even like them. One of the pressing issues people of color face today are drugs. It doesn't matter whether they're being sold, or used. The bottom line, drugs not only arrest the development of generations, but also creates aggression in behavior. That's a problem. Opposed to contributing to the problem, I choose to be a part of the solution."

"In what way?" she urged him on.

"For one, curb the flow of drugs coming into the community."

"But that's an unrealistic goal for anyone. For you, it's an impossibility." she said.

"Walt Disney once said, 'The only way to achieve the impossible is to believe it is possible.' If you recall our deal was struck on a condition? I was paying for information."

"I remember. You wanted to know who I copped from."

"Exactly."

"If you're telling the truth you must be very serious about what you're doing. Ten grand is a lot of money to pay on the premise that I may, or may not have given you the correct information." She paused with hopes that he would expand on the intricacies of his motive, but he never did. "My guess is, you either know something about me that I'm not aware of, or you're a fool?" She paused once more with hopes of a reaction.

But once again, he left her standing in the dark. "Are there many people like you? People who do what you do?" she reluctantly changed her line of questioning with hope that his answer would shed some light on her previous question.

"I'm sure people like me are many, oppose to being few. As corny as it may sound, our youth need real men and women to look up to. At the moment, all they have are thugs and gangsters."

"Interesting concept."

"What I really find interesting is, drug-dealers and gangsters are the most violent people in our communities. Not to mention the most sought after by our young women. For some reason, they find a thug's life more attractive than your average nine-to-fiver."

Robin couldn't help noticing the way he was looking at her. "Why are you looking at me like that?" she asked with a guilty conscience.

"And how am I looking at you?"

"As if I'm one of those women who run around chasing hustlers." He smiled. "Although I have to admit," she continue, "Most drug-dealers do have a certain quality that a lot of females find attractive. I guess it's the danger factor?"

"Present company included?" he asked.

"Present company excluded. I personally would never have anything to do with a hustler. That you can be sure of."

"Personally, I think most women find the money attractive, not the person making it."

"I guess that's what happens when you have no aspirations of your own. When your only dream in life is to 'bag' a hustler, athlete, or recording artist I guess they're looking for someone who can improve the quality of their life - financially, professionally, or just socially."

"I couldn't agree with you more."

She smiled. It was kind of nice sitting with the opposite sex having a serious, intelligent conversation. Normally, a man could care less about what a female thought. Maybe Tyrone was right about him being different? she decided. "Do you perceive me as being that type of female?" she surprisingly found herself asking. As if his perception of her mattered.

The sudden change in his expression led her to believe, he too was surprised at her unexpected question. "That's not a fair question because I don't know you well enough to make that kind of assumption. But... if I had to guess, I'd say, no. You strike me as the type of woman who likes having your own, and being on your own."

She smiled again, this time with relief. "Tell me about yourself?" she asked, getting comfortable.

He leaned back in the recliner and propped his feet up. "I'd much rather hear about you. Besides, I'm not that interesting."

"That's a matter of opinion. I personally find you very interesting. You're not like anyone I've ever met. Most guys would have been all over me by now. I haven't once seen your eyes roaming to my breasts, or ass. You're not gay, are you?" she giggled lightly while anxiously awaiting his answer.

"Hack no!" he quickly replied. She giggled again at the way he replied. The effects of the drink and weed had her feeling a little giddy.

Once she had composed herself. She tried to get serious. "Why did you put your life on the line for me?" she asked with a straight face.

"You needed help."

84

"Yeah but... you didn't even know me. I don't know anyone who would have done that. What you did was nothing short of courageous, or stupid. Still, if I haven't already thanked you, I'm thanking you now."

"Just goes to show you, chivalry isn't dead," he replied with a soft smile.

She returned his smile. "My hero," she whispered. 'SHIT!' she silently thought. 'Did I just say that out loud? Fuck! He must think I'm whack as hell?' She giggled. It was an uncomfortable giggle. She wanted to say something witty. Anything to clean up that "My hero" shit that accidentally escaped her lips but found herself at a loss for words.

It was SunRise who finally broke the silence, "It's getting late," he said, "Come on... I'll show you to your room."

Robin reached for her boots before standing to follow SunRise in back.

That night, Robin went through SunRise's entire room trying to find something. Anything that would tell her something about the man-child who foolishly chose to be her protector. But there was nothing to be found. No photos, no identification of any sort. Not even a piece of mail. It was as if he had checked her into a hotel room because there were no personal effects of any kind.

As she laid awake staring into the darkness she tried to figure out his motives for become her protector. And what role, if any, did Tyrone Sharp play in all this? She desperately wanted to believe the reason he gave, but her suspicious nature would not allow her to accept such an unlikely story from someone she knew absolutely nothing about. No one, she concluded, could be that stupid to put their life on the line for a complete stranger. So why did he do it? She continued asking herself until finally drifting off to sleep.

A group of young hustlers began to gravitate back in front of building four. They had not too long ago left the area once they heard Big Keys and his crew was coming through. They didn't know Big Keys personally. But throughout the years, have heard stories told.

Punchie angrily stepped from the shadow of the building yelling, "Y'all some bitch-ass-niggaz! Fuck you run for?"

"Big Keys came through. You ain't heard? Nigga ain't taking my shit," said one of the hustlers.

"Man you bitch-ass-muthafucka'! You got heat on your hip and as soon as one of these niggaz holla', stick-up-boyz', y'all jet. That nigga ain't even from around here. We should be stickin' his ass up, you feel me?" said Punchie.

"Naw, fuck that. I left 'cause I had to take a shit. I don't know what that nigga talking about."

"That's bull-shit, Wreak. You the nigga that hollered Keys was coming through. Shit, you jetted before me, yo'," complained a huge young teen called, Big.

"Both of you niggaz' pussies," said Punchie. She looked at Big and said, "And you! Nigga we should call you big-for-nothing, 'cause you worthless. I can't wait to see that nigga, Mike. Let 'em know what kind of bitches he got working on his team."

"Mike! Nigga I don't work for no muthafuckin' Mike," said Wreak.

"Yeah," Big was quick to set Punchie straight. "Mike ain't got no dope up in the C.C.P. Spivey got this shit on lock, you heard. Every since 'Fly got pushed last year, them Jamaican boyz' done took over. Mike might have up the hill, but Spivey run this shit down here."

"You talking 'bout that nigga from North Third Street?" asked Punchie.

"Yeah. Why? You wanna a nigga to plug you in, yo?" asked Wreak.

Punchie looked at him as if he was crazy. "Yeah. Picture that. Um' out, son." Punchie left the two young hustlers and proceeded through the courtyard. Moving fast as if she had been in a hurry, she stepped in building three and came out the back.

As she moved through the court-yard between buildings three and two, she entered building two through the back and immediately emerged through the front. As she headed towards building one, she stopped in the middle of building two and one's court-yard and looked around.

"What's good, cuz'?" someone asked from behind. Punchie went for her gun even before turning around. "Slow down, yo.

It's me," said Asmar West.

"Damn, nigga! You 'bout to get got sneaking up on a 'G' like me." She looked around and asked, "Where the rest of them niggaz' at?"

"In the car. Come on." Asmar said while leading the way when a female caught his attention. "Hold up, yo'," he said while eyeing the young, bow-legged beauty. "Damn, yo'. You know her?" he quickly asked.

"That's one of the Matthew girls. Debrah's lil' sista'. That bitch might be fine, but trust me, son. You don't wanna fuck with that. Ol' girl got issues, yo'."

As the young beauty walked past, Asmar spoke. "How you doing sweetheart?"

She looked at him briefly and smiled, but did not stop.

"Yeah. She's feeling me; I can tell."

"Ol' girl sick, yo'. I told you, son. Keep thinking with that thing between your legs. Shit gone get you killed one day. You lucky I was here to save your ass, boy. You running 'round here like shit sweet. This the C.C.P., son. Niggaz' 'round here feast on their kills. You feel me?"

"I don't give a fuck. Bitch fine as hell. Just have to double up on the rubbers. See-what-um'-sayin'?"

Man, you crazy as hell. Where big Keys and 'em? We 'pose to be getting paper and you out here casing some contaminated bitch." Asmar laughed.

"Right behind you, lil' nigga." Punchie quickly turned and was startled when she saw Bomani and Ghost standing there. "Oh shit! Fuck y'all niggaz come from? Y'all niggaz gonna' get enough of sneaking up on a joker. Specially a nigga like me. I was about to bust-off on you niggaz, yah' heard?"

While the two men stared at the young thugged-out female, Asmar laughed, then introduced Punchie. "Yo, Fam'. This my cuz', Punchie. If she don't know who got it, it ain't out here.

You feel me?"

"Mannn! I know who the fuck big Keys is. I probably knew the nigga before you," she told Asmar.

"Whatever, Punchie. Just tell my people Bomani what you told me about them niggaz' from yardy', yo."

"Who the fuck is Damoni?" Punchie quickly asked. Ghost and Bomani couldn't help laughing.

"Bomani, nigga! Big Keys!"

"Oh. Yeah," Punchie began while looking at Bomani. "This nigga on North Third holding like Michael Henderson, yo."

"Holding what?" ask Ghost.

"Weed, coke and dope, yo'. Every since 'Fly got pushed, Mike ain't been able to hold it down like he use to."

"Who is this joker?" asked Ghost.

"His name Spivey, yo'. Nigga from Jamaica. These young niggaz' 'round here moving product for him."

"What type of nigga we talking about?" asked Bomani.

Is he gonna' be a problem? What kind of weight he got behind him and what's the best time to hit him up?"

"The nigga thorough, yo'. But anybody can be got, you feel me. As far as him being a problem? If you cool with going up against about twenty of his soldiers, than you don't have a problem. The nigga got that whole block up there lock down."

"What whole block?" asked Asmar.

"Between West Broadway and Temple Street on North Third. Them niggaz' up there rocking assault rifles, yo'. Damn near every house on that block work for that nigga. You got to hit him between 12:00 p.m. to 6:00 p.m. That's the only time the nigga sleeps. Drive down there right now. You'll see what um' talking about. The nigga live in a chipped up dark green house. You can't miss it. It's the smallest house on the block."

"How he look, yo'?" asked Bomani.

"Short, dark-skin cut-up nigga with thinning dreads. He a old-head like you." Punchie looked Bomani up and down then smiled. "'Bout your age, yo'"

"A'ight. We gonna' check him out. See if he's do-a-ble. If we decide to move on him, you and Asmar can share ten percent of the take off the top. You cool with that?"

"Ten percent! Fuck umma' do with ten percent? And you talkin' 'bout sharing it. Man that's only five percent? Fuck we gonna do with five percent?"

"If the nigga holding like you claim? You can do a lot with it," said Ghost.

Bomani looked at Asmar and asked, "You got a problem with your cut, too?"

"Hell no, nigga. It's all gravy baby."

"Man! Y'all niggaz' full of shit! Probably all talk away," Punchie said before leaving.

CHAPTER 7

Johnny had been on the phone all morning trying to track down his men, Smitty and Wells. It's been four days since he'd seen, or heard anything from them. Angry and frustrated, he left home early this morning and headed straight for the lounge. Unlike home, the lounge was the one place he knew he could be alone to think.

Inside the office, Johnny fixed himself a stiff drink and then took it straight to the neck in one gulp. After fixing himself another, he took the drink along with the entire bottle over to the sofa. "This is where it all happened," he mumbled while visualizing the woman who played him for a fool. The more he thought about it. The more infuriated he became. And not being able to find his men only added to his frustration.

He knew the chances of him ever recovering his product were doubtful and was beginning to realize it would probably be better to cut his losses and move on? Until he thought of his bartender, Rob. If anyone knew where Smitty and Wells were, that would be Rob.

After downing the last drop in his glass, he rushed over to his desk and was about to make a call when all of a sudden, the phone began to ring. Anxious for some answer, he quickly snatched up the receiver and was surprised when the very same person he had intended to call, was on the other end of the line. Before he had a chance to ask about Smitty and Wells.

Rob told him he had just seen something on the news he could not discuss over the phone.

"Stay put!" Johnny shouted into the receiver, "I'll be right over."

Rob was standing at the curb, directly in front of his rooming house building when Johnny pulled up. "You ain't gonna' believe this shit, Johnny," Rob shouted excitedly while getting into Johnny's car.

After pulling off, Johnny quickly asked, "What was so important that couldn't be discussed over the phone?"

The slim, middle-aged man quickly began. "You remember that antique dealer I told you about a few days ago?"

"Yeah...what about him?"

"He's dead!"

"Dead! Nigga, you sure?"

"Positive. They found him yesterday morning in some flea-bag motel," the bartender said with certainty. Johnny paused in deep thought before asking what happened. "I don't really know, Johnny man. They said some maid found him butt-naked.

Lying tied to the bed. Whoever killed him didn't leave any traces behind."

"So the police don't know who's responsible?"

"Not that I know of. I think they said something about him being a patron of prostitutes. One detective told some news-people that the victim probably retained the services of the wrong working-girl."

"How was he killed?"

"Asphyxiation," said the bartender. "Those white-boys love that kind of shit. You read about it in the newspaper all the time. Some crazy ass white-boy done strangled his wife to death while hitting the booty. The shit is crazy, man. Some people will do anything for a nut."

After learning how the old man had died, Johnny paid very little attention to anything else Rob had to say. "Do you know if they found any I.D. among his things?"

"They must have because they definitely identified him. They said his name, and mentioned the fact that he was the owner of a small shop on Atlantic Avenue here in Atlantic City. That's how I knew who they were talking about." He paused before asking, "Do you think that girl had something to do with his death?"

"I don't know, Rob. I appreciate the heads-up. I'll see you later on at the lounge," Johnny said just before pulling up in front of the building where the bartender rented his room.

"Yeah. Later on, man."

Johnny headed straight back to the club. As soon as he sat at his desk It occurred to him he had completely forgotten to ask Rob about Smitty and Wells. Considering the news he had just received from Rob. He was more desperate now than ever to find the two men. As much as he hated to admit, it was becoming painfully apparent that Smitty and Wells were more than likely the ones responsible for the death of the old man which made him worry even more because he knew if they were caught, they wouldn't hesitate to implicate him.

Johnny was just about to roll a spliff to calm his nerves when the phone began to ring. It was his long-time girlfriend, Linda. She had called to inform him that BigButt Lee stopped by the house claiming she had something important to tell him.

Because Linda didn't believe a word of BigButt's story. Johnny had a very hard time trying to convince her he was not cheating. After arguing with her over the phone for the next twenty minutes he finally got in his car and headed for the Boulevard in search of BigButt Lee who was not too hard to find in her signature dirty, white pants.

BigButt was Standing in front of a bar soliciting winos when Johnny beeped his horn to get her attention. As soon as she saw his car, she immediately rushed over.

Johnny quickly rolled down the window. When she stuck her face into the car, he angrily yelled, "Get in, bitch!"

Still grinning, she happily hopped into the car, and was about to speak when he yelled, "Shut the fuck up, hooker!" while pulling off into traffic. "First of all," he continued, "what the fuck you doing rolling up at my crib like you know a nigga?"

"I heard you were looking for those two fools that work for you?"

"Yeah? And?"

"I seen 'em Tuesday nigh'. They bust in on me while I was with this trick," she said with a thick southern slur that was so bad, it was a little hard understanding her.

"Wait a minute!" he interrupted. "What did you say?"

Irritated, she smacked her huge, chapped lips and rolled her eyes while raising her voice a couple of octaves. "I said... I seen them the other nigh'. They made me leave...."

"No, bitch! Before that!"

"They bust in on me while I was with the trick?" she asked, unsure if he was referring to that particular part of her statement.

The rate of Johnny's heart-beat sped up. "Where?" Even though BigButt had just confirmed his worse fears, he had to be one-hundred percent sure.

"Same place all the girls take 'em. The Dunderbird Motel."

"You mean, Thunderbird?"

"Yeah. That's what I said. The one righ' 'cross the bridge. Them dirty bastards kicked me out the room and told me to walk back. I ran 'round back and heard everything. They beat that poor man something terrible. I know where they at righ' now," she added with the same wide grin.

Johnny cut an eye at her. "She don't know?" he thought to himself. He knew he had to do some fast thinking before it was too late. Once she found out the trick she took to that motel was dead. She would put two and two together and run straight to the cops to spill her guts. Smitty and Wells had managed to get him caught up in a nightmare that kept getting worse with each passing moment. He had sent the two men on a simple mission that turned into a homicide which meant, he too could be charged with the actual murder. The police would never believe he had no fore-knowledge of Smitty and Well's intentions. Desperate, Johnny took BigButt back to the club.

Something told him she was holding out. He had to squeeze the right information out of her. To do that, he knew he had to play his cards right. Otherwise, she would write her own songs and have him dance to the tune of it.

Once they arrived at the club, Johnny immediately locked the door behind them.

"You want something to drink?" he asked, walking behind the bar to fix himself a stiff drink.

BigButt sat on a stool at the bar, grinning. "Hell yeah, nigga! And a couple of them reefers you got, too!" Johnny sit a glass of gin and tonic in front of her, and then stepped into his office. Moments later he returned with a dime bag from his personal stash. BigButt smile when he tossed the small bag of weed on top of the bar-counter in front of her. "How the hell um' 'pose to roll this shit!" she yelled while snatching it off of the counter.

Johnny frowned then yelled back at her, "Hold your voice down, bitch! We ain't on the subway!" BigButt busted out laughing and fell off the stool. Johnny stared at her as if she had lost her mind while thinking, "it wasn't that funny". Still on the floor, BigButt continued to laugh and carry on as if she had a front-row seat at a 'Richard Prior' Concert. She never noticed when Johnny walked off into his office leaving her sitting on the floor, still laughing. When he returned with the rolling-paper BigButt was sitting on the stool just catching her breath. He sat the paper in front of her. Then sat on a stool next to her and watched as she quickly snatched up the small pack of cigarette-paper and began rolling spliffs. Once she had the first one rolled. She stuck the entire thing into her mouth and twirled it around, licking it thoroughly. With the spliff completely soaked with her saliva. She offered it to him. He frowned at the thought of placing the spit-soaked thing into his mouth. "That's okay... um' good," he told her.

She shrugged before placing it between her own lips and lighting it. "So what did you hear after they kicked you out of the room?" he casually asked.

While puffing on the spliff, she said, "I heard them fools beating on that man. It was terrible!"

"Cut the shit, bitch and give it to me straight!" he warned.

"Whaz' in it for me?" she asked, trying her best to look sexy while pulling on the spliff.

"Tell me everything you know, and I'll give you a fifty spot. Fair?"

She thought about it and then pointed at his crotch. "I want some of that, too?"

Johnny frowned. "Bitch!" he shouted, "I'd rather fuck a water buffalo and burn in hell!"

"Then let me give you some of this head. I know you done heard how good I am?"

Johnny stood and walked behind the bar to fix himself another drink. After downing two double shots of Rum. He yelled, "Look, bitch! You want the fifty, or what."

BigButt face contorted into an ugly frown before angrily snatching up her bag of weed and standing. "Hell no, nigga!

Let me the fuck up outta' here!" She rushed over to the door and began trying to open it.

Johnny rushed from behind the bar to stop her. "Calm down, Lee," he pleaded, gently grabbing her by the arm in an attempt to lead her back to her stool.

But she would not be smooth over so easily. Half way back to her stool, she stopped and slapped both hands on her massive hips. Her eyes glared wide, watery with hurt. "Well, nigga?" she angrily asked with booming bass in her voice.

Johnny knew she wasn't bluffing about leaving. Not after the scene she had just displayed. He looked at his watch. It was almost 2:30 p.m., and getting later. He couldn't afford to allow her to leave. Not with the information she had. "A'ight, bitch. You got that. Now give me the 411?"

"Not 'til I get mine!" she yelled back with a grin.

He gritted his teeth in anger. "Well come the fuck on, stupid! Let's get this shit over before I change my mind!"

"Righ' here?" she asked with growing excitement gleaming in her eyes."

"Just take your big ass in my office. I'll be there in a few."

Overwhelmed with joy she grabbed her drink off of the counter and made a pathetic attempt to walk sexy, switching her gigantic behind while heading for the office.

Once Johnny heard the office door close behind her, he angrily slammed his fist down on the bar counter while mumbling, "I must be out of my damn mind agreeing to this shit." Sitting three triple-shot glasses on the counter in front of him he began looking for the strongest whiskey he could find. Once he found what he was looking for. He filled each of the shot-glasses to the rim and gulped them down one by one without so much as a chaser. As he sat behind the bar, waiting for the alcohol to kick in. He thought about what she had told him and began to feel depressed. But once the effects of the liquor kicked in, he felt a little better. Initially, he had started drinking around 9:30 this morning without so much as a bite to eat. By the time he stepped into his office, he was drunk as hell and feeling no pain.

Johnny spotted BigButt lying on the sofa, butt-naked. Under normal circumstances, he might have found the sight of her repulsive. Now, he was seeing her in a much different light. A light he had never seen her in before. As he slowly approached her with one hand gripping his crotch to subdue his growing excitement, he stood over her and began to undo the buckle of his belt. BigButt purred with a seductive smile and whispered, "That's righ', daddy. Let me see what you got."

The moment Johnny pulled down his pants. She dove off of the sofa and landed on her knees, directly between his legs. With both hands, she made a desperate attempt to rip away his jock which was the one thing that stood between her huge, chapped lips and Johnny's man-hood.

"Wait a minute, bitch!" he cautioned while pushing her hands away. Even though he had not intended to completely undress, he found himself eagerly striping until he too was completely nude.

Once she saw the thirteen inch 'gun' she had heard so much about. She stared at it before shouting "Wow!" then licked her lips to lubricate them before having her way with him.

Johnny was sitting on the sofa watching with a smile as she tried to swallow every inch of the massive, deformed member.

Bobbing her head up and down, she made slurping sounds with her mouth that excited Johnny so much, he found himself grinding his hips into her eager face. Damn she good," he silently thought. He wasn't sure if it was the liquor he consumed, or just her technique. But at that very moment, she was probably the best 'headhunter' he had ever had.

It was almost 5:00 p.m. when Johnny finally woke from his drunken slumber. It took a few seconds before Johnny realized he was lying on the sofa butt-ass-naked. But when he saw whose arms he was cuddled up in. He immediately jumped to his feet, yelling, "Bitch! Get the fuck off of me!" sending BigButt flying to the floor, head first.

"What's wrong with you?" she asked, rubbing her head while slowly rising to her feet.

Johnny raced to his clothes, which had been scattered all over the floor. He wasn't quite sure what had happened between the two of them, nor did he care. As long as no one found out about what took place, he was good. Still, he tried to recall what actually happen between them. The last thing he remembered was her smiling up at him afterwards. He remembered frowning at the fluids that ran from the corner of her mouth.

He also remembered her trying to kiss him. He couldn't actually remember whether or not she had succeeded? At the moment, his main concern was finding out everything she knew about Smitty and Wells' connection with the old man's death, then getting her out of his club as quickly as possible. "Okay, Lee, you got yours. Now give me mine," he demanded while slipping on his shoes.

Still rubbing her head, she replied, "Um' not sure if I wanna tell you shit. Not after the way you just treated me?"

He looked at her as she stood in the middle of the room, butt-naked with her bottom lip poked out. "Just get dressed, bitch! Rob will be here in a few. I ain't got all day to be fooling around with you," he angrily said before rushing off into the bathroom.

"Gimme' my money!" he heard her shout.

About five minutes later when he came out of the bathroom. She was fully dressed and standing by his desk. "Bitch! If anything's missing from my desk, umma' fuck you up!"

"Nigga! Ain't nobody been in your stupid-ass desk. Gimme' my damn money so I can get the hell outta' here!" she yelled with an extended open palm.

"Bitch! You ain't going nowhere. Not until you tell me where the fuck I can find Smitty and Wells?" Sensing his anger, she backed away just in case she had to make a run for it.

"You betta' be nice to me, or umma' tell Linda I got my swerve on with you," she warned.

He peeped at his watch then stared at her without saying a word. It was at that moment when she realized, his patience were running thin. The last thing she wanted to do was press her luck. "They was asking the trick all kinda' question about some bitch," she finally said.

"Yeah... and what did the trick tell 'em?"

"He told them stupid ass fools her name was, Robin Hood!" she said before busting out laughing.

"Did they believe him?" he quickly asked while bogusly laughing along with her.

"Hell yeah them stupid ass fools bo'lieved him! They bo'lieved everything he tol' them," she said with a roar of laughter. Catching her breath momentarily to add, "They gotta' be the dumbest niggaz' in the world. Where the hell you find them stupid-ass-niggaz? They dumb as hell," she continued while laughing some more. After she had calmed down she told Johnny that the trick had sent Smitty and Wells on a wild-goose-chase to New York City. "What happened next?"

"Shit, nigga, it started getting cold! I ain't have time to stand 'round listen to those two fools all nigh'. I had to hitch ma' black ass back 'cross the bridge... shit."

Once Johnny was certain she had told him everything she knew. He threw her out of his office, then out of the club.

CHAPTER 8

Johnny was on his way out of the lounge when Rob came in to set up for the night. "If I'm not back by eight," Johnny told him, "open the lounge without me."

"No problem, boss. Shouldn't I know where you're going? Just in case someone ask?"

"I won't be long, Rob," Johnny told him without going into details. As a result of what he had learned from BigButt Lee, he wrote his stolen property off as a loss. As for Smitty and Wells? He considered them fired the moment he learned they disobeyed his orders and took matters into their own hands. His only regret was allowing his pride to get in the way by not leaving well-enough alone. At least, he thought, the old man would still be alive.

Racing against time, Johnny jumped in his car and left the city. At the moment, his biggest fear was BigButt Lee. Not because she was the only person who could link Smitty and Wells to the murder of the old man. The way he saw it, the police would be more incline to implicate her. After all, it was she who brought the old man to that motel in the first place. Besides, the police had already concluded a prostitute was responsible for the murder. In a sense, she would be hanging herself. His main fear was word getting back to his girlfriend, Linda. The last thing in the world he wanted to deal with right now was rumors of his intimate encounter with BigButt Lee.

The woman couldn't hold water, more or less a secret. Once word got out about the two of them Johnny knew Linda would surely leave him. This was something he could not allow to happen.

Not because he loved her, but because everything he owned was in her name. Losing Linda meant losing everything he had worked so hard for. And he wasn't about to let that happen. Not if he could help it.

❖ ❖ ❖

It was late in the evening when SunRise returned to the apartment. Robin was reading one of his books while lounging on the sofa wearing his black, cotton robe. And from the looks of it, it appeared to be all she was wearing. As he approached carrying the clothes he promised to have dry-cleaned for her.

She looked up at him and smiled. "You have a nice smile?" he said, placing the dry-cleaning over the arm of one of the recliners. He then sat on the sofa next to her bare feet.

"Thank you," she said, boldly placing her feet in his lap. The robe she was wearing slid all the way up her thigh, confirming his suspicion. He gently grabbed her small, pedicure feet with both hands and began skillfully massaging them. Feeling a little self-conscious, she forced a weak smile.

"Have you been good while I was gone?" he finally spoke.

"Of course," she laughed a little before suddenly realizing there was something on his mind. "What's wrong?"

"When are you going to tell me about the men who tried to abduct you?"

Her pleasant smile quickly changed to a frown of annoyance. "What makes you think there's something to tell? I don't know who those men were anymore than you do."

It was obvious she wasn't ready to trust him. So instead of pressing the issue, he removed her feet from his lap and stood. "I had your entire outfit cleaned."

"So that's why I couldn't find my clothes. I was beginning to think you hid them so I wouldn't leave? You've been gone all day?"

"Now why would I do that?" He suddenly produced her hand-bag from under his coat and tossed it into her lap.

"My bag!" She blurted while sitting up straight to thoroughly go through it. As far as she could tell, everything was still there, including the cocaine.

"Your car had been pretty badly shot up. I had a friend of mine take a look at it. He owns a body-shop and has assured me it'll look as good as new in a week or so."

"What about the deal we had?"

"What about it?"

"Is it still on?"

"That depends?"

"On what?"

"On you. You have to trust me," he said before walking off into the bedroom. She knew he was upset with her and with good reason, too. After all, he not only put his life on the line for her. He had been straight-up with her from the very beginning. Yet, she just couldn't bring herself to open up.

SunRise emerged from the bathroom wearing a large, white towel wrapped around his waist. When he saw her in the kitchen cooking, he sat quietly at the dinning-room table and watched.

"Hopefully your car will be ready by Monday. Until then, you can stay here under the protective wing of my FOLD, or leave whenever you like. I will also honor our deal under the same terms." He stood to leave when she called out to him.

"If it's all right with you," she slowly began. "I'd like to stay here... with you." She was hoping he'd say something. That way, she would at least know how he really felt. Instead, he said nothing. "Also... about the other night," she continued, pausing briefly to clear her throat. "Can I trust you to keep what I'm about to tell you between the two of us?"

He thought about it. He didn't want to commit himself to a promise he was unsure he'd be able to keep. "Tell you what," he said. "Why don't we discuss it over dinner? No more secrets, okay?"

She smiled, "No more secrets."

He walked up to her and leaned over the stove. "Smells good?"

103

"Thank you," she said with a smile. "It's an Italian surprise."

"I've never really been big on surprises. But from the smell of it, I don't think I'll be disappointed," he said before walking off into the back room.

All through dinner Robin managed to avoid discussing the incident. Instead, she chose to pursue an area that had been on her mind the moment she walked into his apartment. Once she learned he was not involved with anyone, she quickly changed the subject.

After dinner, SunRise helped her clear the table. Once they had all the dishes in the washer. He sat her down in the living-room and began casually questioning her about the men who tried to abduct her.

Robin began by explaining how the owner of a small lounge in Atlantic City tried to play her as, easy. "I guess I showed him who was being played," she said, making light of the situation. But SunRise was not amused, or impressed.

"While you were robbing this guy did you ever consider the consequences? I mean... did it ever occur to you that this guy just might come after you?"

"Hell no! This guy was a joke who thought between his legs.

He was so concern with getting between mine, he didn't have time to get my name. He was a pig that got just what the hell his hand called for."

"So he never found anything out about you?"

"Not even my name."

"So how did his men track you all the way to Brooklyn?"

Because it was a question Robin was unable to answer, she looked away, but not before he noticed the change in her previous smug expression to that of concern. He knew there was something she was not telling him. "Is there something you forgot to mention?"

In another attempt to avoid eye contact, she stood and turned her back to him. "Talk to me, Robin. You should know by now I'm here to help you."

"I do trust you," she softly said. "I just don't understand why you feel the need to go out of your way for me? Especially when you don't know anything about me?"

"I knew you were someone who needs my help. And yes, I don't know anything about you. But the little time we've spent together gave me an opportunity to understand you." She sat next to him and buried her head in the comforts of his chest.

He was nurturing, and emotionally supportive. "Would you like to go out?" he asked. "I know a nice little jazz club I think you'll enjoy."

She looked at him and smiled nervously. "Can we just stay here and talk?"

"About what?"

"Something I didn't mention before.

"And what's that?"

"I told you about my reasons for going to see my friend, Rossi. But I never told you why? Or what I do for a living?"

She paused with hopes that he would say something. Instead, he just sat there waiting for her to continue. "Never mind," she finally said with an awkward laugh. Let's just talk about something else. I enjoy conversing with you. You're not like anyone I've ever met. Most guys would probably take advantage of my situation. You didn't. As a matter of fact, you have been nothing but protective and nurturing. Your friend, Tyrone is lucky to have a friend like you."

"Personally I think you were lucky to have a friend like Tyrone."

She smiled bashfully. "Actually, I feel a lil' guilty for assuming he was just another typical black man doing nothing with his life."

"Why would you think that?" he asked.

"A recent observation. Apparently he likes to spend a lot of time at that god-forsaken bar, J's Corner? The only number he ever gave me to contact him, turned out to be the number of that bar. When I called yesterday morning I didn't really expect to find him there. I was expecting someone to tell me where I might be able to find him or, at the very least let him know I called. But he was there. It just made me wonder what kind of person spends all morning hanging out in a bar. If he's not working, he should at least be trying to formulate a plan to do something about his current situation."

"I'm sure he had his reasons for being there so early in the morning. As far as whether or not he has employment? I believe he's self-employed. As far as his line of work? That's something you would have to discuss with him."

"Then I guess he's the exception."

"Every rule has one. But I do see your point. Too many of us waste valuable time standing around doing nothing about our current situation. And until bruthaz' and sistaz' want something better out of life; something significant to pass on to their seeds. There can be no real change. No real growth until, not just their basic perception of reality is transformed. But their vision of self is changed into something positive. Because without a positive frame of reference. Their perceptions of what is, and not what can be, become the habitual frame of reference within which they act and react. When you have something to believe in your efforts seem significant and worthwhile. Your devotion to this life task rises you above the pettiness that often devour our otherwise meaningful lives.

When you have nothing to believe in, much like the individuals you witnessed yesterday at the bar, you're left to the pursuit of sensations; looking for new ways to get off; new ways to break the monotony and boredom of an otherwise stagnant life. Because without meaning, what else is there? Except maybe a cheap thrill in a desperate attempt to escape the moment. We have to find a cause to believe in, or spend the rest of our lives finding ways to escape the fact that we are failures."

When Robin yawned, he thought he was boring her.

"Well... I'm very happy to have met someone who is an active participant in the productive activities of constructive work. Our youth, and good available women are in desperate need of responsible men like you." SunRise looked at his watch. It was a quarter to eight. When she yawned again, he knew she was tired. But it wasn't until she stood and stretched before he suggested she get some rest.

As SunRise lay in bed just about to drift off to sleep, he thought he was dreaming when she appeared in his doorway.

Without saying a word, he watched as she stepped into the room and slowly approached his bedside. When he sat up, she slowly removed the white Tee she had been wearing. As he lay there, transfixed on her beauty, she held out her hand, SunRise took it and guided her into his bed.

Ninety minutes after Johnny left the lounge, he returned carrying two large suitcases. When Rob asked him what was going on? He zoomed straight to his office without saying a word, slamming the door shut behind him. Rob checked to see what time it was. He had a whole hour before opening. With everything in order and nothing to do until then, he decided to try and score a few points with the boss.

Once he thought Johnny had enough time to cool off. He casually knocked on the office door. "Yeah?" Johnny yelled.

Because Rob was unable to discern whether, or not Johnny was still upset, he quickly spoke up. "It's me, Johnny. Can I come in?" When Johnny told him the door was unlocked. Rob took that as a, yes. Johnny was sitting on the sofa with a drink in his hand. A half filled bottle of imported Tanqueray sat on the wooden table in from of him. "Yeah, Johnny man. I heard what that lying tramp said about you. If I were you, I'd put my foot in her ass," Rob encouraged. Unresponsive, Johnny just sat there nursing the half filled glass. "But I know that's not your style," Rob continued. "For the right price I know a couple of girls who would love to straighten that dirty bitch out for you. Know what I mean?" he smiled while joining Johnny on the sofa.

Johnny downed the last of his drink and sat the empty glass next to the bottle, then stood. "You know something, Rob?" he spoke with a faint smile. "I have something in the works for Lee as we speak." The faint smile slowly turned into an angry grin. "Coming between, Linda and me was a big mistake. Umma' see why I can't come between her and that welfare check she gets every month."

"That's cold, Johnny man. That money is for her kids?"

"Yeah... but you and I both know that hooker don't use the money to take care of those kids. Hell... she ain't even home most of the time!"

"Well..." Rob thought while standing. "... I don't know what you have planned, but I'd sure hate to be in her shoes right about now?"

"She did it to herself, Rob. I just don't know why Linda, the mother of my two kids, took that bitch's word over mine?"

"I wouldn't worry about it too much," said Rob. "Linda and my sista' are best friends. I'll get my sista' to talk to her for you. She'll come around. Just give her a lil' time."

Johnny smiled. "Thanks, Rob." He quickly glanced at his watch and changed the subject. "Smitty and Well are done working for me. I had to hire three other niggaz'. They should be here any minute now. It's Saturday night. You know how these niggaz' like to get?"

"Yeah, drunk as hell. Well... I better get back out front so I can let them in."

"Good idea," Johnny agreed.

On Rob's way out of the office, he stopped short of reaching the door and asked, "Do I know any of 'em?"

"I hope not. When they show, send 'em straight to my office."

While Rob was behind the bar tending to his duties. Someone began banging at the entrance door. Upon opening it, he saw three, big, greasy hicks standing before him. He wasn't quite sure what they wanted until the three men began explained why they were there. It was then when

108

Rob realized they were the three Johnny spoke of just moments ago. Once Rob showed them to the office, he immediately excused himself.

The three men were all from a small, predominantly black town called Port Norus, also known as 'The Shell-Pile'. About thirty miles north of Atlantic City, Port Norus was known for its alcoholic men and feisty women whose weapon of choice was said to be a straight-razor. Those living in neighboring towns considered most of the residents of Port Norus, slow witted and country-as-hell. Which was one of the reasons Johnny hired the three men. The other reason was, if the rumors he heard told about them were true? He knew they would work for virtually nothing. But to get them to agree to come, Johnny told them they were going to be his new bouncers; when in fact, he had something else in mind.

"So when the lounge opens, just hang around and try to look tough. If you want something to drink just ask Rob, the guy who let you in. All drinks are on me." Johnny studied the three men closely before adding, "I don't want you niggaz' getting drunk, you hear?"

Wearing a wide grin, all three men nodded. "What about that girl you 'pose to hook us up wit'?" one of the men asked.

Johnny looked at the man with a sense of confidence and said, "I got everything covered. Just don't forget to take her around back, in the alley," he reminded them. The three men looked at one another somewhat confused. Johnny noted their reaction and silently thought, "Maybe they weren't that stupid after all?"

"When you said, out back, you mean outside?" another one asked.

"Hell yeah! You didn't think I was gonna' let y'all bang that bitch up in my lounge, did you?"

The three men looked at one another dumbfound. "But it's cold outside?" the third man protested.

"Yeah... but when you see this bitch? She's got a backyard everybody wants to play in!" Johnny used both hands to describe the size of her derriere. Beaming with anticipation, the three men jumped up and down in their seats like children, while nodding to one another in agreement.

Johnny smiled. He couldn't have been more pleased with himself for conceiving what he considered, a clever plan. He tossed the men a ten dollar bag of Marijuana and warned them to only smoke it outside the lounge.

All three men stood at the same time and all but ran out of the office. Ranging in ages from thirty nine, to forty five, the youngest of the three lived with his girlfriend who was a welfare recipient with seven small mouths to feed. All of which had different fathers. None of which were his.

The other two still lived at home with their aging parents not because they felt a sense of responsibility to take care of them, but because they weren't responsible enough to live out on their own.

Once the three men were out of the lounge, Johnny joined Rob out front. "Everything alright, boss?"

"It will be if everything goes according to plan," Johnny replied.

"Where the hell you find those fools?" Rob tried to make conversation. When Johnny didn't answer, he continued. "Mannn', those fools can't be from around here?"

"What? Oh... no... no.... They're from Port Norus."

"PORT NORUS!" Rob yelled. "Damn, Johnny man. I didn't know you knew anyone from, Port Norus?"

"I got plans for those fools. Check it out, as soon as they get back. Start pumping drinks into them. Just don't give 'em the real shit. Water the shit down. I ain't got nothing to give away."

"Sounds like you've got a serious plan cooking? What's up?"

Johnny smiled to himself. "Like I said Rob, if everything goes according to plan? You'll be the first to see it unfold," Rob was about to speak when someone began banging at the entrance. "Here they come now." The moment he slid off his stool to let them in. Johnny vanished into his office and slammed the door shut behind him. When Rob unlocked and opened the door.

The three men almost knocked him down rushing in. "You guys a'ight?" he apprehensively asked while locking the door behind them. The three men stumbled over to the bar and began banging on the counter in demand of something to drink. Rob rushed behind the counter asking, "What's wrong with you guys?"

"We want something to drink!" one of them demanded while the other two began snickering.

As Rob fixed their drinks, he noticed them whispering while glancing at him. Fearful of their so-called unpredictable mood-swing, Rob sat the drinks in front of them and eased off into Johnny's office. "Yo, Johnny man," he cried.

"What's wrong now!" Johnny irritably asked.

"Those fools are crazy, man! I ain't going back out there! Not while they're out there acting stupid!"

"What happen?"

"Mannn'! They keep ordering drinks and complaining about how weak the liquor is. I know they're use to drinking that moon-shine shit, but damn!" Rob lied.

"Yo', man! Tell those ass-holes I said to get the fuck in here. NOW!" A minute after Rob left, all three men stumbled into the office and stood directly in front of Johnny's desk.

"Yo', man! What the fuck I tell you!" They looked at one another confused. Each waiting for the other to respond, but neither one said anything. "Didn't I tell you not to start drinking until we open?"

"But that's a half hour from now?" one of the men complained.

"You have a problem with that?" Johnny leaned forward to make sure he heard their response. The three men looked at one another again before shaking their heads, no. "Get the fuck back out front and start looking tough; the lounge is about to open."

Shortly after the three-man left Johnny's office, Rob returned shouting, "Yo', Johnny! Those...."

"Damn, man!" Johnny interrupted him. "Haven't you ever heard of knocking?"

"Yeah, but Lee is right outside the lounge with those three fools you hired?"

Johnny's brows shot straight up. "Don't let that bitch get away, Rob! Get her in here and give her whatever she wants.

I want her drunk."

"What about those fools? You know they gonna' be all over her?"

"Them too! Give them the real shit. The strongest shit we have. I want everybody drunk. Now go before she gets away.

Johnny was about to make a phone-call when Rob hurried out of the office only to return seconds later. "Damn, Johnny man. They're gone?"

"Gone! What the...." Johnny slammed the receiver down and rushed out of his office with Rob trailing close behind. When they stepped outside and looked around. BigButt Lee, and the three men were nowhere in sight. "Check the alley," Johnny instructed. Without his coat, the bartender ran around the corner and returned two minutes later babbling about something Johnny wasn't quite able to understand. "Slow down, Rob! I can't understand a damn thing you saying!"

After collecting himself, the bartender continued. "Johnny man, you ain't gonna' believe this shit!"

"What? what? WHAT!!!"

"Mannn... those country ass fools are dogging the shit out of that bitch! I mean... she ain't got no shame, word-up!

She...."

Before Rob could finish filling Johnny in, Johnny ran into his office and called the police. Once he was done explaining what was going on behind his lounge. He immediately called Human Service and gave them BigButt's address. After he was through, he walked back out front and found Rob looking out the door.

Curious, he joined Rob and found a crowd of people standing around watching BigButt Lee being led to a squad-car in hand-cuffs by two policemen. The three hicks he had hired were sitting in the back seat of another squad-car. When they heard BigButt yell, "Let me the hell outta' this damn car!" both Johnny and Rob burst out laughing.

"Yo', Johnny? We open, or what?" Rob asked while holding several people off at the entrance.

"It's still early, but yeah. Let em' in." he replied before returning to his office.

CHAPTER 9

SunRise found himself lying in bed alone when he woke the next morning. His first thoughts were, Robin had decided to decline his offer and leave. He was disappointed, mostly because she never gave him the opportunity to talk her out of it.

As he laid there for a minute thinking about the moment they shared last night. He finally got out of bed. As soon as he stepped out of the room, the pleasant smell of fresh hot coffee brewing led him into the kitchen where he found Robin cooking breakfast. "Good morning," she greeted with a light kiss on the cheek. "I was just about to wake you with a hot cup. You do drink coffee, don't you?" she asked, surveying his hard nude body approvingly.

"I do. Thank you."

She smiled. "It's the least I can do for such a satisfying evening."

"I'm glad you've enjoyed yourself."

"She looked at him with bedroom eyes and replied, "You have no idea."

"I see you really enjoy cooking," he said, leaning over the stove.

"Let's just say I enjoy cooking for you. Now why don't you take a nice cold shower?" She looked at his crotch and added without taking her eyes from it, "That thing still looks hungry, and I don't have the strength to feed it. If you know what I mean?" she giggled, edging him out of the kitchen.

"Can I at least have a cup of coffee before you chase me away?"

She sighed irritably. Then poured him a half cup of black coffee and told him breakfast would be ready in ten minutes.

While SunRise took a shower, Robin was about to set the table when she heard a knock at the door. Before answering it, she quietly looked through the view-hole. There was a dark-skinned man standing on the other side of the door. Robin wasn't sure what to do. Instead of answering it, she ran into the bathroom. "SunRise!" she whispered. Some guy is at the door. Are you expecting anyone, or should I just ignore him?"

"Let him in," he said while stepping out of the shower dripping wet. Robin handed him a towel and rushed back to the door and opened it, but no one was there? She looked down the hall and saw the man standing at the elevator.

"You looking for SunRise?"

"Yeah!" he replied. "He up?" he yelled while approaching.

"Yeah... he's up." Robin held the door open as he stepped into the apartment. "I'll just hang your coat up for you. SunRise will be out in a moment." She took his coat and hung it into the closet. Before stepping back into the kitchen, she asked, "Would you like to join us for breakfast?"

"Sure. Why not," he said. As the two of them waited for SunRise, he made small talk while she set the table. "Why don't you come sit at the table. Everything is ready. SunRise should be out any minute now," she glanced towards the back rooms. "Let me see what's taking him so long," she added, leaving the dark skinned man sitting at the dinning-table only to return moments later with SunRise.

"What's up, Joey?" SunRise asked the unexpected guest.

"You already know, 'Rise. It's all good," Joey replied.

SunRise was wearing a silver-gray, single-breasted Stonegate suit and black mock-neck sweater. It was one of the many things Joey admired about the man-child who made the best formal wear look casual. "You wanted to see me?"

"I did. I just didn't think I'd see you so early?"

"What about?"

"That can wait," SunRise said before sitting. He looked at Robin, then at Joey, and asked, "Have you two been properly introduced?"

Robin and Joey looked at one another and smiled. "Not formally, no." Robin said with a pleasant smile.

"Then allow me. Joey, this is sista' Robin Hoods."

Still smiling, Robin nodded.

"Robin, this is Joey Lemon, a very good friend of mine."

"Pleased to meet you, sista' Robin."

"Likewise Joey and please... call me, Robin. I don't know where SunRise got that, sista' thing from?" Robin briefly glanced at SunRise with a playful frown before smiling at Joey again.

"Anyway..." SunRise continued. "... Robin is my house-guest. She'll be staying here for awhile." Joey nodded in acknowledgment.

As the two men talked while eating, Robin commented on how nice it was to still see such a genuine friendship, and mutual respect amongst black men nowadays. She then looked at Joey and asked, "How long have you two been friends?"

Joey looked at SunRise and smiled.

"A few years, or so. Actually, I never really thought about it. He's such a straight-up, brutha'. Sometime, I feel like I've known him all my life."

"Only a few years? Wow!"

"Yeah; one day he just showed up out of nowhere." Joey looked at SunRise and smiled. "To tell you the truth," he looked back at Robin and continued. "I can't even remember how we met."

He looked at SunRise and asked, "You remember, 'Rise? How we met, I mean?"

"BeeBop, remember?"

Joey smiled, "Oh yeah. That's right. We met through, 'Bop."

"Who's 'Bop?" Robin asked.

"One of the women who saved your life the other night," SunRise quickly said. "Don't worry. You'll get the chance to meet her."

Robin looked at Joey and asked, "So, Joey. You live around here, too?"

"The next building over," he nodded his head towards the window indicating the building that could be seen from the window across the court-yard.

"So what's your take on the drug game?" Robin asked. She had assumed because SunRise was some type of drug activist, Joey was, also.

Not quite understanding what she meant. Joey asked, "How do you mean?"

"Are you an activist?"

Joey smiled. "I don't know if I would call myself that. Am I against drugs coming into our community? Absolutely."

"Have you ever felt as if you were fighting a losing battle?"

"Every day I try to tell a lot of guys thinking about getting into the game, you can't win. Any fool can sell drugs. Not because he's capable, but because he's allowed to. The moment he becomes successful at it - the moment he starts making real money - the government steps in and take it all; blood, sweat and tears. Mean while he's destroyed countless lives, including his own, all in the name of his quest to 'come up'.

Unfortunately, those hustlers out there can't, or refuse to see the drug game for what it really is. There is no future in the drug game. Not with Mr. Gilmor out there watching. They're either too blinded by the need and greed to get paid, or they just don't care about filling grave-yards and state, or federal prisons."

"Who's Mr. Gilmor?" Robin asked.

Both Joey and SunRise laughed a little. "It's just a metaphor, sista'. Not an actual person."

The moment Robin thought Joey had finished making his point she got up from the table and began collecting the empty plates.

She liked him and thought he was right on point. For some reason, he reminded her of Rossi. Listening to him speak was like listening to one of Rossi's lectures. Not that she was comparing Joey's point with anything Rossi ever had to say. Rossi would never concern himself with the psychological slavery that had been imposed upon people of color in this country. Nor would he concern himself with the plight of their struggle to reverse the process. She couldn't wait to meet some more of SunRise's friends if for nothing else than to acquaint herself with their thought process.

As she continued clearing the table, SunRise signaled Joey to the living-room where Robin served them more coffee then returned to the kitchen to give the two men some privacy. After ten minutes, or so SunRise stepped in on her. "Joey has to make a quick run to Brooklyn for me. I asked him to drop you by your spot so you can pick up some fresh clothing, and whatever you think you may need."

"Why can't you take me?"

"I have a few things to take care of here. By the time you return, I should be ready."

"Ready for what?"

"South Jersey?"

"You're going to let me go with you, right?"

"I haven't decided yet. Now go get dressed, Joey is waiting."

"Okay," she replied while drying her hands. SunRise left her in the kitchen to continue his conversation with Joey in the living-room. Inconspicuously, Robin watched him with a sense of admiration and puzzlement. He seemed more concern about her problems than she actually was. Not that she mind. In fact, she was kind of hoping that it would last. On her way to the bedroom, she walked pass the two men and looked directly at SunRise and gave him a smiled. Not just any smile. It was much deeper than that; much more profound.

SunRise unconsciously gazed back at her. Joey looked at Robin, then at SunRise. He couldn't help noticing the obvious chemistry between the two. "If I didn't know any better, I'd say you two were in love?"

"I don't know about that because I've never been in love, but she does kind of grow on you, I'll give her that. Tye' introduced us."

"Tye? He ever tell you how he met her? The two of you make a nice couple." SunRise was silent. "Tell me something," Joey proceeded to pry. "Is she the same girl you were with at the Corner the other night?"

"Yeah. How you know about that?"

"'Bop mentioned it. I don't think they know you brought her home with you?"

"Someone's tried to abduct her. What else could I do?"

"What Tye say when you told him about it?"

"As far as I know, he has no idea."

"What she say about it?"

"She thinks Tyrone is the reason she's here. I told her Tyrone asked me to look out for her."

"He didn't?"

"He asked me to see to it that she gets home safely. Of course that was before I met her. Tyrone left the bar before she and I could close our deal. I'm not even sure if he knows what happen to her the other night? I'm pretty sure he's heard by now, though. Anyway, she was in trouble. There was no way I was going turn my back."

"So how you want me to handle this?" He changed the subject.

In fear of Robin walking in on them, SunRise glanced towards the back before speaking. "First... I want you to drop Robin off at her spot. Go in with her and make sure she's safe. If she wants you to wait until she's done. You wait."

"And if she doesn't want me to wait?"

"That just means she wants some privacy. Make the run at J's Corner. Tyrone will be there waiting for you, but don't leave Robin alone too long." He peeped at his watch. Then glanced towards the back again while wondering what was keeping her.

"Also, if you run into Sweet, or Bop, bring them back with you. If not. Leave word with Tye that I need them."

Joey was about to speak, but was interrupted by Robin's sudden reappearance. "Nice!" Joey complimented on her outfit. It was the very same outfit she had on the night SunRise met her.

"Thanks," she apathetically replied while dusting lent from the legs of her pants with the back of her fingers.

"You a'ight?" SunRise asked after noticing her behavior.

"A little nervous; other than that, I'm fine," she replied while sitting on his lap.

Joey immediately noticed their need to be alone and excused himself before stepping off into the bathroom.

As soon as SunRise heard the bath-room door close, he asked her was she all right again. She held her head down and slowly nodded, indicating she was fine.

SunRise gently lifted her chin forcing her to look at him. "What's wrong?" he asked her again.

She hesitated at first but then admitted that she was afraid. "I don't know what, or who's out there waiting for me," she said in a child-like manner. There was a certain kind of sincerity in her voice. He wasn't sure if she was exercising her charm to manipulate him, or actually being straight-up about her fears. He was sure of one thing, though. One cannot be a master thief without first mastering the art of sincerity.

With that in mind, he had to assume the former. "Joey is more than capable of looking after you. If I thought for one minute he wasn't. I would never trust him with your well being. You trust me?" he asked her.

"With my life," she whispered just as Joey reappeared.

"Good. I'll see you in a few hours, or so." He slid her from his lap as he stood.

While in route to New York Robin, tried to learn as much as she could about SunRise, but Joey wasn't giving up much. In fact, the only information she had managed to obtain. Had been what SunRise himself had already told her. Which made her wonder if Joey actually knew SunRise as well as he thought? When she inquired about SunRise's current activities? Joey told her that SunRise was basically an activist trying to help restore the black community to what it used to be.

"I don't understand?"

He glanced at her briefly before explaining. "SunRise is a nationalist. He's convinced that black people need not be poor, disadvantaged, or exploited. He thinks we have a problem going for self. He's right because unity has always been and we will always be the strength we need for political and economical power. Those who are all for themselves have been programmed to destroy themselves. Poor people in this country desperately need something, or someone to give them hope. Because without it, the subsequent result produces delinquent behavior, drug abuse, or spousal abuse, brought on by a state of worthlessness, child abuse, brought on by a constant state of frustration, cause and effect. The parents become depended upon some kind of substance, or just an abusive relationship. As a result, the children become uninspired and eventually drop-out of school. I mean, what's the point of going to school if you're just gonna' end up like your parents any. It's a vicious cycle that just keeps repeating itself. This is what they see all day every day; the result of a lost generation. The few from the 'hood who are fortunate enough to have certain advantages in life, couldn't begin to understand their brutha's pain and frustrations.

"What kind of advantages are you talking about?"

"The kind when your only worries are what university of higher learning will be better suited for your child's needs. Oppose to worrying about sending your child to school hungry every day or whether or not they'll make it to, or from school safely."

"I see your point, but how does that excuse the rowdy behavior day in and out where you live?" Robin asked.

"Misplaced aggression and frustration often shows up as anger. This is exactly what I've been talking about. It's the main reason why there's a lot of black on black crimes and domestic violence nowadays. We have to stop hurting one another, and start coming together as each other's keeper. If we don't, we'll end up killing ourselves. That is, if substance abuse, or the judicial system doesn't get us first?"

Robin glanced at him suspiciously. She was beginning to wonder if SunRise and Joey were some kind of black revolutionaries left over from the sixties. "That's all I need," she silently thought. "to get mixed up with someone the FBI could be watching?" She looked at him and asked, "Can I ask you a personal question?"

"Knock yourself out."

"How do you feel about law-enforcement?" she tried to get a better understanding of where his head was.

"The same way they feel, threatened." he replied. "That's not to say I don't respect authority. Realistically, I believe rules have to be enforced. Otherwise, people won't follow them. If people don't follow the rules, what's the use of having them? Back in the day, we had, 'officer friendly'. The cop who walked the beat making sure the neighborhood was safe. Those days are long gone. Law enforcement nowadays mean, an armed contingent of men patrolling the black communities to monitor the people - primarily the youth. The police force today consists of nothing more than the front line for the state. Their only objective is to tag-and-bag a black man. For obvious reasons, black men seem to be held as the crown-jewel for the criminal justice industry. Call it what you want. I call it genocide."

Robin frowned. "Genocide? What about the war on drugs? Has it ever occurred to you crime might be the reason they're there? It takes an army to deal with these young fools out here running around with guns bigger than the one the police carry."

Joey shot her a hard look. He was beginning to wonder who side was she on. "Look, sista'..."

"It's, Robin." she quickly corrected him.

"... Robin all that stuff about the "War on Drugs" was instituted only to legitimize the increase of police surveillance and to get the people to stand behind that decision. Not to mention intimidation. We all know that the target is the black youth - the purpose, imprisonment, or death. Have you ever wondered why black men and women constitute over forty percent of the jail and prison population in this country? The bureau of Statistics revealed that whites are arrested at a far greater rate than people of color. Yet, blacks make up the national average of forty percent of the prison population. Numbers never lie. Blacks make up 38.9 million people, as compared to the 197.3 million whites in the U.S. To me, these facts indicate one of two things? Either the entire African-American race in this country is inherently criminals, or there is something more evil at play? Any one of those wasted souls sitting in prison, given a second chance, could have easily been a contributor to society, probably humanity. But the system's solution to the problem, a problem created by the system, has always been build more prisons. Lock 'em up and throw away the key as if people of color are incapable of change."

"So you think a lot of blacks shouldn't be in jail just because they're black?" She quickly asked.

"I'm saying something is very wrong. Like I said before, numbers don't lie. Even if they did, jail shouldn't be the only alternative. Unfortunately, the system seems to think otherwise which tells me a lot about how they feel about us. That's why it's important to try getting through to our youth before it's too late."

She became very quiet, as if she was reflecting upon his last statement. He glanced at her and noticed she was in deep thought. He smiled; pleased to see if nothing else, at least she was thinking.

Joey parked on the block of Robin's rented apartment and was about to get out of the car when she stopped him.

"Don't you have something to do?" she asked.

"Yeah... but...."

"If you're not going to be long, I should be ready in no more than twenty minutes. Can you make it back by then?" Joey was about to speak when she cut him off. "I'll be fine. Go handle your business. The sooner you take care of whatever it is you have to do. The sooner we can head back."

"You sure you don't want me to walk you to the door? You know, make sure you get in safely?"

"I'm sure. Now go!" she insisted before getting out of the car. Joey waited until she was safely in the house before pulling off.

Joey Lemon was an easy going nineteen year old student at a local community college. Unlike SunRise, he grew up in the C.C.P. and since he could remember, it has always been a dangerous place, even for its residence. Although he had to admit, it has never been as bad as it was nowadays. He could remember when old-heads use to talk about, 'back in the day' when disputes were settled with the fist. At the very least, you got to walk away to fight another day. Now, you should be so lucky. Stick-up kids with reps were cautious of getting stuck-up, or worse. Joey had a severe dislike for drug dealers mainly because of his sister, Wendi and her three small children. Because Wendi was addicted to crack-cocaine, the responsibility of taking care of her children had been thrust upon him. Not that he mind. He loved those children as if they were his own. One of the hardest things he had to do was watch them suffer because of their mother's addiction. At their age, which ranged from three to nine, they had to witness their mother's madness on a daily basis. He knew, what their mother was subjecting them to would stay with them for the rest of their lives, which was why he refused to leave them alone with her. If for nothing else, than to expose them to some form of sanity.

Tyrone Sharp was standing in front of J's Corner talking with two other men when Joey arrived. As soon as he saw the silver-gray Jaguar, he rushed over thinking it was SunRise.

"Joey?" he asked the obvious while leaning in the car window to put a little security on their conversation.

"'Rise couldn't make it," Joey began. "He said you had something for him?"

Tyrone reached into the inside pocket of his over-coat, pulled out an envelope. "Tell 'Rise he has one week to make his move. After that, it'll probably be all over the coast," he said while handing Joey the envelope.

"I'll tell him. You didn't happen to see Sweet, or Bop, did you?"

"No, but you might be able to find 'em at the projects."

"Redhook?"

"Yeah."

Joey thought for a moment. "I don't have time," he thought out loud. "If you happen to see 'em?"

"Say no more, baby-boy. I already know," Tyrone assured before backing away from the car. Before Joey closed the window, Tyrone shouted, "Don't forget to tell 'Rise what I said."

It didn't take Joey long before he was pulling up in front of Robin's place of residence. "Right on time," he mumbled when he saw her coming down the steps carrying more luggage than he had anticipating her bringing.

After parking he quickly got out of the car to gave her a hand. "You sure you're not moving in?" he jokingly asked.

She smiled before explaining, "The thing is... I'm not sure how long I'll be staying. I don't wanna have to keep running back and forth, you understand?"

"Of course," Joey said with a knowing smile while helping her placed the luggage into the trunk. Before pulling off, he told her he had to make a quick stop before heading back.

"I have to stop by J's Corner." He looked at her and asked, "You gonna' be a'ight with that?" The last thing he wanted to do was re-open old wound for her. He didn't exactly know what happened to her that night? But from what he heard, he figured it had to be traumatizing for someone like her.

"I'll be fine."

"Are you sure?"

"I'm sure, Joey," she assured him. He studied her for a moment trying to detect the slightest bit of uncertainty.

Once he was convinced she was actually all right with it. He pulled off. He wasn't sure if he was making the right decision by dragging her back to a place she clearly had no desire to go. One thing he was sure of, though. He definitely couldn't afford to leave her alone a second time. When they pulled up in front of J's Corner Robin quietly yelled, "Ain't that one of the women who helped me the other night?" Joey quickly looked in the direction she was pointing and saw TooSweet, one of the women who saved Robin's life. She had just got into her car and was about to pull off when Joey blew the horn, catching her attention before getting out of the car. As he approached her car, she rolled down the window.

"Joey!" she said with a sense of excitement and surprised. "What brings you over here?"

Joey rushed around to the passenger side, and got in. "'Rise is looking for you. I think he may need you and 'Bop for a trip he's suppose to be taking. You seen, 'Bop?"

"I'm on my way to pick her up now. You wanna ride along?"

"I can't. I have to get back to Jersey, but I'll tell 'Rise you got his message."

As TooSweet watched as Joey returned to the Jag. She noticed a female sitting in the car with him. "Bop ain't gonna' like that," she muttered.

CHAPTER 10

Parked directly in front of BeeBop's building in the lot of the Redhook Projects, TooSweet sat waiting in the car when she noticed a small child approaching. Barely able to walk in his unlaced Timberline boots, baggy jeans and over sized Snorkel hooded coat. He took slow, deliberate steps while stomping in her direction until coming to a complete stop outside her car-door. Before speaking, he motioned for TooSweet to roll down the window. "Yo', you 'Bop's, partner, 'Sweet?" he asked with a natural 'screw-face'. His child-like voice told her he couldn't have been no more than seven, or eight years of age.

And by his demeanor, she already knew he was a hustler who had no idea what a childhood felt like. The streets were a dangerous place for a child. But if you were unlucky enough to come from the 'hood, you eventually became that danger even if it came in the form of a child.

"Yeah. What's up?" she asked.

"'Bop told me to' tell you to slide on up 'cause she ain't ready yet." He looked around suspiciously before adding, "Watch your back. Niggaz' wildin' 'round here." TooSweet nodded, rolled up the window as he turned and headed back towards the building in which he came. She waited until she could no longer see the child before getting out of the car.

As she hurried towards the same building the small boy had disappeared into. She passed a flock of addicts waiting to cop while gun totting soldiers-in-training eyed everyone suspiciously. As TooSweet swiftly moved through the crowded lobby she heard someone say, "That's 'Bop's partner." It was the voice of the child she had just spoken with. She looked into the flock of angry face's that carefully sized her up, but didn't see the young boy.

Known to hold her own in any given situation, Audrey 'TooSweet' Strong was a fearless statuesque who had been preying on her own people since she could remember. Now thirty-three years of age, she was the youngest of seven brothers. Five of which were dead; three from a drug over- dose. The other two were killed during a shoot-out with the police in the course of a robbery. The remaining two were currently doing a life sentence at New Jersey State Prison. TooSweet was originally from the 'Prince Street Projects' in Newark, New Jersey where she use to spend a lot of her time. Now, she spent most of her time in Brooklyn with her partner, BeeBop, or in Paterson working with SunRise. As a former stick-up artist who specialized in robbing hustlers. She made the mistake of trying to rob SunRise after mistaking him for a 'Fleetwood-Kid'. A term made famous during the mid 1970's by a journalist who did a story on a fifteen year old Harlem drug-lord who had just retired before his sixteenth birthday. But SunRise, who was always aware of his surroundings, had already gotten the drop on her long before she had a chance to make a move. Surprised and impressed, she laughed. "You find death amusing?" he asked her. Before she could reply, he took her weapon and gave her his watch. "It's worth eighteen grand. The right people will give you no less than ten. It was a gift to me. Now it's a gift to you," he told her before leaving.

A month and a half later TooSweet finally tracked him down to return the watch. When he asked her why she hadn't pond it?

She simply said, "I only rob hustlers."

"You didn't rob me. I gave it to you as a gift, remember?"

"And now I'm giving it back. You got a problem with that?"

They both laughed. After formally introduced themselves. He invited her to take a ride with him? "Why not," she replied before adding. "I ain't got shit else to do." Since, she had been absorbing everything he had to convey. Things that made her realize she had been creating her own problems; problems that would eventually land her in prison, or six feet deep.

He forced her to think about her future which was something she had never considered until meeting him. TooSweet's partner, and friend, Betty 'BeeBop' Gibson, was also a former stick-up artist. But unlike

TooSweet, BeeBop saw everyone as a potential victim. Born and raised in Brooklyn, BeeBop had been in and out of jail since the age of eleven. Throughout her younger years, she had managed to personify the phrase, 'Brooklyn takes' by stacking bodies. Somewhat of a ghetto-star, BeeBop was a legend in her own 'hood. At twenty six years of age, she managed to survive nine bullets that placed her in a coma for eight months. That was two and a half years ago, but hardly her last brush with death.

After meeting TooSweet, who later introduced her to SunRise, BeeBop also turn her life around. The reputation she had established by instilling fear into the hearts of her peers, and victims remains as strong today, as her will to live was back in the day.

Evenly matched with her partner TooSweet in height, skin-tone, and heart both women were blessed with strong Africa genes most black men could not appreciate. They were considered too ruggedly hard-looking to be beautiful. Still neither one of them cared about improving upon their outer appearances. They had more important things on their minds. Like improving the mind-sets of what they considered dead-heads. The long, thick dreadlocks they both sported were not a fashion statement. But to reflect a growing third world conscious. When SunRise created a bond with the black community known as FOLD, which was an anagram meaning Family, Oath, Loyalty and Dedication.

Both women became his right hand.

"Where are we going in such a hurry?" BeeBop asked as the two women boarded the car.

Before answering TooSweet started the car and turned the radio on. The urbane beats of 'Boogie Down Production' blasted from the sound-system of the '89 Marquis. "Jersey," she said while adjusting the volume.

Twenty-five minutes later, both women were sitting in the living-room of SunRise's apartment. Once SunRise explained the situation without betraying Robin's trust. Both women were opposed to the idea of putting their plans on hold for someone they knew absolutely nothing about. "Wait a minute, 'Rise," BeeBop interrupted. "With all due respect, what kind of trouble you getting ready to involve us in? Does this have anything to do with what happened to her the other night?"

"Yeah, 'Rise!" TooSweet cut in. "What's she still doing here anyway? We don't have time to solve her personal problems. We have our own to deal with."

"We also have a week to do so. In the mean time, the sister needs our help?" He waited for the two women's reply.

While BeeBop waited for TooSweet's response, TooSweet stared at him indecisively. "Is that the only reason you're helping her?" she suspicious asked.

SunRise had to think about it for a moment. He wished he could give her a straight answer. The thing was, he didn't have one. "Look, 'Sweet," he said, avoiding the question. "That was a lot of coke she was trying to pass off," he hesitated before continuing while glancing towards the back room. "I'd like to meet the man she got it from. I thought we had agreed on that after Tye brought her to our attention?"

Both women frowned at the idea of going up in unfamiliar territory. "We have no idea what to expect once we get there," said TooSweet.

"She's right, 'Rise," BeeBop quickly cut in. We have people in Camden, but not Atlantic City."

"Than what do you propose?" he asked the two of them.

TooSweet made sure Robin wasn't in the area before speaking. "Look," she began in a low whisper. "You just met that woman. Let her work her own problems out."

SunRise looked at BeeBop. "You feel the same?" he asked.

BeeBop glanced at TooSweet before replying, "Whatever you wanna do, is fine with us, 'Rise."

He looked at TooSweet, who reluctantly agreed. "Good," he said. "As soon as Robin is ready, we can all leave."

"How long is this gonna' take?" asked BeeBop. Before SunRise could answer, Robin appeared fully dressed and ready to leave.

Two hours and thirty-five minutes later, SunRise and Robin were pulling into the lot of a small motel just outside of Atlantic City. Moments later, TooSweet and BeeBop pulled onto the motel-lot behind them. As the four of them exited their prospective cars, SunRise rented a single room and instructed the three women to stay put while he crossed the bridge into Atlantic City to check things out. Even though Robin had given him specific directions on how to get to Linda's Lounge. He still had trouble finding it.

The lounge was loud, crowded, and extremely dark inside. SunRise saw an empty stool at the bar and headed straight for it. While waiting on the bartender, he looked around. There was a lot of dancing, while others sat at their tables talking and drinking. All and all, everyone seemed to be having a good time. Once the bartender noticed SunRise sitting at the bar he did a double-take and came right over. "What can I get you, chief?" the tall, skinny, middle aged man asked while looking SunRise over.

"A club soda, thank you," SunRise yelled over the loud music.

Once the bartender rushed off, an attractive young female who was also attending bar, came over and leaned on the counter towards him.

SunRise leaned forward as she whispered in his ear. "Are you being taken care of?" It wasn't what she said but the way she said it that told him she was not referring to drinks.

"As a matter of fact, I am," he replied.

She smiled and slid a small piece of paper in front of him and said, "The moment you get bored, give me a call." She winked with a warm smile before attending to another patron.

SunRise looked at the piece of paper. The woman's name and phone number had been scribbled on it. He briefly glanced at her once more and smiled to himself. It was the first time he had ever received a proposal from a woman. folding the note, he slipped it into his coat-pocket without giving it anymore thought.

The skinny bartender sat SunRise's drink on a coaster and slid it in front of him. "Sorry I took so long. When I saw you talking to Donna, I took the liberty of taking my time."

"I'm Sorry, you say something?"

"Donna? The girl you were just talking with."

"Oh, the barmaid; yeah... nice woman," SunRise said while standing to take off his over-coat in an effort to get more comfortable.

"I don't know about all that," the bartender said, leaning over the counter to get a better look at SunRise. "One thing is for sure. She don't usually give a joker any rap unless she smells money," he paused when SunRise sat down again and reached for his drink. When the sleeve of his suite-jacket and shirt rose, the gold watch he was wearing was briefly displayed. "And from what I can tell," The bartender continued, "it wouldn't surprise me if you already had the keys to her new condo'?"

SunRise smiled. "Close," he replied. "She voluntarily gave me the digits."

"That's probable because you were still wearing your coat at the time. She didn't get a chance to check out that nice suit you're wearing. Not to mention the watch. Is that real gold?"

"Yes. It was a gift from someone who felt I would be naked with anything less."

"I gotta' admit," the bartender laughed a little before continuing. "When I first saw you sitting there on the stool I was about to ask for your ID?"

SunRise smiled. "It's okay. I get that a lot."

What's your name, brutha'?"

"SunRise."

"Nice to meet you SunRise, I'm Rob."

"Nice to meet you too, Rob."

Rob looked around suspiciously, then leaned towards SunRise's ear and whispered, "You a little over dressed, ain't you?"

SunRise took another sip of his drink before casually sitting the glass back on top of the coaster. "Or everyone else is a little under dressed," he replied. The confused bartender stared at him for a moment. Then burst out laughing while nodding in agreement.

SunRise smiled and paid for his drink.

"Shall I ring it up, or let it ride?" he asked with his palm over the bill.

"Keep the change," SunRise told him.

The bartender's mouth dropped a little. "Damn! Thanks, man," he said, stepping over to the cash-register. Upon his return, he leaned up close to SunRise trying to make conversation. "You can't be from around here. Not dressed like that?"

"I'm from up north,"

"New England?"

"Not that far; North Jersey."

"Oh! Okay," he said, feeling a little foolish for assuming. "I know one thing," he proceeded to change the subject, "dressed like that? That gold digging bitch, Donna ain't gonna' be the only female on you. These bitches around here ain't use to a guy with class."

"If you say so."

"Um' serious about these bitches, though. They gonna' be sweating the shit out of you. Watch what I tell you."

As the bartender quickly rushed off to the other end of the bar, SunRise glanced at him with a critical eye while standing to leave. He wondered how long women would have to tolerate men like the bartender. Men who thought it was macho to use derogating terms when referring to women. As he proceeded to put on his coat he noticed a loud female eyeing him from a nearby table. The last thing he wanted was to encourage her. So he quickly left.

Back at the motel, SunRise found Robin in the bathroom with a towel filled with ice wrapped around her ankle. Somehow, she had managed to sprain it. After SunRise examined it, he saw no other alternative but to send her back up north. Robin, however, relentlessly protested. "Listen to me," he told her. "TooSweet and I will handle your business. You just have to trust us."

"But why do I have to go all the way back? Why can't I just stay here, at the motel?" she argued. TooSweet and BeeBop stood in the bathroom doorway watching.

"Because it's too dangerous," he told her.

"Yeah," TooSweet explained. "Suppose we have to make a run for it? You can't walk, more less run."

"She's right," SunRise agreed. "If we have to move out, you could put all of our lives in danger. Trust me, it's better this way." Robin angrily glanced at TooSweet and rolled her eyes. She then looked at her swollen ankle while trying to move her foot. "Sweet and I will handle things on this end. And we won't leave until this thing is settled," he stroked her cheek gently with the back of his hand. Both TooSweet and BeeBop looked at one another, confused.

"Ahhhh', isn't that cute," TooSweet sarcastically said while checking the clip in her Glock. When SunRise looked up at both women, they quickly left the area. He then told Robin he needed the cocaine, and a little more information on her friend, Rossi. After Robin gave him everything that was needed, he helped her with her shoe. Then carried her out to the parking-lot where BeeBop waited behind the wheel of TooSweet's car. SunRise gave BeeBop the keys to his apartment. Then instructed her to stop by Robin's apartment to pick up the rest of her things and settle up with her landlord. "If she needs anything, it's your responsibility to see that she gets it."

BeeBop acknowledged before pulling off.

CHAPTER 11

It was a little after ten when Robin finally woke. Between the throbbing pain in her ankle, and stressing about SunRise, whom she haven't seen or heard from in almost two days now, she was really worry and hadn't been getting very much sleep.

As she made her way to the bathroom she stopped by the guestroom to peek in on BeeBop. To her surprise, the bed was made and BeeBop was nowhere to be found. She called BeeBop's name while hopping off to the bathroom. When BeeBop didn't answer, Robin automatically assumed she stepped out for a moment and was probably on her way back.

Inside the bathroom, Robin found a note taped to the mirror over the sink. The note was signed by BeeBop and read, "Robin, just stepped out for a change of clothing. I won't be long." Robin noticed the time on the note indicating BeeBop left over two hours ago.

After running warm water in the tub with the intentions of soaking her ankle, she washed her face and brushed her teeth. By the time she finished, the tub had filled with enough water to soak her entire body. She was about to get in, when the phone rang. Her first thoughts were of SunRise. Anxious to hear his voice, she quickly hopped into the bedroom and snatched up the receiver. "Hello!" she all but shouted into the caller's ear.

"Robin. It's 'Bop."

"BeeBop?"

"Did you get my note?"

"Yeah. Just now."

"Um' on my way back."

"You still in Brooklyn?"

"No. Paterson. I had to stop off to take care of something. You need anything before I come in?"

"My ankle is killing me. I was just about to soak it when you called. If you can find me some pain killers that would be nice."

"I'll see what I can do. In the mean time, soak it in hot water. As hot as you can stand."

"Okay. Thanks, BeeBop." Robin hung the phone up and hopped back into the bathroom when someone began knocking at the door.

"That can't be BeeBop?" she thought out loud. "Who is it?" she yelled just before reaching the door.

"'Sweet!" a familiar female's voice yelled back.

Hoping SunRise was with her, she quickly open the door.

A haggard looking TooSweet slowly dragged herself into the apartment, alone.

"Where's SunRise?" Robin immediately asked her.

"If he doesn't make it back by tonight, he'll probably be back tomorrow. He sent me ahead to take care of something,"

TooSweet replied while easing out of her coat. "Where's 'Bop?" She asked while hanging her coat in the closet.

"She stepped out for a change of clothing. She should be back any minute now. Did SunRise take care of that for me in Atlantic City?" Robin quickly asked without looking at TooSweet.

When TooSweet didn't answer, she turned and found the tall woman reared back in one of the recliners. Her eyes were closed as if she had fallen asleep. "TooSweet!" she shouted.

"Yeah? What?" the tall woman asked without once opening her eyes.

"You a'ight?"

138

"I'm fine. Just tired, that's all."

"Did SunRise straighten that guy out?"

"Yeah, Robin. We straighten him out," she said, coming out of her nod.

Robin sat on the sofa with hopes of getting the 411 in details, but noticed TooSweet reaching for the phone. Out of consideration, she told the tall woman she was going to take a bath before leaving the area.

The bath water had cooled off but was still warm enough for her needs. After disrobing, she eased in slowly, lying back with just her head above the water. She closed her eyes and thought of SunRise. How she had first met him at that god-forsaken rat-hole called, 'J's Corner'. She smiled thinking how smooth he was with his words and actions. She thought of the time they made love. He was so caring, and attentive to all her needs but also aggressive in a gentle sort of way.

While lying there, lost in thoughts of the man she couldn't seem to stop thinking of. She began caressing her breast the way she had remembered him caressing them. When all of a sudden, there was a hard knock at the bathroom door. Robin immediately snatched her hands from her breast and abruptly opened her eyes yelling, "Yeah?" while sitting straight up in the tub as if she had gotten caught doing something wrong.

"I put those pills on your bed," BeeBop shouted through the closed door.

"Okay. Thanks, BeeBop!" she yelled back while getting out of the tub. After drying off, she noticed the swelling in her ankle had gone down considerably. Careful not to put any unnecessary pressure on it, she hopped out of the bathroom and heard the two women in the guest-room whispering. She knew they were discussing something they obviously considered private. Which why she hopped to her bedroom, sat on the edge of the bed and began reading the label on the pill bottle BeeBop had just brought her. Moments later, she heard both women come out of the guest-room and walked into the living-room. They were still whispering. Robin couldn't help feeling she was just being tolerated by the two women. After all, she was an outsider who had insinuated her way into their lives and until she proved herself worthy, neither TooSweet, nor BeeBop would accept her into their FOLD.

Robin quickly lotioned up and threw on a pair of cotton pajamas. She then took a few pain pills before joining the two women out front.

TooSweet had just hung up the phone when Robin walked in on them. "I have to make a run," TooSweet said. "I should be back in a few hours."

"Damn, 'Sweet!" BeeBop cried. "You know I need the ride!"

"I'll be right back, 'Bop. This can't wait."

"Oh...yeah...right! What you gotta' do is more important than what I gotta' do?"

"As a matter of fact, yeah," said TooSweet, waiting for BeeBop to give her the car-keys.

"You know what? Here," BeeBop tossed her the keys, and rolled her eyes in frustration.

TooSweet smiled, "I love you, too," she said before leaving.

Totally confused by the two women's behavior, Robin looked at BeeBop and asked, "What was that all about?" while sitting on the sofa.

BeeBop looked at her briefly, then walked over to the window and began staring out. The expression on her face told Robin she would be wise to just leave it alone. Robin curled up on the sofa with the book she had been reading the night before. Once she found the page she had left off from. She began reading quietly when out of nowhere BeeBop began ranting and raving to no one in particular.

"She makes me sick with that, "I gotta' make a run," shit!"

Robin stopped reading to listen with a sympathetic ear. The last thing she wanted to do was be rude by ignoring her. She didn't know BeeBop very well, but as a con-artist, she was a very good judge of character. BeeBop struck her as an unstable time bomb ready to go off at the drop of a dime.

When BeeBop noticed Robin watching her, she suddenly stopped in mid sentence and angrily shouted, "What the hell you staring at me for, yo?"

"Oh, I'm sorry," Robin said with a nervous smile. "I was just checking you out."

"Checking me out?"

"Yeah... you know... you got that look?"

"And what look is that?"

You know? Like a sista' straight up out of the 'hood. Like you don't take nothing from nobody."

"You mean like a ghetto bitch? A 'hood rat?" BeeBop sarcastically asked while staring at Robin intensely.

"Nooo! I'm talking about a continental African warrior. Like the magnificent Queen Nzinga." Robin quickly pulled the name out of her memory-bank. Having just read about the warrior queen of Angola from one of SunRise's African history books just yesterday. The data on the warrior queen couldn't have come at a better time.

BeeBop's expression eased. She tried her best not to smile, but failed miserably. "You really think so?" she asked with a hint of doubt in her voice.

Robin sat the book down. "Absolutely!" she said. "Your flawless, blue-black skin tone," Robin said while trying her best not to stare at the scares. "The thick dreads along with the fact that you're always no-nonsense. It's intimidating, yet, attractive on you. Why do you hardly ever smile?" Robin asked.

BeeBop shrugged. "For me, it's a sign of weakness. Besides, people might think I'm soft. At least that's the case in my 'hood. You ever been to prison?"

Robin did not have to think about that one. "HELL NO!" she replied as if the question was an insult. When BeeBop looked at her strangely, Robin knew she spoke too quickly. "But when I was young, the state of

New Jersey placed me in a home for troubled girls?" she added in an effort to identify.

BeeBop's expression softened. "I know what that's like, too, but um' talking 'bout prison."

"I've never been in prison. Guess I was lucky. So what's it like? Tell me about the horror stories," Robin asked.

"What damn horror stories?"

"You know... the stuff you normally hear that goes on in prison. What's it like in there?"

BeeBop became distant while reflecting upon the time she spent 'behind the wall'. "It's a slave camp," she flatly stated.

"It's a horrible place that succeeds in making big money through our failures. When I say our, I mean repeated offenders; people who keep coming back to jail. The up side is? A lot of bruthaz' and sistaz' doing time often focus on education and consciousness. It's never easy because you always have someone, somewhere in so-called society crying the blues 'bout how prisoners are getting free education. Whereas, in society they have to pay for it; even the prison administration tries to kill college and vocational programs."

"Why?' Robin asked with an interest of concern.

"Because they have this poison perception that comes from their narrow-minded, self-interest. They know they will stay in business as long as people keep coming back to jail. And they're right; that's why politicians did away with vocational and educational programs. The last thing they want is to help prisoners prepare for the outside. Ain't no more rehabilitation. Nowadays, prison is strictly for punishment."

Robin paid very close attention as BeeBop elaborated on the realities of the prison systems.

"And after you've served your time, they throw you back into society as a social misfit. Those who go up for parole armed with the proper tools to help them make it on the outside, are denied parole. You have no idea how happy I am meeting TooSweet and SunRise. They literally saved me from myself. If it wasn't for them, I'd probably be in some prison right now doing the rest of my natural life. I'd give my life for either one of them without question because before they came along, I used to be a stone-cold-fool. Straight up and down, I thought I was the shit. A bullet to the head didn't even slow ma' fast ass down." BeeBop paused in thought as she remembered. "At least not until I was introduced to the, FOLD," she said calmly as she remembered. "'Rise kicked it to me straight-up, without a chaser. FOLD open my eyes to what's real. And now, I try to open the eyes of other bruthaz' and sistaz' by winning over their minds and hearts. I don't want them to go through what I've went through by getting caught up in the same vortex of stupidity."

Robin sat speechless. Expecting to hear stories of brutality and rape, the machination of the judicial-system turned out to be more horrible than anything she could have ever imagined.

CHAPTER 12

Brooklyn's Prospect Park was all but abandoned when TooSweet first arrived. She looked around, but there was no sign of her contact anywhere in sight. "Damn! He's late," she thought aloud, hoping she had not been stood-up. When she looked around again, she spotted an old man wearing a familiar white, wrinkled trench that was clearly too big for his small, fragile frame. As he approached with a newspaper tucked neatly under his left arm, she smiled. "I thought you stood me up?" she said as the two of them sat on an empty bench.

The old man sat the news paper on the bench between them and calmly said, "This better be good, Audrey. What's so important that you had to drag me out here in the cold?"

TooSweet crossed her legs, and folded her hands on top of her knees. "You remember those two men who were killed outside of J's Corner the other night," she began.

The old man stroked his salt and pepper mustache. "Yeah, what about it?"

"I found out they were from Atlantic City and wanted for the murder of a sixty-seven year old man by the name of, Thomas Rossi," she whispered confidentially.

"Tell me something I don't already know!"

She looked at him oddly, "You knew they were wanted in Atlantic City?"

"No, but that might explain the rolodex we found on one of the bodies," he said. Adding, "Aside from learning they were indeed from Jersey we also learned both men were presently on parole."

"What about the rolodex you mentioned?"

The old man studied her for a moment. "They probably took it off of the man they murdered in Atlantic City. You know anything about it?"

"What? The rolodex?"

"Yeah, the rolodex." He carefully watched her for any signs of deception.

"No! Why should I?"

He stared at her as if he was actually able to tell whether or not she was lying. Satisfied she didn't know anything. He pulled a small pad from his coat pocket and began flipping through the pages. "The rolodex we found was stuck on the name, Robin Hoods. It probably broke when the victim fell on it," he said, still flipping through the pages of his small pad.

"Here we go," he stopped on a page with a list of names. "Robin Hoods. Hell-of-va name, huh?"

"A first for me; who is it?"

"That's what we're trying to find out. Do you know anyone by that name?"

"From Atlantic City?"

"No. This one is from right here, Brooklyn. At least that's what we think."

"I don't understand?" TooSweet said.

He put his pad away before continuing. "As I said before, the name along with a partial Post Office Box number was the only information we were able to access."

"Is she a suspect, or something?"

"She?" said the old man, staring at TooSweet suspiciously.

"Robin is a girl's name. Ain't it? At least I always thought it was. I mean, I don't know any men with a name like, Robin. Do you?" she quickly asked.

"Robin Williams?" he quickly said.

"I was thinking more on the line of, Robin Givens?"

He smiled. "Look, Audrey, if you know anything, come straight. We just want to talk with her... or him," he stood with his paper in hand.

"If I hear anything, I'll be sure to give you a call."

"I wanna go out in style. Make me look good. Give me something I can work with," he said, tucking his newspaper neatly back under his left arm before walking off in the same direction he had came.

TooSweet sat there watching as the soon to be retired lieutenant, Al Sheets slowly walked off with both hands tucked comfortably in his coat pockets. She smiled as she watched the old man and began reflecting upon the very first time they had met.

It happened about a year and a half ago when he had rushed BeeBop to the county hospital the last time she had gotten shot.

She could still see his face. Like a worried relative, he impatiently waited for word on BeeBop's condition. He had been so concerned about BeeBop. She actually thought he was a relative. But later learned, the old man who paced back and forth in the waiting room for hours, was an off duty lieutenant of the 81st precinct. She also learned, if he hadn't brought BeeBop in when he did, she would have surely died. It was not because he saved BeeBop's life that sparked TooSweet's friendship with the lieutenant. Any decent human being would have done no less. It was the fact that he remained at the hospital until BeeBop was out of surgery which told her something of his character and because of that act of kindness. Lieutenant Al Sheets and Audrey 'TooSweet' Strong had become very good friends sharing an unspoken bond that brought them together like a father to his daughter. With his access to police files on drug-dealers of interest and her access to privy information on the streets they aided one another when necessary. Neither SunRise, nor any member of the FOLD knew anything about their relationship.

TooSweet wanted to tell her comrades and friends about her connection with the lieutenant, but knew they would never understand the importance of having someone on the inside inadvertently helping them with their cause.

Robin had just hung up the phone from speaking with SunRise when TooSweet stepped into the apartment.

"Hey TooSweet, that was SunRise."

"What did he say?"

"That he won't be back until sometime tonight."

"Did he say anything else?" she asked.

"Well..." Robin began while stretching out on the sofa with a book she had been reading. "... he talked to BeeBop."

TooSweet took that as a, no. Then walked over to the sofa and stood directly over Robin. "He didn't say anything about your friend?"

Robin did not take her eyes from the book, or display any emotions when she said, "He told me Rossi's lawyers were trying to find me."

"Did he say why?"

"Nope, he just told me not to worry. He would explain when he returned." TooSweet walked off to hang her coat up in the closet. "So what you think of, Johnny Williamson?" Robin asked with her eyes still glued to the book.

"Not very much," TooSweet simply replied. She knew Robin was anxious to know every little detail that took place in Atlantic City. She also knew if she didn't find a way to change the subject. Robin would be asking a host of questions. Most of which she wasn't sure she would be able to answer. "Where's 'Bop?"

"In the guest-room. Did you find out how his men found me?"

"Whose men?"

"Johnny Williamson's," she said, finally lifting her head from the book to make eye contact with TooSweet.

"Yeah. But I'll let 'Rise explain," she said, turning her back to Robin. "He's the one who did all the talking to that, Johnny guy. I was just there to watch his back." She turned around and noticed how oddly Robin was staring at her. "What's wrong with you?" she asked, trying her best to appear nonchalant.

"SunRise told me what happen to my friend," she said.

TooSweet didn't know what to think, or how to react. She couldn't be sure if Robin was being straight, or trying to bait her in divulging information. "So what did he tell you?" she asked while sitting.

"He told me Rossi was found dead. Johnny's two thugs killed him to get to me."

TooSweet flinched with shock. "He said all that?" she quickly asked in disbelief.

"Is it true?"

"Yeah...but damn! I thought he'd be a little more sensitive in handling it."

"I asked him to give it to me straight-up."

"That, he did. You don't seem too broken up over the lost of your friend?" TooSweet curiously observed. Robin rolled her eyes and buried her head back into the book she had been previously reading. "You're one cold, uncaring bitch!"

Robin abruptly looked up at her and stared at the dark skinned woman with piercing eyes. "Why the hell should I grieve over the death of someone who sold me the fuck out?" she yelled.

"If it hadn't been from you all coming to my aid, I'd be six feet deep right along with him."

"What makes you so sure he sold you out?"

"Can you explain how the hell Johnny's men found me? I sure as hell can't." she sat up straight with the book in her hand. TooSweet stared at her without saying a word. Robin stared back. "Well?" she asked, waiting for TooSweet to offer a more plausible explanation.

"If someone tortured you, would you talk?" TooSweet finally said.

Robin's brows shot straight up. "They tortured him?" she asked, horrified by the mere thought of it.

"Let's just say he died real ugly, Brooklyn style." Robin held her head down. She felt terrible about some of the nasty things she said and thought about the man who had often told her she was like a daughter to him. She was beginning to think TooSweet was right about her? Maybe she was a cold, uncaring bitch. Which really made her wonder would she ever be capable of caring for someone besides herself? "Personally," TooSweet began, "I don't think he just gave you up so easily. I mean...why would they resort to torturing him if he did? They could have just killed him. Think about it?"

Robin looked up at the tall woman. "If you don't mind, I'd rather not talk about it." She sat the book on top of the coffee table, stood and walked off into the kitchen.

"Oh yeah... I almost forgot," TooSweet shouted behind her.

"I heard the police found a rolodex on the body of the man who tried to 'nap you. The rolodex belonged to your friend. That's probably how they found you." Robin rushed out of the kitchen wide eyed, and stood directly in front of TooSweet. "I thought that would get your attention."

"They who?" she quickly asked with obvious anxiety in her voice.

Before TooSweet could answer, BeeBop emerged from the bathroom. "What's all that shouting I heard?" she asked, eyeing both Robin and TooSweet simultaneously.

"Nothing for you to concern yourself with," TooSweet said, tossing her the car keys. BeeBop snatched the keys out of the air, and began putting on her full length leather coat.

"Did Robin tell you 'Rise called?" BeeBop asked.

"Yeah... she told me,"

"Good!" said BeeBop, "It's your turn to baby-sit." She then glanced at Robin, who did not find her statement amusing.

"No offense, Robin."

"None taken," Robin coldly replied. Despite the fact that the two women were amiable towards her, she had always suspected they viewed her as being too refined to understand their world. She also knew if she wanted to be accepted as a member of their FOLD. It would have to come from the result of her own merits, and not SunRise trying to force her down the two women's throat.

"BeeBop?" Robin quickly stopped her at the door. "Why don't I go with you? My ankle went down some. As long as I don't wear any heels, I can walk on it."

TooSweet looked at BeeBop and quickly spoke up. "That's not a bad idea, 'Bop. It'll give you the opportunity to show her the real world; Harlem World. Besides, I'm too tired to watch my own back, more less anyone else's."

BeeBop looked at Robin indecisively. "If you coming, you betta' hurry up and get dress. I ain't got all day." Robin smiled and rushed off into the bedroom to dress. "And wear something casual," BeeBop yelled. "We ain't going to no fashion show."

TooSweet laughed a little and waited until Robin had left before asking, "So what 'Rise had to say?"

BeeBop made sure Robin was where she was suppose to be before answering. "He told me to go see the 'Barber'. Tye gave him an address to a stash house in Queens. I have to see if Reggy can validate it."

"The house in Queens is supposed to be something big?"

"Rise told me they have enough weight to supply the entire Coast."

"And if Reggy doesn't validate the address?"

"Then it's a wash," she said, staring at TooSweet strangely.

"Damn, 'Sweet. You look worn out."

"I feel worn out," TooSweet lazily replied.

"Why don't you take a nice hot bath, and get some sleep in the guest-room before 'Rise gets back.

"So how big is this Queens thing?" TooSweet asked while slipping off her boots.

"From what 'Rise told me, about two thirds of a ton."

"Good luck, and be careful!" TooSweet said while lounging back in the recliner with her eyes shut closed.

"You'd be much more comfortable in the guest-room, 'Sweet," BeeBop tried one last time to convince her friend. But TooSweet just laid there mumbling incoherently. It was then that BeeBop realized she had fallen asleep. BeeBop walked off into the guest-room, and returned with a large blanket. She carefully placed it over her friend, and turned off the lamp-light next to the sofa.

As the two women were leaving the building, they were approached by two young boys. "Yo', shortie," one of them said while staring at Robin. "I got that 'Devastation' over here?"

BeeBop shot the both of them a cold stare and kept it moving with Robin tagging along close behind. Robin waited until they were in the car before asking, "What the hell was that kid talking about?"

"That's what they call their dope. They can't be from around here; I ain't ever seen 'em before. All these lil' stupid-ass-fools you see running around hustling for another joker. The name is the brand. It lets the dope-heads know what they're getting and who they're getting it from. It's how they know if it's good, or not. Everybody wanna cop from this joker named, Henderson. A lot of the dope you see those fools pushing is his. His main thing is heroin. I guess he's trying to expand by breaking into the cocaine trade now."

"But devastation means ruins, or destruction?"

"Yeah... so now you understand what it's doing to our community. Not to mention the minds of the fools who manage to get strung-out on it." Robin glanced at the angry looking woman who never smiled and saw something she had not noticed before. A profound, unconditional love for her people and community. Not just the community she lived in, but all communities that have been overwhelmed by drugs and violence.

The moment they were officially out of Paterson. Robin tried to make conversation by asking, where they were going?

"Harlem," BeeBop said.

"Harlem!" Robin murmured. If she had known of BeeBop's plans in advance she would have never volunteered to come along. She had never been to Harlem mostly because she never had a reason to. Since coming to New York, she always thought of Harlem as a forbidden zone. A concept she adopted from all the stories she had heard told. Stories that made her skin crawl with fear.

Unfortunately, there was no turning around now. At least, she concluded, she was with someone well known and respected.

BeeBop parked on the corner of 116th, and Lennex Ave. As Robin looked around with part fright and part aversion, she couldn't understand how people could live in such conditions.

Every apartment building in sight appeared to be abandoned. Yet, she kept seeing people coming and going as if someone actually resided in the abandon looking buildings. As children played happily in the street and on the side-walks, Robin couldn't help but to wonder whether they were actually capable of seeing what she saw. She figured they were either blind to their own condition, or so use to having less than nothing, it was their norm. Everyone she had passed went about their business as if everything was fine. But from where she stood, it wasn't. Harlem was a city within a city. One big ball of misery that somehow managed to touch Robin in a way she was unable to describe. As she followed BeeBop down the street, horrified not just by what she was seeing and hearing, but by what she was now feeling. It was the cry of the wounded; sounds of an oppressed segment of society that had been ignored and forgotten. Robin wanted to cover her ears, but she knew it would not drown out the sounds of screaming babies or the wailing of sirens from emergency vehicles, or the occasional pop and bang of gunshots all of which came in an even roar.

She couldn't help from staring as throngs of men, women and children rushed by in a desperate attempt to go nowhere. The very thing Rossi had been trying to shield her from, was becoming all too real.

BeeBop led her into a small barbershop and told her to have a seat. "I be right back. I just have to see someone in back." Robin acknowledged with a nervous smile. BeeBop noticed how closely Robin had been clinging to her the moment they got out of the car and asked, "You gonna' be a'ight sitting here by yourself?"

"I'll be fine," Robin replied with a forced smile to mask her fears.

BeeBop stared at her for a moment with searching eyes. "Welcome to the real world, lil' sista," she said before disappearing behind a black curtain in the back of the shop.

Robin nervously looked around and found herself sitting in the company of several old-timers. Most of which had no hair to cut. Which led her to believe the small barbershop was the one place left for them to come and congregate. As the only female in the company of men old enough to be her grandfather she began feeling a little out-of-place, but not at all uncomfortable. Aside from an occasional glance, the men paid very little attention to her as they went on with the usual grumbles about everyday life. Two old-timers who sat a few feet from her, talked about who got shot last night, and why. She also overheard another conversation from an old man who was having his hair cut. "Yeahhh, it's worse today than it was ten years ago," the old man told the barber. "Them damn dope dealers tearing up this community. Folks don't have no place to go no more." Can't even much sit outside your house without fear of getting mugged, or shot by some damn stray bullet."

The Barber nodded in agreement while running his comb through what was left of the old-timer's chemically relaxed hair. "You right, man," said the barber. "Pretty soon, the only thing that's gone' be left, is a bunch of young zombie-looking muthafuckaz'!"

"TOM!" shouted the old-timer sitting in the barber's chair.

"Can't you see we got a young lady sitting in here? Watch your mouth, man!"

The barber thrust an open palm to his mouth, covering it as if surprised by the presence of a female. "I apologize, young lady. I truly didn't see you sitting there." Robin smiled. "My eyes ain't what they use to be," he added with a heavy grin.

"Your eyes betta' be what they use to be! 'Cause if you mess up my head, I know som'en!" replied the old man who sat under the barber's comb.

"Com'on now, Mr. Bill; I can cut your hair with my eyes closed."

"You should be able to, you've been cutting it for over twenty years now?"

"And gone be cutting it for another twenty, too!"

Robin looked up and noticed BeeBop approaching. "Come on," BeeBop said without stopping. Robin quickly stood and followed her out of the shop.

On the way back to the car, Robin noticed something she had not noticed earlier. Four out of every five shops were owned and operated by non blacks. Which was very strange, sense Harlem was considered the largest black community in the United States.

Yet, blacks seemed to own and operate nothing but a few shops here and there. As they raced back to Jersey, Robin had been silent the whole time. She couldn't help but to feel sad by some of the things she had just seen and heard; things that were not so easy to forget. What hit her hardest was a child prostitute she saw. She wasn't sure the child's actual age, or how long she had been hooking. Judging from her mannerism and speech, which was that of an aged old hustler. She could only assume the child had years into the life which was more saddening than anything she had witness thus far. That little girl, who was someone's baby, could have easily been her. She thought of the women she saw. Women who were also trying to sell the only thing they had left, their bodies; bodies that were too worn and used-up to be of any use to a real man. Then there were the crack heads and dope addicts, the pimps and pushers, winos passed out in the gutter with no hope of crawling back out any time soon. Robin felt a smothering sadness come over her. Not because of the people who were all struggling in different formations to escape their private miseries. It was because deep down, she knew she was no different from any of the individuals she had witnessed in Harlem. The more she thought about it, the more she realized. She too had been caught-up in her own private misery. She was just thankful she wasn't too far gone to realize it.

CHAPTER 14

SunRise and TooSweet were sitting in the front room talking when Robin and BeeBop returned. Even though Robin was happy to see SunRise, she knew he was in the middle of an important conversation. She quickly gave him a warm welcome, then excused herself and stepped into the back to freshen up. A few minutes later when she returned to the front room, the two women were gone.

"Damn!"

"What's wrong?" SunRise asked while rising from the sofa to see if she was all right.

"No baby, I'm fine."

"You sure? How's your ankle? You didn't re-injure it, did you?"

"No. Just a little fired-up."

"About what?" he asked, sitting down in one of the recliners. Robin sat in his lap and told him she wanted to talk with TooSweet about something she had said earlier.

"What did she say?"

"Something about a rolodex with my name on it," she said while scratching her head.

"Oh... that." He stood. "You hungry?" he asked, walking off into the kitchen.

"You knew about it?" she followed him. When he didn't answer, she pressed on. "Well?"

"Well what?"

"What did she say?"

SunRise began looking in the cabinet until he found what he had been looking for. After retrieving some plates and napkins, he began setting the table. "Not much," he finally spoke before turning off the oven.

Robin couldn't help getting the feeling neither he, nor TooSweet considered the rolodex important. She, however, felt differently. For all she knew, the police could be looking for her right now. "Is that all you have to say? Not much!" she frantically yelled.

SunRise opened the oven and removed a large vegetarian pizza. He sat it on the dining table and told her to have a seat. Robin angrily sat and watched him sit two large glasses of ice water in front of her before sitting next to her. It was after his second bite when he realized she wasn't eating.

"What's wrong now?"

She stared at him for a moment before yelling, "I'm still waiting for you to answer my question!"

"About the rolodex?"

"What else?" she yelled in frustration.

SunRise calmly sat what was left of the slice of pizza on his plate and wiped his mouth with a napkin. Leaning back in his chair, he quietly began. "When my people searched the body of Johnny Williamson's men, they found a piece of paper with the word, Mystique and a phone numbers on it."

At that point, Robin became extremely irritable. "I don't give two shits about that! I'm only concern about me, Robin Hoods!" she snapped before he could finish what it was he was trying to say.

"That's obvious," he calmly snapped back with less volume, but equal impact.

Feeling a bit insulted by the implication that hit just a little too close to home, she quickly asked, "What's that suppose to mean?"

"Look!" he continued, "I'm not going to play cat and mouse with you. As I was about to say before you so rudely interrupted, besides the word mystique your name and P.O. Box office number was also found on that slip of paper. We figured they got the information from the rolodex. Unfortunately, my people never got the chance to thoroughly search the two bodies which is why the police now have the rolodex. I was told by an inside source that it was broken when they found it, but they were still able to get your name off of it.

"Oh my god!" Robin sighed in horror. "So I guess the police is looking for me now?"

"Yes," he confirmed. "I was told they want to talk with you, but not for the reasons you think. The rolodex belonged to your friend in Atlantic City. The Brooklyn and Atlantic City police already know who was responsible for his death.

What they don't know is, why? He wasn't robbed? I guess they want to know how you fit into all it?"

"What the hell do you mean? You know damn well what happened! I didn't have a damn thing to do with it! Rossi was my friend!"

"Is that so?"

"Yeah, that's so!"

He stared at her. She was clearly upset, and obviously frighten. Never has he found her more attractive then at this moment. Each time she inhaled, her little nostrils flared, making her appear even more attractive. "That's funny," he said, manipulate her emotions. "You don't seem too upset to me about the news of your friend. Why is that?"

"Let me tell you something, Mister!" she shouted in total rage. "I don't have to justify my feelings to you, or anybody else!" She quickly got up from the table, and rushed into the kitchen. He could have sworn he saw her eyes beginning to water.

Realizing he may have been a little too hard on her, he decided to let up. Robin was standing over the sink, holding a glass filled with ice. She was about to fill it with water from the faucet when he approached her from behind. Gently, he grabbed her by her tiny waist and whispered into her ear, "I'm sorry for being so hard on you, but I found something out in South Jersey that has me a little confused."

"Such as?"

"Well... for one thing. Your friend was an old white man.

A very wealthy old white man?"

"What's your point?" she coldly asked, prying his hands from around her waist.

"The point is," he continued, spinning her around to face him. "His Attorney has been trying to locate you since he learned of your friend's death. Why the hell would your friend's lawyer be looking for you?"

"How the hell should I know?"

"That's what we're going to find out," he said, reaching into his breast shirt pocket, he pulled out a small business card.

Robin's eyes lit up when she saw the card. "That's the same card he gave me!"

"Who? The lawyer?"

"No! My friend, Rossi!" she said, taking the card out of SunRise's hand. "He said something about how important it was to contact the people on the card if something should ever happen to him?"

"Then that's what you should do. We're picking up your car on Monday. If you can wait until then, I'll drive down with you. In the mean time, stop worrying about that rolodex, and the police. Neither one can hurt you."

"One last question, and I'll try not to mention it again," she said in a much softer tone now.

"I'm listening?"

"How did you know about the rolodex, or that the police were looking for me?"

"TooSweet has people at the 81st, in Brooklyn. Which was why I told you not to worry," he smiled, adding, "She has no idea I know. Unfortunately I know more than I care to, and some day she will, too. I just hope it won't be too late. Do me a favor. Don't mention anything about it to her. Sometimes people have to reveal themselves before others can see them for who and what they really are. So keep this between the two of us."

Robin smiled and took his hand into hers. "I'm sorry," she softly whispered, holding her head down in shame. "I've been a selfish bitch, and after all you've done for me."

"Apology accepted," he said, kissing her on the forehead.

"You a'ight now?" he asked. She nodded with a closed smile.

"Good. Let's eat before the pizza gets any colder."

A few hours later while Robin was watching television, SunRise told her they needed to talk.

"Okay," she said, sitting the remote down.

SunRise sat on the sofa next to her and began. "Look. I've been thinking. I'm not sure if I'll be able to go with you to see that lawyer." Her eyes widen with disappointment, but she said nothing. "I have too much to do here. Besides, you have all the information you need. You'll be fine."

"You're not coming?"

"I can't, but I'll be here when you return. It shouldn't take you long to clear up your business." She sat there staring at him. Hurt and disappointment reflected in her eyes. "If you're worrying about going down there alone, I can arrange to have 'Sweet go with you. It'll give the two of you a chance to get to know one another.

"The woman doesn't like me. Besides, we have no idea why that lawyer wants to see me? For all we know, he could be trying to involve me with Rossi's murder!"

He smiled. "I seriously doubt that. And as far as 'Sweet not liking you, she's just a hard woman to understand. She doesn't dislike you, she just doesn't know you. Getting to know someone takes time. She hasn't spent any time around you. Not like 'Bop," he tried to reassure her before changing the subject.

"Now... Tell me about your friend, Rossi? I want to know all about him."

Unsure where to start, she thought about it for a moment before speaking "He was a good man," she said, pausing before continuing. "Do you remember when I told you I ran away from that state home for girls?"

"Yeah... I remember," he said, holding her gently in his arms.

"Well... I ended up in Trenton, New Jersey which was where I met this older girl who took me under her wing."

"Lucky you."

"Not really. She had me boosting clothes from malls. Every time I stole something, she would sell it to some jerk who fancied himself as a 'fence'. One day, we brought some goods to him and he started asking me all these questions about my past. I didn't like him, and I damn sure didn't like the questions he asked. I began thinking maybe he was trying to set me up, or something? After all, I was on the run, you know?

So I told Tina, the girl who took me in, that I didn't like or trust him. But she told me he was cool. I think she said something about knowing him for years, so I let it go. One day Tina and I stopped by his house with some clothes I had just stolen. Rossi was there. He was really nice and seemed to take an interest in me right away. I don't mean anything perverse.

It was more of a genuine concern for my well being."

"Why do you think that was?"

Robin thought about it. "I've often wondered about it."

"And your conclusion?"

"Probably because he saw how Tina and that ass-hole of a fence was treating me. He took me to the side and told me if I continued to deal with them. Eventually I was going to get caught. There would be no one around to protect me. As young as I was, I knew he was right. Getting caught meant going back to that state home. There was no way in hell I was going back there."

"What did you decide?"

"Well... Rossi offered to feed, house, educate, and teach me everything I needed to know about being a thief.

"You said something about educate?"

"Oh... he hired a private tutor for me. Being with Rossi, I didn't have to worry about anything, or anyone. The money I made stealing for him, I banked. Once I had enough to live comfortable, I stepped off. That was about a year and a half ago, but I still stole for him. As a matter of fact, that was the reason I went to see him; it was strictly business."

"What kind of business?"

"The usual. He had me hit the safe of this beautiful Cape-style home in Litchfield, northwestern Connecticut.

Despite what others may think, he was a good man. I just never allowed myself to become too attached, he did."

"If life with him was so good, why were you in such a hurry to leave?"

"Because he was too damn overbearing and protective of me; he was the same way up until the day he died. He probably meant well, but damn."

"Have you ever asked yourself why a stranger would offer to do so much for you?"

"I think he was just lonely. The only family either of us had was each other," she sadly replied.

"And you don't have a clue why his lawyer is trying to find you?"

"Not really. The last time I saw him, he told me I was the only family he had. That's when he gave me his card and made me promise to contact the person on it if something should happen to him." She paused. With her head resting comfortably on SunRise's chest, she looked up at him. "There's something you should know. I wanted to mention it before I found out about Rossi, but it just didn't seem important at the time."

"What didn't seem important at the time?"

"What I was commissioned to steal? That last job I did for Rossi was clearly a sham. Normally, he'd tell me exactly what to take. This time, he told me to take everything in the safe?"

"What's so odd about that?" SunRise asked.

"Because what I took out of the safe wasn't worth taking - at least not to me; it damn sure wasn't worth the money he paid me for taking it...unless he was just being generous?"

"What exactly did you take?"

"Low grade diamonds worth no more than twenty, or thirty grand and some legal papers."

"You sure the legal papers weren't what he was paying you for?"

Robin thought about it. "Could be?" She looked up at him again and asked, "You not gonna' let me go all the way down there alone, are you?"

"You don't have any idea why he asked you to contact his lawyer if something should happen to him?"

"No. He just gave me the card and said something about the people on the card will know what to do. He also tried to get me to retire and take over his ethnic art business. He probably wanted to retire himself; god knows he didn't need the money." After hearing her story, SunRise knew, deep down she really did cared about her late friend and couldn't help wondering if she felt responsible for his death. "Baby, you'll have to excuse me. My hair is driving me crazy," she said while getting up from the sofa.

"You need some help?"

She smiled mischievously, "Only if you intend to wash my back?" He chased her into the bathroom with her giggling along the way.

CHAPTER 15

When Robin woke-up the next morning, SunRise did another 'disappearing act'. It was the second time he got that off.

She hated that about him. No matter how late she kept him up, he'd still manage to sneak out without waking her.

Robin was lounging in the living room reading a book when SunRise returned several hours later. "Hi. I didn't hear you get up this morning?" she said just before standing to get a glass of juice. "You'd probably make a hell-of-ah creep-thief in another life." She glanced at him and giggled before asking, "You want me to fix you something to eat?"

"What I want," he said, easing up on her from behind, "Is already prepared. I just have to warm it up a little." He held her waist from behind and began kissing her on the side of her neck.

She giggled while hunching her shoulders. "Stoppp," she softly purred. Not because she really wanted him to. It just seemed like the appropriate thing to say. Stopping was the last thing she wanted. He was the one man whose touches made every nerve in her body tingle with anticipation. "Stoppp," she repeated with a sensuous moan while closing her eyes. She tilted her head back losing herself willingly in his embrace. When her lips found his, he swooped her up and carried her off into the bedroom.

No words were spoken as they tore each other's clothes off between kisses. When he began nibbling on her neck, she felt a shiver of fire run down her spine as he slowly eased inside of her taking his time with short, even strokes at first while building a momentum that slid her all the way up to the head-board. She cried out his name in a fit of passion while digging her nail into the blade of his shoulders. She loved the way he was giving it to her and wanted even more of him.

Lost in a sea of passion, she showered him with long kisses that lit a fire of hunger that brought out the beast in him. In a single motion, he flipped her onto her belly and began giving it to her from the back while whispering all the things she wanted to hear. When she felt her muscles twitch, she rocked her apple bottom to and from to meet his thrust. In the heat of the moment, she turned and looked at him. His face was tight while his eyes rolled into the back of her head. With her bottom tilted up, she gave it to him just as good as he was giving it to her. And when it was over, he collapsed on top of her back. The scent of sex, and the sound of heavy breathing was all that there was to fill the space between them.

It was well into the evening when TooSweet and BeeBop arrived. "What's good?" SunRise quickly asked.

Both women took off their coats before sitting. "That address you gave me to check out was a private home in the Rego Park section of Queens." said TooSweet.

"Is that all?"

TooSweet stood, pulled an old, torn envelope from her pants pocket and handed it to SunRise before continuing. "The names on the envelope are the occupants of the residence. I also saw a van parked in the drive-way. I had a friend run the plates for me and he came up with..." She produced a piece of paper and began reading from it. "... Alberto Torrez, age 42. Married to a Maria Elizabeth Torrez, age 36, no children. Mr. Torrez has ties to a Washington Heights hood that goes by the name, Teflon. Teflon owns an apartment building in Washington Heights and is rumored to have strong ties to the Dominican Cartel.

We think he's Michael Henderson's connect. You might be on to something, 'Rise."

Still examining the name on the torn envelope, SunRise asked, "Did you have a chance to check out the apartment building?

"'Bop can fill you in on that," she said, handing him the information from the license check.

Just as BeeBop was about to speak, he interrupted her while going over some notes TooSweet had just given him. "What's this about crates being unloaded from the van into the garage?"

"Oh yeah!" TooSweet said. "I almost forgot. While watching the house, I saw two men unloading what appeared to be crates. They took them out of the van and loaded them into the garage. It took about forty-five minutes to unload them. A half hour later, I followed one of them all the way to Midtown Manhattan where he purchased four tickets to some Broadway show that premiers tonight."

SunRise smiled with his eyes while staring up at the ceiling in thought. "So what's up with the apartment building, 'Bop?" he finally asked.

"It's just an old, run-down, five story building. The occupants are mostly Latinos. The only people I saw coming or leaving were the people who live there. But the entire block was filled with drug-dealers, or addicts…mostly from Jersey."

"What makes you think they were from Jersey?" he curiously asked.

Before BeeBop had a chance to elaborate, Robin quickly spoke up. "Washington Heights is a known drive-by drug market for Jersey. The Jersey license plates are a dead give-away for state-troopers. The unfortunate poor people who live in the Heights, are literally being held hostage in their own communities by Dominican drug-lords. At any given time of day, you can see the Port Authority police making arrest on the George Washington Bridge, or the New Jersey Turn Pike, all coming from Washington Heights." TooSweet and BeeBop stared at Robin somewhat confused. They then looked at SunRise as if they couldn't have said it any better.

SunRise tossed the torn envelope and slip of paper on top of the coffee table and glanced at his watch. "'Sweet, I want you to continue watching the house. I want to know if those tickets they purchased are for opening night."

"And if they are?" TooSweet asked.

"Then you report in."

"And if they aren't?"

"Then they probably won't leave the house. Report in."

She frowned. "But that doesn't make sense, 'Rise?"

"I have something in mind," he assured.

TooSweet stood and began pacing. "Look, 'Rise," she said.

"Whatever you have in mind, we have a right to know?"

"'Sweet's right, 'Rise." said BeeBop.

He studied the two women and then stood. "If the owners leave, I'm going to send someone in to check it out."

"I have an idea," Robin interrupted.

"And what might that be?" SunRise asked while sitting again.

Robin's face lit up excitedly. "Why don't I go with TooSweet? If the owners leave, we can go right in. This way, we'll have much more time to search!"

"We?" TooSweet asked while staring at Robin oddly. "Um' sorry, baby, but that's not my line of work. I'm a soldier. Not a thief."

"Even better," Robin calmly said. "You can watch my back. Just in case something should jump off, you know?"

"Forget it, Robin; too dangerous. You can get hurt, or worse," SunRise told her.

A little surprised at his reaction, Robin frowned. She didn't mind him being protective of her, but not in front of the girls. Especially when this might be her only chance to prove herself worthy. That is, if she ever wanted to be truly accepted as a member of the, FOLD. "That's why TooSweet will be there watching my back," she explained. "I know you're trying to protect me, but I can do this. You know I can. Besides, who else is more capable? Creeping is what I do best. They haven't built a spot I couldn't get in, or a situation I couldn't get out of."

As SunRise was considering Robin's offer, BeeBop quickly spoke up on Robin's behalf. "At least give her the benefit of the doubt, 'Rise?"

"Wait a minute!" yelled TooSweet. "Don't I have something to say about it?'

SunRise looked at her, then at Robin. "'Sweet's calling shots on this one, Robin. If it was up to me, I'd say no." He looked at TooSweet again and asked, "Do you wanna work with Robin?"

TooSweet looked at Robin and rolled her eyes smugly before looking at her again. "Look!" she began. "No offense, but robbing some two-bit loser of a drug dealer for less than a kilo doesn't make you capable enough for me to trust you with my life. Um' sorry, but ..."

"Suppose you don't have to trust me with your life?" Robin quickly interrupted. "I mean... suppose I go in alone? You can wait for me in the car."

"Assuming they actually leave the house," SunRise inserted

"Of course," Robin said. While all eyes were on TooSweet waiting to hear her decision TooSweet looked at SunRise, whose eyes seem to be pleading with her to say, no. She then looked at Robin, and smiled arrogantly.

"Give her a shot, 'Sweet. She might just surprise you?" said BeeBop.

TooSweet stared at Robin indecisively. "I'll tell you what," she finally spoke. "You can go with me on this one. If they happen to leave and you still wanna go in, I'll wait one hour for you... in the car. Hopefully you won't take that long."

Robin smiled. "You have a deal," she said while smiling at everyone in the room. She was excited about finally getting the opportunity to do something positive for the FOLD. But mostly, she was excited about finally getting the chance to prove to the girls, she was more than just a well kept, stuck-up bitch.

While Robin was getting ready BeeBop looked at SunRise and asked, "You have anything in mind for me?"

"'Face and his wife are coming over tomorrow."

"Do I know them?" asked TooSweet.

SunRise crossed his legs. "Joey put me on him. He said they owe FOLD a favor. I later find out from Official, "Face and his wife single-handedly took out Butterfly and the three men Big Moon sent and then pushed Big Moon and his crew for trying to push him."

"I heard about that last year," said TooSweet. "But I heard it was some huge female from D.C.?"

"That would probably be his wife. They call her, Nemesis.

And I doubt if she's from D.C." SunRise pointed out.

"How you know all this, 'Rise?" asked TooSweet.

"From Official, but it's public knowledge now that 'Face was responsible for the Massacre on Bunker Hill. He also told me Nemesis saved his life at Butterfly's that night."

"I wonder why he never said anything to me about it." complained BeeBop.

"If that kind of information was public knowledge, 'Face and his wife would have probably been dead shortly after Mike found out. Butterfly was one of Mike's top producers, remember? Everyone is under the impression Big Moon pushed 'Fly which is why Mike hasn't moved against 'Face. The way he sees it, 'Face did him a favor getting rid of Big Moon; saved him the trouble of doing it himself." SunRise never mentioned anything about Nemesis sister who have been in a FOLD safe-house for more than a year now.

"Well if this guy and his wife is suppose to be all that. Why we haven't heard anything about them?" asked BeeBop. "More importantly, why we haven't tried to recruit them into the FOLD?" TooSweet couldn't help asking.

"'Face is young, but obvious not new to the game. So far, he and his wife manage to stay off of the radar," SunRise said while thinking. "Something had to happen; something that forced them to reveal their talents?"

"Didn't you tell us Joey said they owe us a favor?" asked BeeBop.

"I talked to Joey, but he seemed reluctant to say too much about them. Anyway, you all will have a chance to meet them when they arrive tomorrow."

"What kind of business do you have with them?" asked TooSweet. Before SunRise had the chance to answer, she asked another question. "Do they know who we are and what we do?"

SunRise quickly changed the subject. "What's this animosity 'Bop and I detect coming from Robin and you?"

"Robin and I are cool. I just have to check her every now and then. Keep her real, you know what um' saying?" She glanced at BeeBop, then back at SunRise. "We know the two of you are a couple, and we think it's nice which is why I'm so hard on her. I don't want her thinking what we do is a game. I want her to understand, if she's going to roll with this FOLD? It has to be for four reasons - Family, Oath, Loyalty, and Dedication."

"I get it, and you're absolutely right. This isn't a game. It's real, as are we. Regardless of her reasons for wanting to be down. Don't leave her. You know as well as I do what would happen if she's caught," he warned.

TooSweet smiled. "I wouldn't think of leaving her. She's my little sista' whether she realizes it or not. And I will protect her with my life just as I have in the past."

"Just as who has in the past?" Robin asked, walking in on them completely dressed in black carrying a duffel bag.

"Who you 'pose to be? 'Alexandra Monday'?" TooSweet sarcastically asked with a snicker.

Ignoring the question, Robin sat down on the sofa next to SunRise. Who stood, grabbed her by the arm and pulled her off to the side. "Look, Robin," he whispered. If the occupants leave, I want you to check out the garage. I wanna know what was in those crates TooSweet mentioned earlier. If the opportunity presents itself, check to see if a safe is in the house. If I'm right, they should be keeping books. I need to know who their suppliers and distributors are." And whatever you do. Don't take

175

any unnecessary chances." Robin nodded, indicating that she understood. She then looked at TooSweet and told her she was ready.

TooSweet studied her without displaying any emotions. "We'll see," she simply replied while leading the way out of the apartment.

CHAPTER 16

It was dark outside when Robin and TooSweet arrived in the Rego Park section of Queens. Inconspicuously parked across the street from the targeted house. Robin looked around and noticed a public school down the street before asking, "Which house is it?"

"Right there," said TooSweet, staring at a house across the street directly in front of them.

Robin looked at the house, then at TooSweet and asked, "Why the hell did you park right in front of it?"

"So you could get a good look. Where you want me to park?" she asked while attempting to start up the car.

Still staring at the house, Robin stopped her. "Wait a minute. No one's home." she uttered under her breath without taking her eyes from the house.

TooSweet peered over her shoulder. "You know something," she whispered. "I think you're right."

Though the van was still sitting in the driveway, all the lights in the house were turned off.

"What time is it?" Robin asked.

TooSweet glanced at the clock on the dash board, "Almost seven. Why?"

Without taking her eyes from the house, Robin began to formulate a theory. "If your man was going to take you out to an 8:00 p.m. show, you'd probably want him to take you to dinner first, right?"

"Yeah... I guess so. I mean, if he' going to splurge for some extravagant show. He better be buying me dinner first," TooSweet offered, second guessing the situation.

"That makes sense. I mean... anything else wouldn't made sense."

"Exactly," TooSweet agreed. "So what you wanna do? It's your call? I can always tell 'Rise you couldn't find a way in? You don't have to do this if you don't want to, Robin."

Robin gave the situation careful thought before making a decision. "Drive down the street and let me out."

TooSweet slowly drove down the street. Before Robin got out of the car, she gave TooSweet specific instructions. Once she was out of the car, drive around the block. "If you don't see me standing on the curb when you come back around, leave the area and come back in a half hour. It shouldn't take any longer than that."

"Are you sure you want to do this?"

"Don't worry. I'll be fine."

"Who said I was worried!" TooSweet replied with a smile.

After Robin was out of the car, TooSweet did not pull off until Robin had disappeared into the night. It didn't take her long to get into the house. Having bypassed the cheap security system, she was in before TooSweet, who, instead of circling the block once as Robin had instructed. Drove pass twice before finally leaving the area.

The first thing Robin did was make sure the house was clear before starting her search. When she did not find anything out of the ordinary, she headed straight for the garage by way of the kitchen. Aside from your usual garage junk, she saw nothing that resembled crates which was disappointing. She had hoped to make everyone proud of her by hitting the mother-load. Instead, she was beginning to feel as if she had let them down. Just as she was about to leave, she saw something that caught her attention. Under the wooden work-bench was a relatively new indoor mat. Curious as to why someone found it necessary to lay a mat under the work-bench was worth investigating. With a little effort, she slid the bench off of the mat.

When she pulled it back, she found a drop-shoot that led directly to the cellar. "That's what probably happened to the crates?" she concluded while trying to open the heavy bolted lock. Unable to pick, or pry it, she put everything back the way she had found it and then stepped back into the house in search of an entrance that led to the cellar.

Robin looked in all the usual places before finding the cellar door behind the staircase that led up-stairs. With a pin-flashlight in hand and nerves on edge, she slowly crept down the dark cellar steps. Even though she knew the owners would not be returning anytime soon. She couldn't seem to shake the fear of getting caught which was the very thing she found so exciting about being a creep-thief'.

Carefully looking around, she immediately spotted what appeared to be crates. Each was stacked on top of the other up against the wall. After taking a closer look, she was blown away by what she saw. Several kilograms of what appeared to be cocaine were neatly stacked in each of the crates. She open one of the packages and tasted it. When the tip of her tongue numbed, she knew it was cocaine. She didn't have time to count each package, or the number of crates. But if she had to guess, she would have to say there were fifty crates, ten Kilograms to each.

As she continued to look around, she remembered SunRise saying something about, records. She left the cellar to take a look around on the second floor and found an office-type setting in the master bedroom.

While sitting at the desk going through each computer disk. She found one that was unlabeled. She placed it into the computer's drive but was unable to access any files. The disk was protected with a pass-word. She quickly removed the disk from the drive and pocketed it. She then turned off the computer and wiped everything down. She wasn't sure how long she spent searching, but somehow knew it was time to leave. Out of habit, she made a quick sweep of the room and found an attaché case hidden under the mattress, a personal stash of cocaine in a table draw next to the bed, and several weapons hidden throughout the room. Robin grabbed the case and opened it. To her utter surprise, it was filled with neatly stacked one hundred dollar bills. The moment she got over the initial shock of what she had found. She quickly placed the money and disk into her duffel before closing and placing the case back where she had found it.

Having stumbled on to something that was bigger than anything she could have ever imagined. She knew they would murder her if she got caught.

Before leaving the house, she peeped at her watch. Five more minutes to spare before TooSweet made her final round.

Robin stood in the foyer waiting for her ride. She smiled nervously while thinking of the money she just found. Estimating each stack contained ten thousand, she began to add it all up in her head "Ten times twenty is two-hundred-thousand," she computed. No matter how hard she tried, she just couldn't stop entertaining the thought of keeping it. She looked at the hefty duffel and knew TooSweet would surely notice. She thought about calling a cab and remembered the recently opened mail she saw sitting on a table in the front room upon entered the house. She looked around and immediately spotted the table. After grabbing the first piece of mail she saw. She headed for the phone she recalled seeing on the kitchen wall earlier. "Yes...can you please send a cab to 654 Westwood drive. I'm in a bit of a hurry; no later than five minutes? Okay, thank you." After hanging up, she immediately left the house. For her, it was a toss-up; whoever showed up first would make the decision for her. She nervously waited on the sidewalk beside a large tree that shielded her from being noticed by nosy neighbors.

She glanced at her watch again and then looked around while trying to come up with a good enough reason why she should keep the money. "Shit!" She began to rationalize. "I'm the one who put my life on the line? Besides," she thought. "SunRise never said anything about finding cash? His only concern was whether or not there were drugs in the house?" She smiled to herself and held the duffel close to her bosom while nervously looking up and down the clean, quiet, residential streets of Regal Park. Having lived in an all white community with Rossi, she knew only too well what type of people resided in Regal Park. She could see them now; sitting in their comfortable safe havens totally convinced that they were insulated from the deplorable social ills of urban society. Those were the very same people who would not hesitate to point an accusing finger at the disadvantage. Who they so desperately believed was responsible for the drug crisis in America. Not once have they stopped to think, if most of the poor in urban society lack the means of transportation. How is it possible for them to transport illegal drugs of this magnetite into the country? And why would they flood their own communities with it especially when clearly all of America's wealth managed to find its way back into the hands of the wealthy one percenters.

While Robin leaned up against the tree wondering whose pockets were going to get lined with profits from all the cocaine she saw in the house. A car pulled up directly in front of her and came to a complete stop. Totally exposed and paralyzed with fear, she stared blankly into the beaming headlights, unable to move.

After watching Spivey for a while, Bomani notice one very important detail. Whenever Spivey left the block, his soldiers relaxed. Still, Bomani knew he was going to need more men which was why they recruited someone special. Three old-heads, two of which were out of Newark, New Jersey and the other one was from Jersey City, New Jersey. Neither of which have ever been big on doing too much planning or talking. Like Bomani, their only concern was who the mark was? Where could he be found and how much could be got. Spivey was said to be holding a little under a million in drugs and cold hard cash stashed in a single locations. It was also said that Spivey was not to be trifled with. A real gangster whose name alone still induced fear into the hearts of his competitive rivals long after leaving the playground he once ruled in Kingston, Jamaica. Spivey wasn't just a drug dealer. He was a blood thirsty beast who clawed his way out of Kingston's ghettos with brute force. While greasing the pockets of dirty political figures that made it possible for him to legally get into the United States.

Not long after arriving on a temporary visa, Spivey settled in Philadelphia where he met a woman - but not just any woman. She was as thorough as Spivey and down for whatever. Her only flaw had been loving him. Six months after meeting, they married.

Once Spivey became a U.S. citizen two years after getting married his wife took a fall for him and was sentence to five years in a federal prison. Instead of 'holding her down', he immediately filed for divorce and moved to Paterson, New Jersey where he began to make his presence known. His only competitor, or so he thought, was Michael Henderson. But Spivey soon realized it would be in his best interest to align himself with Big Mike and reap the rewards Mike's New York connect had to offer. Mike's only requirement was for Spivey to stay on his side of the bridge leaving Spivey with the north and west side of town which was fine by Spivey. Even though the north side was small, west Paterson was vast and predominantly white; rich with untapped resources of potential addicts. While the two men enjoyed the fruits of their labor both of their ex-wives, though separately, were plotting against them.

Spivey was on his way out of the house with his two best men, when Bomani and his crew ran up on him. "Whaz' 'dis! What dah' fuck you blood-clotz' doing comin' at me like yah' gone take som'in!" Spivey shouted without the least bit of fear.

Truth was, he knew if stick-up boys made it this close to him on his own block. Chances are the small army he employed to protect him, had to be dead. With the barrows of two shot-guns aimed at Spivey and his men heads, they were ordered back into the house. "Yah' come at me at me own 'ouse! You know who ya' fuckin' wit'? Me Spivey Wise! Original shatta!" Spivey was beginning to fear the worse and wanted to shoot his own men for not going out in a blaze of bullets.

"Shut the fuck!" shouted Roc'mon, a midium height stocky built man with a loud imposing voice.

"Yeah tough guy, bellies on the floor. MOVE IT!" shouted Shorty, a handsome, forty-seven year old Latino who lived for the game. At four foot ten, Shorty was the loose cannon in the crew. Even with the two Glocks he never left home without, Shorty weight never exceeded a buck twenty but he managed to make up for it in heart.

As Spivey and his two men slowly laid on the floor face down with their hands behind their heads, Spivey's first thoughts were, his own men had set him up. It was the only explanation he had to explain why they didn't go out in a blaze of glory.

That is, until Shorty walk in back of him and cocked his weapon.

Spivey closed his eyes tightly shut and braced himself. "POW! POW!" When the two shots exploded in his ears, he felt something wet spatter on the left side of his face. Still, he never flinched or showed the slightest bit of fear. It was after opening his eyes when he realized his two men had been shot in the back of the head. "OH Shit! Yah' didn't 'ave to shoot me man. Me don't give a fuck about what'cha want. Take it all!

Shit don't mean nothing to Spivey, ya' 'ear me! Nothing! Spivey angrily shouted while foaming from the mouth.

"Where it at, yo'?" Roc'mon asked.

"Yah' come in 'ere demandin' shit like yah' own the place shootin' up me crew and shit! Yah' don't think I know yah' gone shoot me too. You betta' shoot to kill, yah' 'ear! Spivey die me-self before me tell yah' anything, yah ' blood-clot!"

"Oh, you gonna' give up the goods, nigga," said Ghost.

"Let em' up," Bomani told his men while staring at Spivey intensely.

"On your feet, nigga; LET'S GO!" Roc'mon shouted. As Spivey slowly rose to his feet, he stared at Bomani as if he was determined not to forget his face in life or death. Bomani briefly glanced at Ghost, who tossed him a handkerchief to wide his face. "You got one of two choices," Roc'mon began. "Live to hustle another day, or get got like those two clowns lying at your feet."

"You can keep the drugs, brutha'. We just want that loot you got stashed up in this mutha'," said Bomani.

"Me don't believe yah'," said Spivey.

"Well believe this, nigga!" Roc'mon cocked the pump and aimed it at Spivey's head while cutting an eye at Bomani for approval.

Bomani stepped up until he stood eye to eye with Spivey.

"Where it at, yo'?" he calmly asked.

"Me done said what me had to say. Yah' gone dead me, do it. Spivey never gone be afraid to die, yah' 'ear me?"

"Spivey ever been afraid of pain?" Shorty asked while approaching. Roc'mon began laughing.

"Look, bruh'," Bomani began. "You got caught slippin'.

If we came here to push you, you would be pushed. All we want is the money. Fuck the drugs."

Spivey frowned. "What dah' fuck yah' talking 'bout, mon'?

Ya' just murdered two of me best men! Shot 'em dead, in cold blood." Spivey said while staring up at Bomani in disbelief.

"They got caught slippin'. You know the rules. What you don't know is, your rival Mike Henderson hired them to push you and then hired us to push them. How the fuck you think we knew exactly when and where to hit you? You seem thorough, but your crew is whack as hell. If I was you, I'd clean house and start all over again, you feel me?"

"Bomani, man. Why the fuck we talking? Let's just push this joker six feet deep and get this loot, yo'," Roc'mon pressed.

"Word up, yo'. I ain't with all this talk, yo'. Shit make a nigga look soft," said Tree, a tall nappy-headed man with ashy dark skin.

"What's it gonna' be, yo'?" asked Bomani.

The very mention of Michael Henderson's name made Spivey believe what they had said about his men turning suits. The sad part was, they weren't just his best men. They were also his friends, or so he thought. The only issue now remaining concerned his own life. Could the big man with the long locks who called all the shots be trusted to keep his word, was the questing? Spivey studied Bomani expression long and hard before conceding. "Come with me, Bee," he told Bomani. When Ghost, Roc'mon, Tree and Shorty followed, Spivey quickly stopped them.

Bomani looked at his crew and said, "Gimme' a minute. I'll be right back."

"Fuck that!" Shorty spat. "Let's just murder this nigga and take it all!"

"Damn! Calm down, Shorty. Bomani got this," Roc'mon tried to calm the little man.

"Um' just saying!"

"Let Bomani do what he do and chill the fuck out, yo'.

184

You buggin'!" Roc'mon laughed while looking at Bomani. "Go handle your handle, Bomani. Shorty over here buggin', yo."

Spivey quickly lead Bomani to an upstairs bedroom where he took Bomani in his confidence. "Dig this, mon'. Me got twenty bricks of coke, thirty-seven pounds of pif' and four and a half balls in cash. Take 'alf of the weed and coke. The drugs are on consignment. Me need the cash to pay me suppliers, ya' 'ear?"

"I like you, yo'. Don't fuck it up by taking my kindness as weakness. Now, this is how this shit is going down. We take the four-fifty. You keep the drugs to re-up for your suppliers."

"Me can live with that," Spivey said. The last thing he wanted to do was press his luck.

Bomani stared at him coldly. "Like you had a choice; where's the safe." Spivey smiled nervously and walked over to a closet. Bomani watched him closely as he opened the door. "Easy now," he cautioned while coming up behind the short Jamaican shotta'.

When he saw the four foot floor save, he smiled with a closed mouth while motioning with his gun for Spivey to open it.

As Spivey stooped down and began opening the safe, he proceeded to thank Bomani for looking out for his interest.

"Me gone see Big Mike as soon as me get me crew together, yah' 'ear me?"

When Bomani saw the stacks of case, he asked, "You think I can get something to bag all this cash?"

"Yeah, yeah, no problem, mon," said Spivey while rushing over to his bed to removed the pillow casing from a pillow. "Mind if me ask you a question?"

Bomani motioned with his gun for Spivey to bag the loot.

"Whaz' up?" he asked without taking his eyes off of Spivey.

"What made yah' cross big Mike and take sides wit' me?"

To Spivey, it was a contradiction, especially when they could have easily used his men to retrieve the goods before pushing them.

"I don't like Mike. You? I don't know."

"Them blood-clots tried to push me off me earth. Me can't trust none of them blood-clots!"

Bomani looked at him and smiled. "You know what you have to do, righ'?"

"Me already done it."

Bomani stood and smiled coldly. "I'm glad we didn't have to push you. We'll see ourselves out." After Bomani left, Spivey sat on the edge of his bed; the moment he heard the four men leave the house, he made a call. "This is Spivey Wise. Put Khalif on the line, ya' 'ere!" As he impatiently waited, he looked up and saw his ex-wife standing in the doorway aiming a gun at him. "Maria?" was the last word he ever spoke before she pushed him. "POW-POW-POW-POW-POW-POW!"

As casually as she had entered the house, she walked over to the phone and pried the receiver out of the dead man's hand and placed it to her hear. "Spivey? Spivey you 'dere?" she heard a man's voice with a Jamaican accent on the line. "Your boss is dead and you're fired," she said before hanging up.

CHAPTER 17

Parked in the lot of the notorious C.C.P. Tyrone made sure the pearl handle of his .45 was clearly displayed when he tucked it in the front of his trousers before getting out of the car. Because the C.C.P. had a notorious reputation for gun-play. He wanted to let-it-be-known he too, was holding. Like most outsiders, he hated coming to the C.C.P. The last time he was here left a bitter taste in his mouth. Mostly because of the humiliation of getting robbed. If nothing else, it was embarrassing which was why he never mentioned the incident to anyone. Not even SunRise, whose name alone would have probably given him a pass. The last thing he wanted was a confrontation. But if it came down to it, he had no problem giving it to a joker.

Tyrone Sharp wasn't an actual FOLD member. He was a supporter, aiding the cause upon SunRise's request. And like SunRise, he had nothing but love for brothers. Still, there was no way in hell he was about to allow someone to hurt, or rob him again. Not if he could help it. The mistake he had previously made by underestimating the small, low-income housing project was 'his bad'. The next mistake will be the other guy's for confusing him with a victim.

As he cautiously approached building, four, he saw the usual gang of hoods hanging out front. He quickly pulled out his weapon, cocked it back and casually walked pass them with his gun in hand. "I got that 'body-bag', ovah' here! Ovah' here, y'all. 'Body-bag' righ' ovah' here!" he heard some young cats shouting.

At SunRise's apartment, Tyrone was greeted by BeeBop at the door. "Tyrone? I thought you hate coming over here?" she said, totally surprised to see him.

"How you doing baby-girl? Is he in?" he asked while stepping into the apartment.

"He stepped out for a minute. Joey's niece came over crying.

The next thing I knew, 'Rise was rushing out of here to see what was going on. He's been gone a while? He shoulda' been back by now?"

"Where's Joey?"

"I don't know. I saw him earlier. He looked like he was going through something. Can you blame him? That cracked-out sista' of his. 'Rise probably had to go over there to stop him from killing her. If it hadn't been from 'Rise, he probably woulda' killed that bitch a long time ago!"

"Don't do that, baby-girl."

"Do what?"

"Call the sista' the 'B' word. She has problems, true, but she's still a sista'. Not just any sista'. She's one of us, which makes her family."

"Yeah... but...."

"No yeah or buts about it. Instead of judging her, you should be trying to help your man figure out a way to get her some help?"

"My man?"

"You know who I'm talking about?"

"If you talking about Joey? Yeah, I care about him. I care about all my friends."

"Your interest in Joey is a little deeper than just mere friendship." When she looked at him strangely, he immediately said, "What? You didn't think anyone noticed? I've known you since you were a little girl, remember? Just tell the man how you really feel. Who knows, he just might surprise you?" BeeBop shook her head in doubt before lowering it.

"Um' the last person Joey would be interested in. Anyway, you didn't come all the way to Jersey to talk about me and Joey. Why you wanna see 'Rise?" He peeped at his watch and was about to speak when the phone ranged. "Hold that thought," she said before answer it. "Yeah?" she quickly spoke into the receiver.

188

"Oh, whaz' up, 'Sweet. Y'all still in Queens?" She turned her back to Tyrone as she carefully listened to the caller. "Is that right? I'll be damn! Yeah... uh-huh... uh-huh... okay, I'll tell him. Later."

The moment she hung up, Tyrone asked her, was that TooSweet on the phone? "Yeah," she said while sitting. "'Rise sent her and Robin out on a mission."

"Robin who?"

"Robin! The girl you introduced 'Rise to last week?"

Tyrone appeared confused. "You mean to tell me 'Rise pulled her into the FOLD?"

"Worse. They act just like a married couple."

He smiled. "Well I'll be damn!" he was about to ask for details when they heard a key turning in the door before it opened. SunRise, Joey and his sister's children walked into the apartment.

BeeBop looked at Joey, then the three small children and immediately asked, "What happened?" SunRise glanced at her briefly while helping Joey with the children's coats. "'Sweet just called," she quickly changed the subject in an effort to lighten the obvious tension in the room. She wasn't sure what happened between Joey and his sister. But the look SunRise just gave her, led her to believe it wasn't a good time to be inquiring.

"What she say?" SunRise quickly asked without once looking at her.

"Not too much," BeeBop replied while following him around the apartment. "She didn't even mention Robin. She just said something about spending the night at my spot in Brooklyn. She told me she'll be back tomorrow."

For the first time, SunRise looked at her. His attempt to cover his concern was a complete failure. "Is someone after them?" he couldn't resist asking.

"She never said. She just said she'll explain when she comes in tomorrow; it sounded like she was in a hurry."

"And that's all?"

BeeBop shrugged, "As far as I know, yeah," she said while periodically glancing at Tyrone. Who had been preoccupied playing with Joey's three year old nephew, Sekou. Tyrone was crazy about the three year old toddler. Aside from being the quietest baby he had ever known, Sekou was also the angriest. Tyrone have yet to see the toddler laugh, or cry. On occasions he might manage to get a smile or two but that was all. No one actually knew if Wendi, the toddler's mother was using while pregnant with him. But one thing was for sure. Sekou was an old soul who constantly watched everyone with a gaze that was almost intimidating. Like his uncle Joey and his mother, Wendi, Sekou had a healthy blue-black complexion. And for his age, was as strong as an ox.

SunRise looked at Joey and said, "Joey, why don't you take the girls in back and get them cleaned up for bed. "They can sleep in my room tonight. You and Sekou can sleep in the guest-room."

"And what about you?" Joey asked.

"Don't worry about me. The children come first."

Joey nodded, then gathered all the children and took them in back.

With the children now out of the way, SunRise joined Tyrone on the sofa. "On Joey's recommendation, I hire a few outsiders. 'Face and his wife Vicki; you know 'em?"

"Yeah. Doc patched his wife up last year while you were out of the country. Her husband, 'Face' trained her. Joey say she turned out to be a real force."

"They'll be here tomorrow at noon to pick up the details. I need you to follow them. Make sure they don't run into any problems. I also want you to recruit this brutha' who was just released from a Halfway House. If you want, take him with you. Show him how we do." 'Face and Vicki have a message and gift from us for him. So don't panic if you see them stopping by his place."

"I understand. Do I know him?"

"You might. Michael Henderson tried to recruit him, but he turned them down.

"Who is he?"

"A soldier name Sunny Black; got out of prison six months ago. You might remember him by his streets name, Black-Sun?"

"Naw'," Tyrone slowly shook his head, no. "Don't think I know him."

"Back in the day, he used to be a soldier for a North Main street crew ran by a joker name, Joe-boy."

"I remember Joe-boy. Use to get his packages from those country-boys in Harlem back in the 70's. Shit, after Joe-boy got finish cutting it up. Cat's were still dropping like flies from over-dosing."

"So I heard.

"Yeah. That was before your time, 'Rise."

"So it was. We're looking to recruit this P-town legend.

He already declined Mike's offer. And is probably expecting Mike to send his boys over to try and change his mind. But that's not Mike's twist. He don't get-down like that," SunRise replied before changing the subject. "Anyway, go see him. His address is in the envelope with your fee. I have a few more gifts for him. I need one of you to shadow this kid out of Washington Heights. You should be able to find him at this new club in Irvington, New Jersey tomorrow night. It might be better to send Sunny Black. You'll have your hands filled shadowing our contractors."

"What's the name of the club?" Tyrone asked while producing a pen.

"Club X Ray. Everything you'll need to know is in the package."

Tyrone placed the pen back into his inside coat-pocket and asked "How long you want him to shadow this guy?"

"He has to find out as much as he can tomorrow night at the club, because I need him to keep an eye on 'Sweet. I have a strong feeling she's gonna' need help."

Tyrone looked at him confused. "You know something I don't, 'Rise?"

"I do, just not willing to share prematurely. You have the particulars of your assignment."

"I understand." Tyrone said as they both stood. "Well. If there's no further need of my services. I have to be getting back."

"Of course," SunRise said understandingly. "Give me a minute." He walked off into the back only to return with an envelope. "Thanks again. I really appreciate it." He handed Tyrone the envelope and walked with him towards the door. "You'll find everything you need to know inside. If I forgot to mention something, I'll call 'Bop and have her fill you in. Again, thanks."

Tyrone took a quick glance inside the envelope, then pocketed it. "No problem, 'Rise," he smiled warmly while opening the door. Before leaving, he looked at BeeBop. She had been sitting on the sofa watching the whole time. He blew her a kiss and said, "Don't forget what I told you, baby-girl?" BeeBop nodded and told him to drive safely.

"What was that all about?" SunRise asked after Tyrone had left.

"Personal advice. You know how Tye is, big brutha' to everybody." Without giving it much thought, SunRise headed for the back with BeeBop following. Upon stepping into the bathroom, they found the two girls in the bathtub washing. SunRise immediately apologized and left. BeeBop, however, remained to give the girls a hand.

Inside the guest-room, SunRise found Joey helping his nephew with his pajamas. "If you need me," SunRise began. "I'll be in Brooklyn. When I return tomorrow, Robin and I will be taking a short trip for a few days. In the mean time, you and the children are welcome to stay here. There's plenty of food, so make yourselves at home."

"Thanks, 'Rise. We should be out of your way by tomorrow."

"We're family, Joey," SunRise said before leaving the room.

Once BeeBop got the girls out of the tub and into their pajamas she stepped into the living-room and found SunRise sitting on the sofa in deep thought. Sensing something was bothering him, she asked, "You a'ight?"

"I was just thinking."

"About what?" she sat next to him.

"Robin. After I sent TooSweet back I spent the entire day trying to find out as much as I could about her late friend, Rossi. With the help of a private investigator I found out, after an autopsy was done, his lawyer claimed the body and had it sent out of the country. I also found out, and don't ask how, but Robin's friend was an extremely wealthy man who had an affinity towards young women. Young black women." He paused, "I'm curious about the type of relationship the two of them shared."

"You think it was more than just a casual friendship?"

"I don't know. When I asked her about it? She said he was like a father to her."

"But you think it was more, don't you?"

"Thinking constitutes doubt. The only way to be sure, is to go back down there with her to see that lawyer who's been looking for her. Hopefully he can provide more answers."

"She don't know why the lawyer wanna see her?"

"As far as I know, no. The investigator told me her friend's lawyer has been looking for her the moment he learned his client was deceased." SunRise stood when Joey walked into the room.

"Yo', 'Rise. Umma' put the girls to bed."

"Okay, brutha. 'Bop and I are on our way out. I just have to get a few things from the room before leaving." As SunRise headed towards the back, Joey was about to follow when BeeBop called him back to the sofa.

"You don't mind if I stay behind to give you a hand with the girls, do you?"

"I don't, but shouldn't you check with 'Rise first? He may have other plans for you?"

"If he does, he ain't said nothing to me?" When she looked up and saw SunRise returning, she whispered to Joey, "I'll let him know I'm not going with him."

SunRise stood in the middle of the living-room floor carrying his coat and over- night bag. "Remember, Joey," he said, sitting the bag down to put on his coat. "Whatever you do, don't send the children back to your sister's. I know you're concerned about her. We all are, but the children come first. We can't have her smoking those chemicals around them." He then looked at BeeBop and said, "You planning on staying or coming with me?"

"You know where I live. Umma' stay and give Joey a hand with the girls. Joey has classes tomorrow, and the girls have to go to school. Umma' watch Sekou until Joey and the girls get back."

"Not a bad excuse," he replied.

"What? You know what, never mind. Just be careful," she said, edging him out of the apartment.

"Wait a minute, 'Bop!" He reached into his pants pocket, and pulled out a key. "I almost forgot to give Joey my key. 'Sweet has the spare." He was about to hand Joey the key, but paused. "Or should I give it to you?" he asked before handing her the key. "Oh yeah, do me a favor and pick Robin's car up from the shop. It should be ready. I'll give you a call around 9:00 a.m." He was about to leave, but thought of something else. "One more thing," he said while reaching into his inside coat pocket. "Give Nonie, the shop owner this," he hand her a piece of paper with an address on it. "Tell him to deliver the car at that address. And make sure he instilled the phone."

"That reminds me," said BeeBop. "You do know I ain't got no phone in my apartment."

"Don't have, 'Bop. You don't have a phone at your apartment," he corrected her.

"Whatever!" SunRise smiled, shook his head, then left.

After BeeBop took the liberty to read to the children before putting them down for the night, she and Joey sat in the front-room talking most of the night. "I appreciate you volunteering to help out with the kids."

BeeBop saw it as the perfect opportunity to tell him how she really felt. "I like you, Joey. I've always liked you. But you were always too busy to notice."

Taken by complete surprise, he sat up straight and stared at her. "Define like?" he asked, trying to best understand the extent of her feelings toward him. BeeBop turned and looked away. She had hoped he would just take the bait and run with it. Instead, he was forcing her to stand naked and bare her soul. "I'm waiting?" he insisted.

She turned and looked him straight in the eyes. "I'm big on you. There! I said it. Happy now?" she said with nervousness in her voice while toying with a match-book she pick up from the ashtray.

He smiled. "I'm feeling you too, 'Bop."

"Okay, we like each other. You hungry?" She stood and walked off into the kitchen as if his words meant nothing.

Joey followed. "Look, 'Bop," he grabbed her gently by the arm, forcing her undivided attention. "I was serious when I said I was feeling you. If you feeling me as much as I'm feeling you. Maybe we should see where it takes us?"

As BeeBop stood leaning up against the refrigerator. She studied his eyes as if they were truly the windows to his soul. His words were direct and in all seriousness. She couldn't believe what she was hearing, nor was she quite sure just how to respond. Her experience with men had been much different from what Joey was offering. He was a man who understood and appreciated women.

Unlike her pervious relationships with hard-core thugs who had about as much respect for women, as the police had for them. Joey had his head on straight and always treated her with respect. Something BeeBop was not use to getting, especially from a man. As a woman, she was considered hard. It was also the way she liked her men, hard and thugged-out. She smiled as she remembered how she use to think being sweet-talked by a man consisted of the crude comments they made about the size of her ass. Looking back now, she couldn't believe she actually use to find that exciting. That is, until SunRise taught her a little something about self-respect.

"What you smiling about?" He asked, now holding her around the waist.

"Seriously, Joey ain't nothing I'd like better than to get with you. I just don't think it's a good idea right now. You already have your hands filled with your sista', Wendi. You don't need me in your life complicating things even more."

"You're exactly what I need in my life, 'Bop. I was kinda' hoping we needed each other. What you think?"

After the flight back from Miami, Vicki and Londell tooled up to make a quick trip to Wildwood, a summer resort area at the very end of south Jersey.

During their two week stay in Miami Beach. Vicki finally broke down and told Londell why she never made the trip to Camden last year. She told him about her encounter with the two dirty cops who robbed her and tried to murder him. She even told him about running into Kenny-Sam after Moon's two thugs forcefully brought him to the garage on Bunker Hill. But when she told him where she ran into Kenny-Sam? She saw that look in his eyes. A look she remember seeing twice. The first time was at the old apartment. After Londell murdered the three men who raped, beat and was about to murder Vicki. He took her to his home and nursed her back to health. But because Vicki was still in shock, Londell didn't know what to do to help her except what he did best. The mistake he made, was verbalizing his intentions in front of her.

The second time was in Eastside Park after she had neutralized the two cops who tried to murder him. The moment she removed the hand-cuffs, he went completely berserk. It wasn't so much what he did to the cop that frightened her. It was the look in his eyes. They were bloodshot and inflamed with rage.

Two hours and forty-five minutes later, they were crossing the bridge that took them straight into west Wildwood. Neither Vicki nor Londell had a clue where they were going. Vicki had been trying to talk him out of it all day. Reminding him they had a prior meeting with SunRise tomorrow. "I still think we shoulda' waited?" she said adding, "Suppose we can't find him? We can't stay down here until we do?"

"If he's here we'll find him," was Londell's only reply.

"That's another thing," Vicki went on to say. "We're not even sure he's here?" When Londell did not reply, she continued. "I hope you're not upset with me for not telling you sooner?"

He looked at her and smile. It was a pleasant smile that immediately put her fears to rest.

"I wanted to tell you a long time ago. I just didn't wanna open any old wounds. Besides, I was planning on handling Mr. Kenny-Sam myself."

"I'm glad you did tell me," he finally spoke.

She looked at him and couldn't help wondering why he was in such a rush to end Kenny-Sam. "I wasn't going to ask, but I have to know?"

He glanced at her. "Know what?"

"Why they tried to push you that night?" she stared at him waiting for him to answer. She had been hoping once she opened up and revealed all her secretes, he'd do the same. But he never did.

"There go that nigga right there," he said.

Vicki looked and saw the same man she had encountered in the garage lot on Bunker Hill. He was standing on the corner in front of a bar called Bud's talking to two other men.

"Is that the same man?" he asked with hostility in his voice while driving right pass the three men.

She looked at him strangely before answering, "Yeah. That's him. He was one of the men who came to the apartment and got you, right?"

"Naw', he wasn't one of them." He looked at her. "Why?" he asked.

"When I saw him leaving that place they took you to that day. I could have sworn he was one of the men I saw you leaving the apartment with. That's why I moved on him. I'm sorry I never said anything before."

He looked at her and forced a reassuring smile. He could tell she was still under the impression that he was upset with her for not telling him about Kenny-Sam sooner. "Don't worry about it, Vee. Um' pissed off," he finally admitted. "But not at you. I don't think I could ever get upset with you." Because he seemed sincere, she smiled. "It's that nigga who got my jaws tight," he added while staring down the street at Kenny-Sam.

"You wanna tell me why it's so personal?"

Without looking at her he began. "I never told you why Big Moon and 'em tried to push me because I didn't know. When they brought me to the garage that night, I never saw Kenny-Sam there. I always knew he was cool with Big Moon, but thought he was his own man."

"What are you talking about, baby?"

"The nigga hired me for a job. It was a two man job and I wasn't gonna' take it. But because I always liked and respected Kenny-Sam, I did. It was the same job I took Baxter Keys with me on. In fact, it was the same night I followed you from the Cheater's Club. Months later, I found out who he paid me to push. I never confronted him about it, but it always bothered me?" He paused to glance down the street. Making sure Kenny-Sam had not left yet.

"Why, baby?"

"For one thing, he is a soldier like us. He don't distribute hits, he carries them out."

"Didn't you know all this before taking the job?"

"Yeah, I just figured the nigga was doing me a favor by throwing some action my way, you know?"

"I understand, baby." She looked up and saw Kenny-Sam leaving. "Look!" she anxiously whispered. "I think he's leaving?"

When Londell looked and saw Kenny-Sam and his two friends part ways. He fired up the engine and followed. Wildwood and its' neighboring towns were a far cry from where Londell had come from. Similar to that of Vicki's home town in Ocean City, Maryland, The resort area resembled a ghost-town during the winter months, but came alive with tourism during the summer.

As Kenny-Sam casually walked down the street as if he didn't have a care in the world, Londell slowly followed. "Baby, can we just do him so we can go home?" Vicki quickly asked.

"Not until I find out, why?" Londell replied before speeding up. He drove pass Kenny-Sam and parked around the corner. "Wait here," he said while getting out of the car. Vicki watched as he peeked around the corner while pulling out his weapon.

Just as Kenny-Sam came around the corner, he almost bumped into Londell. "Pardon me," said Kenny-Sam before realizing the man he almost bumped into was the man he had been hiding from. "Face?"

"Surprise, surprise, nigga."

Kenny-Sam looked at the gun with the suppresser attached to it and began to plead his case. "Wait a minute, 'Face. I ain't in the game no more. And I damn sure ain't have nothing to do with that shit Moon tried to pull. You know me, yo'?"

Londell was beginning to believe him until Kenny-Sam said something Londell knew was a lie. "In fact, as soon as I heard what was going down. I was on my way over there, but some crazy-ass-bitch split my shit before I could make it inside."

The moment Vicki heard him, she go out of the car and walked up behind him. "Looks to me like you were leaving, if I'm not mistaken," she said. When Kenny turned around and saw her, he smiled. Vicki quickly patted him down, then slowly walked around him and stood by Londell's side.

"Something funny?" Londell asked him.

"I tried."

"That you did." Londell agreed. Adding, "The sad thing is... I was beginning to believe you." Londell said with a smile. "I know it wasn't personal. I just don't know why?"

Still smiling Kenny briefly glanced at Vicki. "You righ'.

It wasn't personal. Last year, you did some work for us. You just made the mistake of taking some lame with you."

"Baxter Keys?" Londell asked.

"That be the one. Moon didn't want to take the chance you running your mouth. We were trying to move against Big Mike. You might say it was a power move. The people we hired you to push were power playaz'. I told them niggaz' not to fuck with you. I told them you were thorough and would never talk, but they didn't wanna take any chances."

"You know my twist."

"I thought I did. But when you took your boy, Baxter with you? You fucked up. And there wasn't shit I could say to make them think otherwise. I tried, they just wasn't having it, you feel me?" Londell just stared at him. "When I saw them bring you in, I got the fuck out of there. I ain't want no part of it?" While Londell and Vicki were silent, Kenny-Sams was beginning to think he had a shot in talking his way out of dying.

"The reason I left the game was because of what they did to you. What I thought they did to you," he corrected himself.

"How you want it?" Londell asked.

At that very moment, a police car drove pass and slowed down while staring at them. Kenny saw his shot and took it. "FUCK YOU LOOKING AT!" he shouted, trying his best to provoke the police-man without going out like a chump.

The cop smiled and gave Kenny-Sam the finger before speeding off.

You've got to be kidding, Kenny-Sam silently though.

"Nice try. Again, how you want it?" Londell asked for the last time.

Kenny-Sam tried to maintain his smile, but his eyes clearly displayed fear. For a brief moment, he actually thought it just wasn't his time to die. Having survived a skull fracture that placed him in a comma only to awaken and find his entire crew dead. He was beginning to think somebody up stairs liked him. "You already know, yo'." Londell walked up to him and showed Kenny-Sam another courtesy by shooting him in the right side of his chest twice, "CLACK-CLACK!" That way, his family could give him an open casket funeral.

CHAPTER 18

BeeBop had already left the apartment when Joey woke this morning. After waking the girls he made sure they ate breakfast before sending them off to school and then waited with his nephew for BeeBop to return. Upon her return forty-five minutes later. Joey told her SunRise had called. "They should be back around noon."

"You better get going, Joey. I don't want you to be late for your classes," she warned. Joey peek at his watch, grabbed his things and kissed her lightly on the lips before leaving.

All morning BeeBop couldn't stop smiling or thinking about Joey. Feeling somewhat like a house-wife, she spent the entire morning cleaning while Joey's three year old nephew followed her around the apartment. It was almost noon before she finally had everything in order, and not a moment to soon. The moment she was able to relax, SunRise, Robin, and TooSweet walked into the apartment and immediately gathered around the television. "What's up, y'all'?" she asked. When no one answered, she joined TooSweet on the sofa with the toddler sitting in her lap. With all eyes glued to the tube. They watched and waited as SunRise played with the remote until he found the news at noon on channel seven. "What's going on?" BeeBop asked again but everyone seemed too preoccupied to have heard her.

During an intermission, BeeBop broke the silence by asking, "Anyone interested in anything from the kitchen while I'm up?"

Without taking their eyes from the television, everyone declined.

As the news resumed, they all waited with growing anticipation for the anchor-woman to give her report.

"Forty million dollar drug stash seized in a New York City raid!"

As the anchor woman continued, BeeBop watched while Robin and TooSweet became quietly excited.

"Police seized nearly half a ton of cocaine... worth an estimated $40 million on the street... and arrested four suspects in what authorities called the city's biggest drug bust in recent history. The four suspects allegedly have ties to Dominican's violent drug cartel, said Queen's District Attorney Carl Williams, who disclosed details of the bust at a news conference earlier, where 400 bundles of the drug were displayed. Williams said the 416 kilograms, (915 pounds) of cocaine were seized by city police narcotics officers in a raid on a private home in the Rego Park section of Queens last night. Those arrested were identified as Alberto Torrez; his wife, Maria Torrez; Ricardo Garcia; and his wife, Luisa Garcia. They allegedly were part of a distribution network based in the Dominican Republic that "Reached all the way into a private home on a quiet residential street in the Rego Park section," the district attorney said. "Because this enormous quantity of drugs had been blatantly stored in the immediate vicinity of a neighborhood school makes this seizure all the more significant." All four were arraigned this morning on charges of controlled substance, which carries a maximum life sentence. Criminal Court Judge Jessica Green set bail at $2 million for Torrez, $1 million for Garcia, and $750,000 for each of the two women. Williams said the raid was the result of a tip received from a Brooklyn Lieutenant, Al Sheets of the 81st precinct who claims to have received his information from a, "very reliable source". Soon after, a search warrant was procured for the private home on Westwood Drive directly across the street from a public school house. In other news today...."

SunRise turned the television off while staring at Robin, and TooSweet, who sat wearing smiles of satisfaction. "Well... that's, that!" TooSweet said while standing.

"Was that the same address y'all' checked out yesterday?" BeeBop asked.

"Yeah," Robin told her while still holding on to the duffel bag she came in with.

BeeBop looked at SunRise, then at TooSweet. "Y'all' gonna' tell me what that was all about?"

Robin stood and shouted, "This!" while emptying the overstuffed duffel onto the carpeted floor.

Staring in disbelief at the massive amount of money scattered all over the carpet. BeeBop quickly shouted, "Damn, y'all'! How much is it?"

"I counted twenty stacks of what I thought was ten thousand each," Robin began. "Which came to two-hundred grand. After TooSweet and I got to your spot in Brooklyn, I found out each stack contained twenty-five thousand."

BeeBop began calculating out loud.

"That's right, girl. A half million tax free!" Robin said excitedly.

"Y'all' shoulda' seen Robin's face when I came back to pick her up!" said TooSweet. "She almost pissed in her pants."

Everyone laughed; everyone but SunRise. But no one seemed to have noticed. They were having too much fun. Once the three women had calmed down some, BeeBop glanced at SunRise and saw the computer disk he was tapping against his chin. "What's that, 'Rise?" she asked.

"This?" He looked the disk over. "Robin ran across it before finding the money. I had someone look at it this morning. We found two files, one in Excel; the other in Word."

"So what was on it?" she continued to pry.

"Everything. Robin had good instincts to take it because it contained a spreadsheet template of their books, suppliers, distributors, sales and some names; three of which I'm familiar with."

"Who name is it?" asked TooSweet.

"Michael Henderson, Teflon Figueroa and Johnathen Crain Junior - a young, rich, New York lawyer who once represented Michael Henderson. I read about Henderson getting off on some drug charges. One of Mike's dealers got bagged leaving the city with ten birds. He cut a deal with the D.A.'s office by giving up Mike."

"I don't know where I know that name, Johnathen Crain but it sounds real familiar?" said Robin while trying to recall.

"Why would some big-time lawyer's name be on that disk?" asked BeeBop.

"I was about to asked the same thing, 'Rise?" said TooSweet.

"I'm not sure, but I have a strong feeling we gonna' find out. I never got a chance to get in the Word file. The people who looked at it was unable to access it. I'm going to have Reggie take a look at it. I doubt if he has any problems gaining access."

"What you think is in it?" asked Robin.

"I have no idea?"

"What you gonna' do with it?" she continued to pry.

"I'd like to use it to shut down the rest of their operations, but something tells me this thing is much more complex than it appears," he said before turning to BeeBop.

"'Bop, when Joey gets back, have him make a copy of it. Put the copy in a safe place and give the original to Tyrone. Tell him to delete the word file and send it certified mail to Vincent. Make sure he warns Vincent not to open the package until instructed. I have a feeling we're going to need this information as a bargaining chip in the near future," he said while briefly glancing at TooSweet suspiciously before looking up at Robin. "If you're planning on making that trip, I suggest you start getting ready. I wanna be on the road by 3:00 p.m."

"You're coming with me?" she asked excitedly.

He looked at his watch. "You better start getting ready before I change my mind." Beaming with glee, she hopped up and rushed off to the back. Once she was out of the room, SunRise told the two women to make every effort to inspire Joey to take control of his situation. "When I left you and Joey last night, 'Bop. I stopped by Wendi's to talk some sense into her. She gave me her word she would seek help."

"You believed her?" BeeBop asked.

"I do." He paused then told them to try and use a little diplomacy. "I don't want him getting the wrong idea... as if we don't care." SunRise was about to speak again when they heard a hard knock at the door. Before answering it, he told the two women to tool-up. After BeeBop gathered up the money and placed it into the closet. SunRise signaled TooSweet, who took a quick look through the peep-hole before opening the door. In stepped a youthful-looking, light-skinned man with unusually large, cherry-red lips. Behind him was a tall, beautiful, caramel complexion young woman with haunting hazel eyes. Both were casually dressed. The male in baggy jeans, white tennis shoes and button-up, three quarter inch white leather coats. The female who cautiously stood a few feet in back of him wore tight skinny jeans, black leather boots and a loose fitting long, black leather coat. With both of her hands folded behind her back, both TooSweet and BeeBop understood the gesture which told them she was not a threat, nor did she feel threatened.

"Londell... Vicki... thank you for coming. Please," SunRise gestured with a wave of his hand. "Have a seat," he said, trying to make his guest feel a little more at ease. Because both declined, SunRise knew they had no intention on staying long. He then looked at BeeBop and signaled her with a slight nod of his head. She quickly walked off into the back room only to return seconds later with two envelopes - a white business size number ten and a large yellow manila. After handing them to him, she resumed her former position. SunRise handed both envelopes to Londell and watched as he briefly examined the contents while his wife, Vicki stared at the toddler who had been sitting on the floor. SunRise looked at the toddler. He was staring back at the tall, attractive woman with equal intimidation. SunRise looked up at her, she looked at him, they both smiled.

After the couple left, Robin joined the crew in the living-room. "Did I hear someone mention my car?" she asked, sitting next to the two women on the sofa.

"Yeah 'Sweet and I was..."

"Were! 'Sweet and I were!" SunRise interrupted.

"Whatever!" she irritably snapped before continuing.

SunRise smiled. He knew the more he stayed on her about her grammar, the more she would be inclined to choose her words more carefully. "... As I was saying," she glanced at SunRise with a stern eye before continuing. "'Sweet and I were just discussing the Nissan Motor Corporation. What made you get a Nissan?"

Robin shrugged. "I don't know; probably because it reminded me of a Lexus. Only... it didn't cost as much," she laughed lightly and asked, "Why?" Both women stared at her as if her answer had come as a complete surprise.

"Oh." BeeBop glanced at TooSweet briefly, then explained. "A lot of people don't know this, but Nissan... their corporation give young black adults special educational opportunities like scholarship grants, internship, and post-graduation jobs. They even train bruthaz' and sistaz' for entrepreneur and decision-making positions."

"Don't forget about what they do for historical black colleges and universities," SunRise reminded.

"Oh yeah!" BeeBop continued, "They provide summer fellowships to professors, too. 'Sweet and I thought you patronized them for those reasons, but it's all good. What you didn't know before, you do now."

SunRise looked at Robin and suggested, "Now that school is out, Robin. You should call that lawyer. Let him know you're on your way."

Robin produced the card SunRise had given her, and sat it next to the phone while dialing the number.

"How long y'all' 'pose to be gone, 'Rise?" BeeBop asked while playing with the baby who was now sitting on TooSweet's lap.

"Hopefully no more than two days, but who knows? It could be shorter, or longer. Just be sure to check your messages, and don't forget to check on Wendi every now and then."

"Yes, hello," Robin quickly spoke into the receiver. "My name is, Robin Hoods. I understand you... excuse me? Yes ... I am. I'm calling because I heard... yes... yes... MY WHO!" she shouted into the receiver. Everyone in the room looked at her as she continued. "Are you sure there hasn't been some kind of mistake?" she asked with a troubling look in her eyes. "Yes...I am well aware of that! Are you aware that I am a black woman?"

SunRise, TooSweet, and BeeBop looked at one another. They were just as confused as Robin appeared to be. "This... I gotta' see. Sure... 9:00 a.m. Mondays. I'll be there."

The moment she hung the phone up SunRise asked, "What was that all about?"

Robin didn't answer right away, she just stared at the phone blankly. It took asking her a second time before she looked up at him and said, "He said I was Rossi's biological daughter and sole beneficiary to his estate." Her eyes were hollow and confused.

"That's good news! Ain't it?" BeeBop quickly asked.

"You don't understand," Robin told her. "Rossi wasn't my father. How could he have been? I met him while on the run. He was a fence who took me in. We were friends, that's all."

"I see what you saying," BeeBop said before adding, "All um' saying is... the man left you everything he owns. From what I've heard, he had a lot to leave. If he wanted to claim you as his daughter, let him. He's dead, o-kay!"

"Maybe they made a mistake," said SunRise. "Or it could just be his way of showing you how much you meant to him." He stood and sat on the arm of the sofa next to her. "We won't know anything until we see what kind of proof he has." He gently rubbed her neck with one hand and asked, "You ready to roll?"

Robin smile weakly while standing. "You ain't gonna' packed?"

"Of course," he said, grabbing her suitcases. "My bags are in the Jag, but we're going to use your ride."

"My car?"

"I guess you didn't notice your ride sitting in the lot when we pulled in. 'Bop picked it up this morning. Nonie did a good job on it."

209

"Thanks BeeBop," Robin said just before opening the door.

"We forgot all about the money?"

"The money is yours. You found it," said SunRise.

"No. We found it, which means it belongs to all of us."

"'Sweet, 'Bop and I have no need for it. Normally when we run across drug money we donate it. Hell House is up for our next donation."

"Donate it! Are you serious? What's a Hell House, anyway?"

Everyone looked at Robin before TooSweet took the floor to explain. "It's like a Foster Home for children whose parents were so addicted to drugs, they couldn't take care of them. Most of the children have been born addicted. Mother Hell, the lady who founded and ran it, died just last year."

"Yeah..." BeeBop interject, "that broke my heart when I heard she passed away. People came from all over the country just to pay their respects."

"If anyone needs this money more, Robin. It's Hell House," SunRise said before continuing. "The place is run by Mother Hell's daughter now, Linda. She gets no help or aid from the Government."

"How in the world is she able to keep the place going?"

"Hell House survives merely through private donations."

"Well... um' down, but I don't want my name used?"

"All FOLD's donations are strictly confidential. 'Sweet will see to it WON'T YOU, 'SWEET?" he raised his voice to get her attention.

Still playing with the baby, she abruptly looked up at him, startled. "What! Oh... yeah... yeah. I'll take care of it."

"Y'all be careful and hurry back," BeeBop said.

"Likewise," SunRise replied, glancing at TooSweet briefly before reminding BeeBop not to forget what he said about the disk?

"Don't worry, 'Rise, I'll take care of it," she assured.

CHAPTER 19

Londell and Vicki sat in their car going over the file SunRise had just given them. Still parked in the lot of the C.C.P., Vicki seemed to be the only one who noticed SunRise approaching the parking-lot carrying several pieces of luggage.

Walking beside him was a woman Vicki did not remember seeing at his apartment moments ago. While the woman got into the passenger seat of a black '93 Altima. Vicki watched as SunRise placed the luggage in the trunk of the Altima, but did not close it. She had assumed he was just being nice by giving the woman a hand with her bags until she noticed him retrieving some more luggage from the trunk of his Jaguar. When she saw him place the luggage in the trunk of the shiny black Altima, then get in behind the wheel. She concluded the woman must have been his companion after all. As SunRise slowly navigated out of the parking lot, she inconspicuously glanced at her husband to see if he had noticed. Satisfied he hadn't, she began reflecting on the prior meeting her husband had with the young nationalist.

The legendary founder of the FOLD. The man she had heard so much about; the man whose connections inadvertently saved her life and changed it forever. He was nowhere near what she had expected. In fact, he was just a boy. At least that's what he appeared to be on the surface.

But she knew better than anyone how deceiving appearances could be, and often were. She looked at her husband and remembered the first time she had saw him. She smiled. "Who you wanna see first?" Londell asked without taking his eyes from the file.

"What? Oh. It doesn't matter." Her mind was somewhere else.

He briefly glanced at her before starting the car and backed out of his parking space. "I guess we'll see Mike last?" he replied, pulling out of the lot.

Double parked in front of a pool-hall on Governor Street.

Londell told Vicki he would be right back before getting out of the car. When he returned moments later. He told her the man they were looking for just left the pool-hall.

"You know this dude, Sunny Black?" she asked while reading the file on the man in question.

"Not really," he replied before pulling off. "Growing up, I use to hear niggaz' kicking his name around."

"What type of person is he?"

"An old school soldier from the '70's; niggaz' out here can't appreciate a nigga like him. During his time, when you put in work, you put it in. If you got caught, you ate it like a man. These young, hungry ass niggaz' out here today can't do no time more less put in real work. That's why I don't fuck wit' 'em. Niggaz' now dayz' will tell just to save their own ass. But catz' like, Sunny Black and Big Keys, those catz' were real thugs."

"Is Big Keys Baxster Keys older brother?"

"Yeah."

"He just got out, too. Didn't he?"

"Yeah."

"How long was Black-Sun locked-down?" she continued as if trying to keep the conversation going.

Londell gave the question some thought before answering.

"Um' not sure? It's been a minute, though. It should be in his file, everything else is?"

She looked at his file again. "He had a life sentence; did fourteen years and eight months and made parole first eligibility. He must have been a model prisoner?" she said with huskiness in her voice. When he didn't comment, she put the file back into the envelope and sit it on top of the dash. "I still don't understand why he wanna pay us to do something he coulda' accomplished with one phone call?"

Londell glanced in the rear-view mirror suspiciously before saying, "You should be glad we getting paid for doing something he coulda' accomplished with one phone call?" He glanced in the rear-view again.

"What's wrong?" she turned in her seat to see who was behind them, but did not notice anything out of the ordinary.

He glanced in the rear-view once more, "I thought we were being followed by this white 'beamer'."

She turned in her seat again, but saw no white BMW behind them. "You said the same shit yesterday about a different white car?" she reminded him.

Five blocks from the pool-hall, they parked directly in front of a run-down apartment building. As they walked towards the shabby building, the strong odor of heavy spices told them the building was heavily influence with Latino residence.

Once inside, they heard loud reggae tong music coming from an up-stairs apartment. Sunny Black's apartment was the first door on the first floor. With an open ear, Vicki lean up against the old wooden door, then knocked.

A dark skin man of medium size and height with short, thick dread-locks snatched open the door as if he had been expecting trouble. But the moment he saw Vicki, his posture eased up. Londell misinterpret his behavior and became extremely jealous. "Can I help you?" he asked with his focus directly on Vicki.

Londell looked at Vicki, then at Black-Sun, who seemed to be ignoring the fact that Londell was even standing there.

Over taken by a combination of jealousy, rage and disrespect, Londell went for his Glock-nine. But Black-Sun already had a Double-O-Seven blade to his throat. "Calm down, young buck," he said with a half smile.

"The last thing I want is a beef with you," his eyes were still on Vicki as if he was anticipating her making a move.

"SunRise sent us," Vicki immediately spoke up. She saw the look in his eyes. A look that told her he was anything but a joke.

"SunRise?" he seemed surprised. "Sorry 'bout that," he released Londell and lowered the knife. "I was expecting someone else? Come on in." Once Londell and Vicki were inside, he closed and locked the door behind them. "Place ain't much," he said while staring at Londell. "But it beats being stuck in a cage and it's mine as long as I can pay the rent."

"This should help," Vicki said while producing an envelope with cash.

He took the envelope and looked inside. "Damn! Must be 'bout ten grand in here?"

"Actually twenty," Londell pointed out while still rubbing his neck. The mere thought of how close he came to having his neck sliced open gave him the shivers. He never had any illusions about getting got. It was the way he almost got it that shook him up.

"I can't accept this. It's too much."

"You'd be a fool not to," Londell continued. "The money is a gift. No strings attached. We were told you have a lifetime of parole. SunRise can make it disappear, giving you a clean start."

"To do what?"

"Start making amends by becoming a constructive member to the community, instead of destructive." When Black-Sun looked at him strangely Londell quickly added, "His words, not mine."

"Look," Black-Sun went on to say. "I had a lot of time to reflect on my past. I'm not proud of the life I use to live, and I damn sure ain't going back there. I lost my humanity long before I got put behind the hall. But there was this young girl from my old 'hood in Asbury who started writing to me. Without the comfort of her letters I don't think I would have made it. She helped me find my humanity by helping me see the things in life that were important. We all have eyes, but that don't mean

216

we able see the things in life that make us weep. I know you're probably saying to yourselves, "this nigga must have lost his mind?" But peep this, you see life in a whole new light when you're able to feel. It don't make you soft. It makes you what you were meant to be, human. And until you can feel, you'll just be stone, cold dead like the people you've pushed. So you can tell SunRise it's a very generous offer, and I really appreciate it. But soldiering just ain't in me no more."

"I don't think you understand. The money is a gift. You don't owe him anything. You were recommended by someone on the inside with you; someone from your old 'hood whose word obvious means a lot to SunRise." Black-Sun tried to think of who it could have been, but hit a blank. "And by the way,"

Londell added. "SunRise ain't no hustler. He's a nationalist. He knows you came home trying to do the right thing, whatever that is. He also understands how hard it must be for you coming home to a whole new world. I guess he don't wanna see you get caught up out of desperation, you feel me?"

"I feel you. But, damn!" he said while looking at the money. "Who is this cat? Some type of millionaire?"

"Why you say that?" asked Vicki. "Because earlier. Some grease-monkey dropped off this muscle car; a real classic. Said it was a gift from, SunRise. I refused to accept the Keys and the title; bad business owing another man; especially when you don't even know who you getting in bed with? But if he's straight like you say I'll consider accepting after we've had a chance to speak?" Londell and Vicki stood. Just as Londell was about to open the door so they could leave, Black-Sun stopped him. "If y'all don't mind me asking what's your names?"

Both Londell and Vicki looked at one another. "They call me, 'Face. This is my wife, Nemesis."

"Look. Nothing for nothing and I hope you don't take this the wrong way. That move you tried to make on me earlier will get you killed. You seem like a nice couple, but in your line of work, there's no room for emotions. Think twice before you make a move that's all um' saying."

"You said in our line of work?" Londell asked.

"I saw you coming. It wasn't hard to tell the both of you were packing weight. That's what made me think you were someone else."

Londell glanced at Vicki. Then told Black-Sun he would try to remember that thing about his emotions.

Recently released from a New Jersey State Prison after serving one third of a life sentence Sunny Black had been a formal soldier for a local drug-dealer name, Joe-boy. Back in the mid 1970's, Joe-boy was one of P-town's many Heroin dealers who supplied users with nickels, dimes, twenty-cent spoons and quarters bags of Scag, now known as, Scramble. Unlike other drug dealers Joe-boy's dope was so good, overdoses were a common occurrence which only made his product all the more appealing to addicts. But with that kind of monopoly on the drug game came a price Joe-boy was not prepared to pay. Not only were there multiple attempts on his life, but random stick-up boy wreaked havoc on his dealers. That is, until he hire a young notorious hood named Sunny Black. Whose retaliation had been so brutal and exact, Sunny Black's name hung like a black cloud over the heads of Joe-boy's competitive muscle; hence the name, Black-Sun.

When Sunny black was arrested for work he put in on behalf of Joe-boy. Joe-boy turned his back, leaving Sunny Black to the mercy of some young public defender. Who, as it turned out, got all three murders to run concurrent. Sunny Black received a life sentence and did his time like a man.

Joe-boy however, became his own best customer by getting hooked on his own product. A few years later he was found dead in his apartment from an overdose. One of his dealers, a young business minded thug name Michael Henderson, took up where Joe-boy left off.

With Sunny Black home now Mike knew his organization could go a long way with that kind of muscle on his team. Which was why he offered Sunny Black an executive position in his organization, but Sunny Black respectfully declined. He didn't know Michael Henderson personally. Mike had been a kid and a nobody when Sunny Black went to prison. But everyone knew of Sunny Black's reputation including Mike. So when Mike sent his boys over to recruit Sunny Black. He respectfully declined.

Explaining, the man everyone called, Black-Sun no longer existed. Still, Mike didn't strike him as a man who would just take no for an answer. And Sunny Black was prepared for whatever came his way.

Because Michael Henderson was a business man, his offer to Sunny Black was merely a business proposition; nothing more, nothing less. SunRise understood the situation only too well.

A week before Sunny Black was released, word from the inside came to his attention that the P-town legend had made parole.

Unlike Michael Henderson, SunRise did some research before making a decision.

A few minutes after Londell and Vicki left Sunny Black's apartment. He got another visit from a representative of SunRise named, Tyrone Sharp.

Michael was lounging in the comfort of his large, brass-frame bed toking on a spliff while impatiently awaiting his young, recently acquired girlfriend who took her time slipping into something a little more comfortable in the bathroom.

Wearing only a full-length, Paisley-printed, Italian silk robe and a pair of Blues Brothers dark shades, he was getting sleepy. "Come on, girl! I ain't got all night!" he shouted before hitting the spliff one more time. "It don't take that long just to get naked." The room was dim, almost dark except for the contour of the light that escaped from the crack at the bottom of the closed bathroom door on the other side of the spacious master bedroom.

He was about to call out to her again, when the bathroom door suddenly opened. Mike immediately sat up in bed and looked at her. Standing in the spot-light of the doorway striking a provocative pose, she was breathtaking. Pleased with his new find, he was beside himself. Wearing a hot-pink lacy bra and panty set that hugged her figure like a surgical glove. Mike smiled approvingly as the ravishing, young, white female glided across the room until she stood in front of him at the foot of the bed with both hand on her thick, creamy hips.

Mike was wide awake now as he laid his six-foot, four-inch frame back on the plush pillows with his hands interlaced behind his head. His pole stood straight up as if waiting to be served. He had to admit. She was a fine piece-of-ass. And the thought of him about to tap it, had him dripping-rock-hard. But because of who he was, he didn't want to appear too anxious. That would only betray a weakness. "Get that ass over here," he commanded. On her hands and knees, she crawled onto the bed between his legs until she came face to face with the head of his rock hardness. Mike closed his eyes and enjoyed the ride as she ran her soft lips from his nuts to the head of his swollen gland.

With the anticipation of having his knob polished, he moaned while grabbing the back of her long blond locks in a desperate attempt to force her to go down on him.

Without opening her mouth, she lightly ran her lips down the length of his swollen manhood, then back up to the gland.

Mike wasn't sure what she was doing, but it was definitely working. He smiled and felt his toes curl when all of a sudden, they heard the door bell.

When Camille jumped out of bed as if she had been expecting company, Mike opened his eyes and asked, "Where the fuck you think you going?"

"Someone is at the door, baby." she pointed out the obvious while throwing on a robe and a matching pair of open-toe kitten-heels.

"No shit, bitch. Let them niggaz' down stairs get it. That's what the fuck they get paid for."

"I would, but you know how they are? In a minute this house is gonna' be filled with some more of your men. I don't like all those strange men running in and out, Mike. Three of them roaming around here is more than enough. Besides, I don't like the way they keep looking at me."

Just then, they both heard the door-bell again. Anxious to continue what she had started, he relented. "Okay! Okay!

Just hurry the fuck up."

"Relax, daddy. I'll be right back," she promised before rushing out of the room while making sure to close the door behind her.

As Vicki and Londell headed for the house of their target, Vicki began going over Michael Henderson's file. Londell looked at her and suggested, "You sure you wanna do this now? We don't have to rush it. We can do it another time." Still going over the file she replied, "This is the perfect time. We know he's home and how any men he has in the house with him. I wanna take care of it tonight so we can lay up all day tomorrow." He smiled at the idea of the two of them relaxing at home, then yawned. She looked at him with concern, but didn't say anything. Once he stared the car and pulled off, she continued. "Baby, I kinda' like working for SunRise. He seems young, yet, knows exactly what he wants, and how to get it. Maybe we should work for him exclusively, you know? He does have a strong crew, and they're growing. We can grow with them?"

He glanced at her briefly, but didn't say anything. "So what's his story? You never told me anything about him?"

"Why the hell you so interested in him?"

She smiled at his obvious jealousy. "Remember what Black-Sun said about letting your emotions throw your focus?"

"Fuck that old-head; prison done made that nigga soft."

"Or wiser. Seriously though, SunRise is interesting, don't you think?" When he didn't answer, she added, "And cute, too."

"And not your type at all."

"How you know?"

"Because I know you! According to Joey, he's a revolutionary; a nationalist. Joey said he heard his mom and pops were members of the 'Black Liberation Army' back in the day. He don't know how true it is. The niggas is a ghost. Don't nobody really know a damn thing about him?" He took his eyes from the road to glance at her. "The nigga do look young as hell, don't he?"

"He sure does," Vicki agreed.

"Ain't no way you gonna' tell me he's as young as they say," said Londell.

"Why you say that? He does look pretty young. How old do you think he really is?"

"Who the hell knows; seventeen, eighteen, nineteen?

The nigga looks like he about fifteen, or sixteen. Personally, I think he's in his twenties. From the shit Joey told me about him. The nigga know too much shit to be that young." He glanced at her again and asked, "You still wanna work for him exclusively?"

"No one's worth our time exclusively."

"I use to think that, too. Now, seeing the paper that little nigga is giving away, um' not so sure?" he yawned again.

"Well... whatever you decide is fine with me." She looked at him and smiled.

"What about Michael Henderson? You sure you feel up to this?"

"I feel just fine. It's you I'm worried about. Why don't you go home and get some rest. I'll take care of it."

He glanced at her and wondered if she actually knew who they were about to go up against. "I ain't that tired!" he said. She smiled, knowing full well he would never allow her to take on such a huge responsibility by herself. Not because he didn't think she was capable, but because he knew every job always have an element of risk. "You sure you're gonna' be a'ight? You're no good to me if you ain't thinking straight."

"Um' fine, Vee," he assured her, adding, "Even if I wasn't, I still wouldn't let you go up against this guy alone," his eyes were warm and caring. "Maybe we should call it a day? We'll get 'em tomorrow."

She snuggled up close to him. "I wanna finish it so we can spend tomorrow all to ourselves," she purred, resting her head on his broad shoulder.

As Camille rushed down stairs to answer the front door she passed through the family-room. There were three men sitting in front of a large screen television, dead. Fresh vomit covered their mouths and the front of their clothing. Without stopping, she rushed to the front door and quickly opened it. A middle aged man of Caucasian decent stood at the door. "Mr. Spurlock," she acknowledged with obvious sarcasm before continuing "Nice of you to finally show up." With one hand tucked in his full length top-coat pocket, he casually walked into the house while cautiously looking around.

"Where is he?" he asked.

"Up stairs in the master; it's at the end of the hall," she quietly directed him. He nodded, then pulled a .45 from the pocket of his top-coat and slowly headed towards the steps that led to the second floor.

As he passed through the family-room, he spotted the three dead men and stopped, turned and looked back at her. "Yeah. As you can see, I've already done most of your work for you," she smiled with a closed mouth while striking a 'ho' stance' with one hand on her hip and purposely allowed her robe to open just enough to give him the view of his life. Instead of welcoming the view, his jaw tightened, he rolled his eyes, turned on his wing-tip heels and preceded up the steps.

Londell parked two houses from the residence of the target and looked around. When he saw the blood-red Ford Mustang Mach III still parked in the driveway, he killed the lights and cut the engine. "I'll go check it out."

"No!" she stopped him. "I'll go. Just give me five minutes to neutralize whoever is in the house."

"Wait a minute, baby! It's too dangerous!"

"I'll be careful, I promise."

"I know this guy. He ain't gonna' be an easy mark like the other."

She nodded, kissed her index finger and pressed it against his huge lips before getting out of the car. Londell popped the trunk and watched as she walked to the rear of the car. Inside the trunk, she retrieved a stilettos knife, and a .380 and a suppresser. Once Londell heard the trunk slam shut, he got out of the car just as she was slipping the stiletto up the sleeves of her coat. She then began attaching the suppresser to the 380. Once she was done, he checked the clip in her gun and cocked it before handing it back to her. Then nodded reassuringly and watched as she casually walked up to the house. He knew she would be all right. After all, he trained her. Still, he knew Michael Henderson would not fall so easily. That was the thing that bothered him most.

Exactly as Camille had pointed out, he found the master bedroom at the end of the hall. Slowly, he eased towards the door while inserting a suppresser attachment to the nozzle of his weapon. Once he reached the closed door, he cautiously listened for any movement inside the room but didn't hear a thing.

Mike was still chilling on the bed puffing on the 'Purple haze', wondering what was taking his young toy so long. He had met her a week and a half ago. But it seemed as if he had known her all his life. Not only was she fine. She also seemed to know how to handle herself in any situation. More importantly, she made him look good by playing her position of being seen, not heard. She was the perfect woman for him. He had even entertained the possibility of making her wifey, but that wouldn't be for some time. After all, he hadn't even sexed her yet. If she could satisfy his sexual appetite, she was good to go. If not? She had to go. Just like Catherine, his previous wife.

Catherine had been perfect in every way except the one that counted the most. She couldn't keep her legs closed. It seemed as though every-time he turned his back, she was flirting with either one of his boys, or one of his business partners. In Mike's line of work, that was considered a no-no. And as hard as it was for him to let her go, it had to be done.

Mike chuckled as he thought about the plan he personally formulated in getting rid of her. He had told everyone, including the men she was sleeping with, that she left him because she couldn't stomach his line of work. They all believed it.

No one actually knew where Catherine was from. Not even Mike himself. So when they asked, and he knew they would. He told them she went back home to Little Rock, Arkansas. He chose the small, mid-western town because no one from the 'hood knew anyone from Little Rock, Arkansas.

He also thought it was clever of him to actually use one of the men she had been sleeping with to murder her. Everything Mike owned was in her name. If something happened to her, as her husband, everything would be left to him. All he had to do now was wait until her body was found.

It had been a month since Mike sent Catherine to meet her maker. He couldn't stop wondering why her body has not been found yet which was beginning to worry him. From time to time, he often found himself missing his Catherine which was his main reason for finding someone new. The funny thing was, his new piece, Camille, actually found him instead. He couldn't quite put his finger on it, but she reminded him so much of Catherine. The only distinction was, Catherine was about eighteen years Camille senior, high-class, and well educated.

Camille, on the other hand, was not high-class. Nor by any means was she low-budget. And even though she didn't have Catherine's Ivy-League education she was far from a dim-wit. Hell, he wasn't even sure if she was actually white. He had just assumed. Rightly so, like Catherine, she had the same golden blond hair and sexy sky-blue eyes. Side by side, she could have been Catherine's little sister. But there was no way they could have ever came from the same parents. Catherine was tall, with nice big tits, but the ass was a little flat.

Camille, however, was a little shorter but had it all. Perfect natural tits and a big, round ghetto bootie. Which was a rarity for a white chick, he thought. As his thoughts drifted back to the moment he couldn't stop thinking about how good she looked in that bra and panty set he had just brought her. He thought about the attention she was about to show his penis and was hoping she had half the talent Catherine had. That was something he really was going to miss about his ex. He smiled at the mere thought of Catherine's 'head-hunting' skills. "That bitch had a head-game outta' this world", he thought aloud and felt himself getting hard again while wondering what the hell was taking Camille so long?

Frustrated, he was about to jump out of bed to see what was keeping her, but was too groggy to move. "Must be the Haze?" he thought out loud.

Before Vicki rang the door-bell she looked off into the night with hopes of spotting Londell. Because it was too dark, she couldn't see him, but had no doubt he was on point and watching.

The moment Mike heard some movement outside the bed-room door. He quickly yelled, "Baby, is that you?" Hoping it was her. He was about to yell again when the door suddenly burst open. In the doorway he saw a dark figure that definitely wasn't Camille.

"CLACK!" The first bullet caught Mike in the upper shoulder. "CLACK-CLACK-CLACK!" The second, third and forth exploded in his chest, killing him on impact. As Mike slummed over on the bed leaking, his assassin was about to walk over and check out his handy-work, but the sound of the door-bell adverted his attention.

CHAPTER 20

Still clutching his gun, Spurlock rushed down stairs and instructed his female cohort to answer the door. Camille took a quick peek through the view-hole to see a young, caramel-complexion, black woman with Asian shaped, hazel eyes standing in the light on the other side of the door. Hoping the woman was someone she could easily get rid of, she quickly opened the door.

"Yes? May I help you?" she politely asked while clinching at the neck of her robe to indicate she was cold and did not have all day.

Vicki stared at her for a moment. Almost as if she was expecting to see someone else. "I'm sorry," she said. "I was looking for a, Michael Henderson. I don't suppose he lives here, does he?"

"As a matter of fact, he does. But at the moment he's asleep. Who should I say came by when he wakes?" asked Camille while staring at Vicki's lips the same way most men often did.

Vicki immediately pulled out on Camille while forcing her way into the house.

Londell watched in shock. "What the fuck is she doing?" he muttered under his breath while nervously looking around to see if anyone else had noticed. With his nine-millimeter in hand, cocked, and concealed under his coat. He glanced at his watch and began to time her.

"Are you crazy? What the hell are you doing?" Camille angrily asked.

"What I came to do, bitch. How many in the house with you besides Henderson?" Vicki quietly asked, nudging her gun up against the back of Camille's head while cautiously scanning the perimeter for any un-anticipated surprises. It was at that moment when she saw some movement out of the corner of her eye. But before she could react, she felt a crashing blow to the right side of her jaw that immediately put her down. Lying on her back dazed and confused. It wasn't until she had a chance to clear her head before she realized her gun flew out of her hand. Camille quickly stepped out of the way.

She wasn't quite sure what was going on, but knew it had nothing to do with her. Still, she did not like Spurlock and couldn't resist the opportunity to signal Vicki to get up. Vicki looked over just in time to see her attacker picking up her gun. She then glanced at Camille. "Your move," said Camille while slightly tilting he head in Spurlock's direction. By the time she made it to her feet, Spurlock was aiming her gun at her and about to shoot. Camille slowly shook her head from side to side while thinking, "What a waste". Even though she had been rooting for the woman who had just threatened her life, she couldn't help feeling it was over. That is, until she noticed a Stiletto knife easing from the right sleeve of Vicki's coat.

Camille smiled when Vicki skillfully flung the knife, piercing the upper part of Spurlock's thigh. "Ahh!" he cried out in pain as the gun went off hitting Vicki in the upper right side of her chest. As she stumbled backward towards the front door, she collapsed, but did not lose consciousness.

While Spurlock took the time to remove the blade from his thigh, Vicki struggled to remain conscious. Badly hurt, she looked around for the young blond, but the woman was nowhere in sight. With the last once of strength she had left in her.

She managed to grip the door-knob and twist while slowly rising to her feet.

Inside the master bed-room, the first thing Camille saw was Michael Henderson slumped over the bed, dead. Ignoring the body, she quickly dressed and wiped down everything she had previously touched. Her job was completed. She had been hired to clear the way to Michael Henderson's demise. A fate accomplished.

After five minutes had elapsed, Londell walked up to the door and was about to try the knob when the door abruptly opened. It was Vicki, but something was wrong. "You a'ight, baby?" he whispered. Vicki took two steps towards him before collapsing in his arms. "Vicki!" He caught her. While his first concern was for her safety, he eased her unconscious body down on the porch. It was at that moment he realized she had been shot and was bleeding badly. He looked towards the house. When he didn't see anyone pursuing her, he made the mistake of tucking his gun in the waist of his pant. He was about to scoop her up when he noticed a pair of black wing-tip shoes stationed in front of him. Realizing he had fucked up. He slowly looked up with bloodshot eyes of rage and saw a middle-aged, pale-skinned Caucasian male wearing a pair of gold, circular frame glasses grinning down at him. In his hand was Vicki's weapon. "Time to say goodnight, motherfucker," said the man before pulling the trigger, "CLACK!" Vicki regained consciousness just long enough to see an obscure figure standing over what looked like Londell's body. She blinked a few time to help clear her vision. It was then when she realized the very same man who had attacked her in the house and managed to use her own weapon against her was now nudging the lifeless body of her husband with his foot. Making sure Londell was in fact dead. In a dream-like state, she helplessly watched in horror as he turned in slow-motion and looked at her. When he realized she was still alive, he aimed the gun at her face. Unable to move, Vicki closed her eyes and felt a tear run down the side of her face.

Back down stairs, Camille was on her way out the back door when she spotted Spurlock's gun on the floor in the foyer. The thought had occurred to her to leave it, but something told her she was going to need it. While reaching down to retrieve it, she heard Spurlock's voice coming from outside the house.

She looked towards the front door that had been left ajar and eased closer to get a peeked. Careful not to be seen, she was just in time to witness Spurlock shooting a young black male in the head. She watched as he began nudging the youth's body with his foot, making certain his victim was no longer breathing.

"He's out of control," she whispered under her breath while watching the ruthless killer who seemed to enjoy his work a little too much.

Camille knew she was supposed to be next on his list. Men like Spurlock and the people he worked for could never be trusted.

When he turned toward the house, she ducked. She was sure he had seen her watching, but it was the wounded black female his attention was now focused on. Once he realized she was still breathing, He aimed the .380 at her face, but before he had the chance to pull the trigger, "CLACK!" a single bullet between the eyes surprised him.

When the assassin's bullet never came, Vicki opened her eyes. Just barely conscious, she looked up at her assassin.

A single stream of blood trickled down the center of his forehead. Shock was the last expression his face cast before he fell on top of her husband's lifeless body.

She looked around confused and tried to move but her body would not respond. She strained to stay awake but was finding it extremely difficult. As she laid there staring into the night, she saw a tall, dark, shadow approaching, but couldn't be sure. Assessing she was still in danger, she tried to move one last time, but black-out instead.

Camille quickly wiped the weapon of her prints, removed the silencer and pocketed it before placing the weapon back where she had found it. She looked at the wounded black female and wanted to help her, but could not risk being seen. Her only other option was calling, 911, but noticed someone cautiously approaching the house. Quickly, she recovered the single spent shell out of habit. Then backed away into the shadows of the house and slipped out the back door.

CHAPTER 21

SunRise couldn't help noticing Robin had not touched her food. Since they left the lawyer's office earlier, she seemed a little distant which was understandable. Rossi's lawyer had revealed some things she didn't just find hard to believe, but was not willing to accept. Providing her with medical records, a birth-certificate, and a video-cassette tape of Rossi's will that proved indisputably, Thomas Rossi was in fact, her biological father.

The will was more like a confession than anything else and Robin had the unpleasant experience of viewing it in the presence of SunRise. Had she known what the tape contained prior, she would have never contested the lawyer's objections of having SunRise in the room while the tape was being viewed. The tape consisted of Rossi leaving his entire estate to Robin, and a detail account of how Robin had been conceived. Which turned out to be a humiliating story, to say the least. According to the tape, Rossi had an affair with Robin's mother that lasted until she became pregnant with his child. After confronting him with what was supposed to be good news. Rossi denied the child was his by accusing Robin's mother of sleeping around. An accusation that gave him the perfect opportunity to sever all ties with his pregnant lover.

After Robin's mother's death, five years would pass before the guilt of abandoning his unborn child began to set in; a guilt that led him to a relentless search for his illegitimate daughter.

In the will, Rossi points out how his search led him to *Foster Care* where he managed to obtain a copy of Robin's blood-type. Having already acquired her mother's full medical-history, he was convinced beyond any shadow of doubt that Robin Hoods was in fact his biological daughter.

In his attempt to legally adopt Robin, he learned it was too late. She had already been adopted, rejected, and thrown into an institution for troubled young girls. Rossi immediately procured a written court order from a local judge to have Robin released into his custody but once again, he was too late. Robin had left the institution, only this time, it was of her own accord.

Still, Rossi did not give up his search. Because the institution Robin had escaped from was located in the south central area of New Jersey, he contacted everyone he had ever dealt with in that vicinity and hired a private investigator. With head-shots he had obtained from the institution Robin left, Rossi made sure the people he employed to find her had a detailed description with specific instructions that no one was to take any actions before contacting him first.

A month later, Rossi got a call from one of the investigators who gave him an address to a low-leveled fence in Trenton, New Jersey.

Rossi's last will and testament described how he felt when he first saw Robin. There was no mistaking it; the young girl he had went through so much trouble to find turned out to be a mirror-image of her late mother.

Robin began to cry when Rossi tried to explain how his fears of losing her was what prevented him from telling her the truth throughout the years. She hated herself for being the daughter of a man who used her mother for his sexual pleasures, then cast her aside after learning his once prized whore was now pregnant with his illegitimate child. He had abandoned her mother when she needed him most, which was the one thing she could never forgive him for.

"A penny for your thoughts," SunRise said when he noticed her preoccupation with a distant thought.

She looked up at him as if he had interrupted something private and apologized for not being very good company. "I just can't help wondering what could have driven my mother in the arms of a man like Rossi?" she said moving the food on her plate in circles with her fork.

SunRise wiped his mouth with a napkin before speaking. "It's senseless to keep beating yourself over the head with questions that can't possibly be answered. Maybe she saw something in him you didn't? From what little we've learned about your mother, she was obviously a kind and trusting person."

She looked up at him with a flash of light in her eyes and said, "I wonder what my mother's parents were like?" She stared at him as if waiting for him to fill in the blanks before realizing that was a question that would probably remain unanswered. She dropped her head and resumed playing with her food.

SunRise wanted to say something to make the hurt go away, but there wasn't anything he could say. He knew this was something she alone had to come to terms with. "Look baby," he said in an attempt to give it a shot. "You've been through hell and survived to tell about it. As far as your parents are concerned, they're gone. Your grandparents are gone. It's over. You have to be strong enough to pick up the pieces and go on with your life."

Still playing with her food, she looked up at him, slid her chair back and stood up. "Yeah... go on with my life," she muttered, pacing back and forth. "How can I do that knowing I was the cause of Rossi's death?" There was a certain sadness in her voice.

"Maybe. Maybe not. One thing you can be sure of though, Rossi was responsible for Johnny's men finding you."

Robin's pacing came to an abrupt halt. She stood in front of him staring with a blank expression.

Anticipating an aftershock, SunRise stared back while silence dominated the room. He knew he shouldn't have made that statement about Rossi, but it was true; Rossi had sold her out. There was no way he was going to let her go on feeling guilty about something she had absolutely no control over.

She smiled and sat in his lap. "I'm so glad you came with me."

"For a minute I thought you were ready to jump all over me for saying what I said about your father."

"Friend!" she corrected him.

"Okay... friend. So I take it you're not upset with me?"

"Hell no! Why would I be? You were right. I tried to tell TooSweet he sold me out, but she called me an uncaring, coldhearted bitch." Robin laughed as she remembered.

"You're kidding."

"Oh no I ain't. Girlfriend had a serious cap on me. I'm glad she decided to let me go with her to Queens. It made a world of difference between us."

"I told you she just had to get to know you. Besides, she was being hard on you for your own good." Robin gently rested her head on his shoulder, then pulled away abruptly "What's wrong?" She took a deep breath and looked at him. "Remember I told you that name sounded familiar? Remember?

"What name?"

"You know? The one on the disk we found in Queens?"

"Johnathen Crain Junior?"

"I remember why it sounded so familiar?" she said before elaborating. "He owns the house on Long Island that Rossi commissioned me to rob. Remember I told you it was the reason I went to Atlantic City to see him?"

SunRise looked at her strangely. "You sure it's the same name? Why would Rossi hire someone to rob the safe of some young lawyer? It doesn't make sense?"

"Young? The man who owned the house I robbed was old; at least in the seventies?"

"And you're sure his name is Johnathen Crain Junior?"

"The difference between me and a common thief — I'm a professional. I study my hits, as oppose to someone who just stumbles in the dark until...."

"Okay. Okay. I get it." he quickly interrupted her. "What can you tell me about the man you robbed?"

"Like I said, he was just some old, white, rich guy living alone."

"Do you have any idea why your friend Rossi hired you to rob him? I also remember you telling me nothing in the safe was worth the fee he paid you?"

"Nothing that we know of."

"What do you mean?"

"The diamonds weren't worth shit but his instructions were specific — 'Take everything in the safe' he said — so I did. Along with the diamonds were some legal papers."

"What did he do when you gave everything to him:" SunRise asked, recreating Rossi's actions in his mind.

"The diamonds were the last thing I gave him. They were what you might call un-set, commercial stones; mostly used to create a cluster in jewelry. The first, were some legal papers he just tossed to the side. The second was a sealed manila envelope. He opened it and peeked inside, then locked it in his desk. The diamonds he emptied out on his desk and took about an hour examining them. After he told me I had to come with him to his crib to get paid. We got into a huge argument about my money."

"Tell me about the envelope he placed in his desk?"

"Oh yeah *that* envelope." Robin smiled. "I was thinking? Maybe that envelope was the reason he became so worried about something happening to him the last time I saw him? Before he locked it in his desk, I asked him about it, but he never answered."

SunRise thought about everything Robin had told him and couldn't help but wonder if there a correlation? He knew the universe dictates, eventually, everything comes full circle, but this was just too weird. "Looks like we'll never know," he said while holding her tight. "I realize your friend was all you had left to call family. I can't imagine how alone you must feel right now which is why I want you to know I'll never leave you, Robin."

"You promise?" she asked in a child-like manner.

"Ankh my heart and hope to die. In fact, I have something for you." He took a platinum chain with a platinum Ankh from around his neck and placed it around hers.

Robin looked at the ancient symbol and toyed with it. "I noticed TooSweet, BeeBop, Joey and Tyrone have the same Cross. What kind of cross is it?"

"It's not a cross. It's an ancient symbol that represents life, righteousness and prosperity. It's called an Ankh. Display it proudly."

"I'll try," she said before changing the subject. "When we get back, can we take a trip some place where we can be alone?"

"Where would you like to go?"

"How 'bout the Caribbean?"

"We'll see. Now get dressed, I'm taking you out tonight."

"Where?"

"You'll see. It's a surprise I think you'll enjoy."

Robin hopped up out of his lap smiling. "Give me a minute to change," she said, rushing off into the bathroom.

For the first time since they met, he finally got her to go out with him and have some fun.

SunRise drove pass Linda's Lounge and was a little surprised when he noticed it was closed. Without giving it much thought, he drove straight to Philadelphia where he and Robin took in a show. Afterwards, they stopped at a reggae' club in North Philadelphia, where Robin did her thing on the dance floor.

Both were exhausted when they arrived back at their hotel suite late that night. SunRise called the desk and asked for a 7:00 A.M. wake-up call.

The following morning they checked out of the luxurious casino hotel in Atlantic City and proceeded to Cane May Court House for Robin's final appointment with the lawyer.

"I have to make a quick stop." he told her.

Heading uptown, he glanced over at Robin and found her napping. They had gotten in pretty late last night not to mention the extra two hours he kept her up putting in work.

He was running late and wanted to find a travel agency before it got any later. It would be nice, he thought, to surprise her when she woke. Unfortunately, there were very few, if any, businesses that were open.

As he navigated the Altima downtown in an attempt to leave the city, he saw the bartender of Linda's Lounge standing outside of a bar talking with a very loud woman. He glanced at his watch; it was a little after 8:00 A.M. He looked over at Robin again; she was still asleep. The last thing he wanted to do was wake her, which meant beeping the horn to get the bartender's attention was out of the question. So instead, he quickly parked the car and got out.

The woman the bartender was talking with gave new meaning to the word 'tacky'. Along with her dime-store fake fur, dirty white pants that were clearly too small for her massive derriere, she wore a platinum blond wig that made her look even more ridiculous. She was loud and had a mouth that was so foul, it would make a sailor frown.

As he slowly approached the sad looking pair, he was tempted to turn and head back to the car, when the bartender spotted him, it was too late.

"Hey, young brutha'! How you doin'?"

Before he had a chance to say anything, the woman shouted, "What's yo' name?"

At the risk of getting trapped off in a chit-chat conversation with the woman, SunRise politely ignored her as if he hadn't heard her and gave his undivided attention to the bartender. "I just drove past the lounge and noticed a government stamp on the entrance. Whaz' up?"

"Oh, yeah, D.E.A. raided the Lounge about three days ago. They confiscated a lot of Johnny's things, including the safe in his office. Before they left, they shut him and the lounge down."

"So he's in jail?"

"Not anymore! After he made bail, ain't nobody seen him since. He left his woman and his kids behind. I heard he was in Mexico?"

SunRise didn't have to ask what Johnny had been charged with; he remembered warning the club owner to give up selling drugs before it was too late. Obviously Johnny had not heeded his warning.

"Damn, brutha'!" the bartender continued. "You didn't come all the way down here just to see Johnny, did you?"

SunRise smiled. "Fortunately no; I'm on my way out of town. Do you know of any black-owned travel agencies that might be open?" SunRise changed the subject.

The bartender glanced at the woman he had been talking with and noticed she was leaving the area with three crack-head winos. "YO', LEE!" he yelled to get her attention.

She turned, but did not stop walking.

"HOLD UP!" he shouted.

She frowned and yelled back, "WELL BRING YO' LIL' SKINNY ASS ON, FOOL!"

Embarrassed, he smiled stupidly before telling SunRise to try Philadelphia. "You'll have a better chance finding one there."

SunRise could tell he was anxious to leave. "Thanks!

"As a matter of fact," he interrupted. "Try Market Street. You'll find all types of agencies there. Travel, Realtors, you name it."

SunRise peeped at his watch. "Well, I better get going if I intend to get my lady to her appointment on time. I appreciate your help. Peace!"

"Yeah... you take care, young brutha'," the bartender said before rushing off to catch up with his female companion.

Before getting into the car, SunRise looked at the woman and noticed for the first time how unusually large her behind really was. Seeing her reminded him of how blessed black women were for being naturally endowed.

Robin woke just in time to find SunRise getting out of the car. Still a little out of it, she looked around somewhat confused before asking, "Where are we?"

"Philadelphia."

"Philadelphia! Baby what we doing in Philly?" she complained while glancing at her watch.

"Follow me and you'll see," he told her.

Reluctantly, Robin followed, vehemently complaining all the way. It wasn't until after Robin stepped into the building before she realized it was a travel agency. Seeing the large posters that advertise the Bahamas made her gasp and smile as she rushed over to get a closer look.

SunRise couldn't help smiling as he watched her; she was like a kid in a toy store, running around trying to view everything all at once.

"May I help you?" a young black woman asked from behind her cubicle desk.

SunRise walked over to the woman while looking around. It would appear that she was the only agent working. "My lady and I are interested in spending a few weeks in the Caribbean. Can you suggest the perfect place for a marriage proposal?"

The woman smiled, then looked over at Robin. She was standing a few feet away, reading some flyers. "Is that the lucky woman?" the agent curiously asked.

SunRise glanced over at Robin and said, "Yes... it is."

The young woman looked at Robin again and noticed her interest in one poster in particular. "If that's her choice, she couldn't have made a better one."

SunRise looked at the poster Robin had been so preoccupied with. It was an ad for Aruba.

"Aruba is a beautiful Caribbean island that's 19 miles long and 6 miles at its widest point," said the young agent. "It has plenty of beaches, and casino resorts and hotels. In fact, this small island has more than 3,000 modern hotels on its palm beaches and a five-mile stretch of white sands. It's a four hour flight from New York or a two and one half hour flight from Miami."

"And what would be the best time to go during the winter season, or does it matter?" SunRise asked, signaling Robin to join them.

As Robin sat in a chair next to him, the woman smiled at her, then continued. The first week of February. This way, you'll have an opportunity to check out their Carnival Celebration. I'm sure you'll enjoy it." She cut an eye at Robin and added, "It's also a perfect time to stroll along the beach under the warm sunlight and set up that special conversation you plan to have with your lady in the evening."

SunRise looked at Robin. She was staring at him with a stupid smile. He looked at the agent and asked about Antigua and Barbuda. The agent expression changed as she leaned in closer and lowered her voice. "I strongly advise against going there," she warned. "Those isles use to be a tropical paradise. Now... they're nothing more than a private headquarters for the C.I.A., and U.S. military."

Without commenting on the woman's accusations, SunRise conferred with Robin about spending three weeks in Aruba. He didn't have to sell her on the idea, she was all for it.

Once the necessary arrangements to leave during the first week of February were made, the agent asked if their passports were in order?

Even though Robin did not have one yet, SunRise assured the woman that both of their passports were still valid.

She smiled, "Just checking," she said. "You'd be surprised how many of our people don't even own a passport. I often try to encourage those who've never owned one, to apply. If for nothing else, it's the best damn form of identification anyone could have."

After concluding their business with the agent, Robin rudely grabbed SunRise by the hand and lead him out of the small building.

"What's wrong with you, Robin?" he angrily asked after they were clear of the building. "That was rude; especially to a sista'."

"Yeah... well... I didn't like the way she was looking at you!" Robin replied while getting into the car.

SunRise slammed the car door shut behind her and walked around to the driver's side and got in.

"You're angry because I pulled you out of there?" she asked, sensing the tension between them.

Without so much as looking at her, he pulled off.

"Look..." she began "If I offended you? I apologize. I was just protecting what's mine."

"Number one," he finally spoke without taking his eyes from the road. "I am not a possession to be owned. I'm a person, just like you. I am assuming the role as your man only because I have given myself to you willingly. That does not mean you own me. It simply means we have an agreement; a committed relationship. No one or anything outside this relationship can ever come between what we have unless one of us allows them or it to. Number two don't ever play yourself like that with me again. If, for some reason you don't feel totally secure with what we have, than I guess we really don't have much."

She stared at him with nervous eyes.

When he glanced at her, she looked away. He knew she was ashamed and embarrassed for acting so childish. He also knew she wanted to say something to make everything all right. The way he saw it, there was very little she could say to justify her behavior.

"I'm sorry." she spoke softly while resting her head on his shoulder. "You know I would never take you for granted."

Instead of a reply, he said nothing as they drove back to Jersey for her final appointment.

CHAPTER 22

Cape May Court House was a small, quiet town in the county of Cape May. Predominantly white, there was something special about this calm little town with its colonial style architecture that gave you a sense of a time long since passed.

SunRise parked in front of the old court house building where judicial proceedings use to be held before relocating a few blocks down the street. As they hurried to make Robin's final appointment, SunRise began to reflect on the meeting they had with the lawyer yesterday. Though he appeared sincere and about the business at hand, there was something about his unspoken behavior SunRise couldn't quite put his finger on.

Inside, they were met by the same pleasant, elderly woman with snow-white hair styled in a tight bun that sat directly on top of her head. After a moment of pleasantries, she informed the lawyer his 9:00 A.M. had arrived.

Shortly thereafter, a short, bold, over-weight, middle aged man appeared. "Good-morning," he said with a wide smile that exposed his coffee-stained teeth. "Please, come right in," he gestured both Robin and SunRise into his office and closed the door behind them.

SunRise sat on a sofa by the door and Robin took a seat next to his desk. SunRise watched the lawyer hand Robin various legal documents to read and sign. Taking her time, she read everything before putting her signature on each. The documents gave her full control over her inheritance, which turned out to be quite substantial. In addition to the small villa in Egg Harbor Township and the ethnic antique shop in

243

Atlantic City, Robin's newly acquired wealth included a beach house and art-gallery in North Beach, Florida, a 4.7 million dollar home in Oak Bluffs, Martha's Vineyard, a villa on the La cote d' Azur, 'the French Riviera', and several other assets in stocks and bonds that brought her entire holdings over $17.4 million dollars.

As it were, Sig. Rossi came from a wealthy family in Milan, North Italy. The death of his mother, over twenty-two years ago, left him the only surviving member of his family. After burying his mother, he left the old country for the Americas.

"My office has represented your father since he first came to this country," said the lawyer. "He was a special man with a special talent for obtaining things otherwise unobtainable. As a matter of fact, a very close friend of mine recently retained his service on the recommendation of my word that he was the best in his field. Unfortunately, your father was murdered before we had a chance to conclude our business."

Robin briefly glanced at SunRise. "Would it be too much trouble to ask if you could check? It's imperative that package be delivered to the person who paid your father a lot of money to procure it."

"Imperative?" Robin quickly asked.

"I know it's a strong word, but your father made a commitment. A commitment I'm afraid not even his death could allow him not to keep."

"Are you threatening her?" SunRise asked as he stood and approached.

"Of course not, sir; merely stating a fact. The last time I spoke with your father, Ms. Hoods, he assured me the package could be picked up the following day at his shop; unfortunately, that day never came for him. It would mean a lot to me, and the people who retained Sig. Rossi's services, if you could check his shop? Maybe he put it up somewhere in his office?"

"I can't promise you anything, but I'll check. If it's there, I'll know where to find it," Robin assured before adding, "But like I said, I can't make any promises."

"Thank you, Ms. Hoods. I'm sure his client will be very pleased. If it's any help, I'm told the package is in a brown, manila envelope marked 'confidential'."

"Like I said, I'll check."

He smiled. "Either way, you will give my office a call to let me know, won't you?"

"Of course. Now, about this P.O.A. You no longer have Power of Attorney over the estate?" Robin asked.

"Legally, no. You're of legal age to do as you see fit with your inheritance. However, I'm quite sure your father would have wanted me to continue representing his estate. Of course, that will be entirely up to you. I'm sure I can advise you on key issues concerning investments." he said handing her the last and final document to sign.

Robin quickly read the document then signed it. The moment she had her copies, she stuffed them into her hand bag and stood to leave. "It was nice doing business with you," she said.

The lawyer stood and opened his mouth to speak, but Robin turned and start walking towards the door SunRise held open for her.

"Ms. Hoods?" he called to her.

She stopped short of reaching the door and turned, "Yes?"

"Would you like this firm to continue representing you?"

She looked around the small office before replying, "Thank you, but I have my own lawyers."

Back in the car, Robin talked SunRise into spending the holiday at the house in Egg Harbor Township before heading back up north. "It'll be nice spending time together, alone."

"And how are we supposed to get in Robin? Even though the place is legally yours, it's still gonna take a few weeks before getting the deeds transferred to your name. Besides, we don't have the keys."

"Oh yes we do! I still have a set from when I used to live there. And as for not having the deed yet, as long as I have these documents claiming ownership, I don't need the deed."

"Is it far from here?"

"Not from here. But I need you to do me a favor and take me back to Atlantic City. I have to get something from the shop. Ok?

SunRise glanced at her briefly while starting the car. "It must be important to send you all the way back in the opposite direction."

"That package Rossi's lawyer kept asking me about?"

"What about it?"

"I think I know what he's talking about. It's the envelop I took from the safe Rossi had me hit in Connecticut?"

"You think it's still locked in his desk? If it's as important as that lawyer made it out to be, wouldn't Rossi have taken it with him when he left?"

"I saw him lock it in his desk," Robin said. "We left together that day, remember? He never retrieved it," she said before adding "Now I know why he was so adamant about taking everything in the safe. I wonder what's in it?"

Twenty minutes later, Robin rushed into the small antique shop while SunRise waited for her in the car. When she returned, the only thing she was carrying was her hand bag.

SunRise assumed she didn't find what she was looking for, which meant whatever it was, Rossi must have moved it.

"It was still there," she said removing the manila envelope from under her coat. "I wonder what's in it?" she said looking it over.

246

"You sure that's it? Didn't he say it was a brown envelope marked confidential? That envelope is white."

"Yeah, but if you hold it up to the light you can see the word confidential in uppercase letters. Rossi placed it in a larger envelope."

SunRise looked at the envelope and asked, "Does it have a name on it?"

"No, nothing.

"You don't have any idea what's in it?"

"Not a clue. Like I said before, I knew something was odd because he was clear about me taking everything in the safe. Normally, he'd be specific. I don't know what that was about and didn't care as long as he had my money after I delivered."

SunRise glanced at her while wondering what kind of man sends his daughter out stealing for him. "You want me to swing back to the lawyer's office? It'll save the trouble of having to swing back later."

"No."

"No?"

"No. Aren't you curious about what it is?" she asked.

"Have you ever heard the term 'ignorance is bliss'?"

"No. Where did you come up with that one?"

"It's true. Sometimes knowledge can be a burden."

"Bliss, burden; I still wanna' know why this thing is so important all of a sudden," she said before placing it on the seat between them.

"If you open it, he'll know."

"Once we get to the house, all I have to do is find a way to open the original. Reseal it and put it in another envelope."

Instead of trying to convince her otherwise, SunRise changed the subject by asking for directions to the house.

As Robin directed him how to get to the house, she went on and on about how much he was going to like the property.

When they finally arrived, she shouted into his ear, "We're here! Just turn right up this road."

SunRise turned off of the main road, onto a gravel driveway that led to what looked like private property.

"That's it! Right there, baby! You see... I told you it was nice!"

SunRise pulled onto the 2.6 acres of professional landscaped grounds and saw the small Italian style villa. He was speechless. Robin had not exaggerated. The entire grounds on which the villa sat was incredibly beautiful. Cruising up the driveway, he took in the scenery before parking directly in front of the house. Before he had a chance to cut the engine, Robin jumped out of the car and hurried up to the front door and entered a security-code on the pad before inserting her key. Once she had the door open, SunRise retrieved the *Confidential* envelope Robin left sitting on the car seat and the luggage from the trunk then followed her inside.

SunRise sat the luggage and envelope down and looked around. The foyer was beautiful he thought before noticing a flight of white carpeted steps. "Where do those steps lead?" he asked.

"To the suites, of course. Come on, I want to show you the rest of downstairs before we go up." She grabbed his hand and led him through huge double French doors that took them to the family room that had a vaulted ceiling and masonry fire place. Large windows induced brightness and displayed a magnificent view of the grounds. When she showed him the kitchen, he couldn't help but to be impressed. It was equipped with forty-two inch wall cabinets, a pantry, center-island with a Jennair gas range and a sunny breakfast area. SunRise noticed another staircase in back of the pantry, and inquired about it.

"Actually," Robin began, "This staircase gives you easy access to the pantry from upstairs in case you want a late night snack or something."

"That makes sense," he muttered admiring the stained custom trim and crown molding.

"Come on! I want to show you our room."

He followed her up the pantry steps and found himself standing in a white carpeted hall. They walked past three guest suites before entering the master suite at the end of the hall.

SunRise stood in the doorway and looked around speechless. It was as if he was standing in the doorway of the presidential suite at some extravagant hotel.

"Come on, baby! Don't just stand there, check it out!" Robin yelled from a brass-framed, king-sized bed.

The first thing SunRise noticed was the twenty foot walk-in closet in which Rossi's clothes still hung. The bathroom was also very spacious. There were his and her sinks, a sumptuous bath with a whirlpool tub that was roomy enough to comfortably fit two large adults and separate showers.

Robin showed him the other three rooms which were not as large but equally as nice. Each had its own bathrooms. Before leaving the last room, she opened two huge sliding-glass doors and took him onto a deck-like balcony overlooking an oval-shaped pool and jacuzzi. "The pool can be heated to a specified temperature unless you'd like to lounge in the jacuzzi?"

SunRise stepped back into the room without saying a word.

"What's wrong, baby? You've been kind of quiet since we got here."

"Just tired, that's all."

"Why don't you unpack while I hook us up something to eat?"

"That sounds good." he said shutting the glass door.

After Robin had left, he walked out into the hall to make sure she had gone back downstairs, then stepped back into the guest suite and made a phone call.

"Hello?"

"Who's this? Joey?"

"Yeah. What up, Rise? 'Bop is right here, you wanna' talk to her?"

"Yeah... let me speak with her."

"Hey, Rise! You and Robin 'bout ready to come home?"

"Let's just say, she's done handling her business but we're still checking a few things out. Is everything alright on your end?"

"Joey and the kids are back at Wendi's. Before you start screamin' at me I think you should know Wendi agreed to enter a treatment center as soon as they can find available bed space. 'Um makin' all the necessary arrangements to speed up the process."

"That's a good idea, 'Bop. I know Joey appreciate you helping his sista'."

BeeBop looked at Joey and smiled. "He better!" she said before changing the subject. "There's something else you should know. I don't want to mention it over the phone, so..."

"What's the problem?"

"It's about your freelance writers. They completed the first article but ran into a problem with the second."

"What happened?"

"Face is no more."

"And the female?"

"Her eyes are closed but our tail assured me that they will open."

"I reiterate. What happened?"

"Well... from what I got from the tail, someone else wrote the second article. Whoever it was, tried to write our freelance writers out of the script."

"By accident or on purpose?"

"It had to be by accident. We think they just happened to be writing the same script at the same time. The unknown publisher hired a professional writer. We have his name but his publishers are still unknown. I was told he was about to close her eyes permanently but our tail wrote him out of the script. We don't have all the details yet but I'll stay on it and try to have somethin' for you by the time you return."

"Good work, 'Bop. By the way, have you heard from 'Sweet?"

"No, but I do know she's supposed to be having dinner with an old family friend tomorrow. Why?"

"No reason. Did Joey make the copy we spoke of?"

"Of course. Why you so worried about that stupid ass..."

"Because I need you to give the original to Tyrone ASAP and tell him I said it's a go. If I'm right, our lawyer is going to need the original as a trade-off?"

"Trade off? What the hell you talkin' about, 'Rise?"

"Look, I probably won't be calling again but I still want you to hang around the phone until I return. Hopefully I'll be back by tomorrow. Do not wait to hear from Tye. Get that message to him immediately. We clear?"

"Okay! I got you. Give Robin the peace, and y'all be careful."

Robin was standing in the doorway watching.

"I was wondering what happened to you?" she said as she stepped into the room.

"Sorry 'bout that. I got caught up on the phone."

"Is everything a'ight?"

"I wish I could say it was. Something happened that commands my immediate attention." SunRise saw the disappointment in her eyes.

"Can we at least stay the night?" she asked.

"How about we talk about it over dinner?"

"Then let's eat, your food is probably cold by now."

"Not from where I'm standing," he teased.

Robin smiled timidly and was about to speak when he suggested she go on ahead. "I have another call to make. I won't be long, I promise."

She smiled and left the room without saying another word.

SunRise, however, did not make the call until he was certain she had gone. The moment someone picked up the receiver, he quickly spoke up. "This is SunRise. Where is she?" While the party on the other end elaborated, SunRise listened with a critical ear.

"Okay," he said, "this is what I want you to do." As he quickly, yet quietly delivered his instructions over the phone, he kept his eyes fixed on the door which had been left ajar.

The moment he was off the phone, he heard Robin call out to him. He quickly rushed down stairs to see what was wrong and found her standing in the kitchen holding the contents from the manila envelope. "Baby, you need to see this!"

CHAPTER 23

Sitting at the bar in the lounge area of the Alexander Hotel, Camille waited patiently to meet her contact. It had been a day since the Henderson hit yet she couldn't stop thinking about the wounded, young female who tied to murder her.

The description given to her by her handler was impeccable. She was to meet a well dressed man in his mid-forties carrying an attaché case. He would be of average weight and height with grayish-black hair.

She was about to order her first drink when she glanced towards the entrance and spotted him walking in; at least she had assumed it was him. As he was the only man to come in fitting the description and carrying an attaché case. He was not bad looking for his age, she thought. Having been warned by her handler to watch him closely, seeing him for the first time she was beginning to understand why — clearly, he was a lady's man, she thought.

Camille was conservatively dressed in a charcoal gray business suit which included a knee-length skirt, matching blazer, a white button-down cotton blouse, black pumps and a matching clutch. Her long, black, expensive extensions that had been styled tightly pulled to the back in a single French braid, could have easily been her own hair. Her make-up was subtle, but the dark liner and shadow that framed the perimeter of her eyes made the light-brown contacts she wore, pop.

Her black wrap-around trench coat had been carefully laid over the empty stool next to her for two reasons — to deter unwanted company and to convince her contact she was not staying at the hotel.

"I almost missed you," someone said from behind.

Camille casually removed a pair of dark designer wrap-around shades, then turned on her stool and saw him standing in back of her. She had been right; clearly he was a lady's man who took very good care of himself in a way most men would never bothered to.

"How's that when I'm the only woman in the lounge," she replied while standing to shake his hand. "Hi. I'm Camille. Camille LaRue." His hands were soft and fingernails manicured. As she looked into his eyes, she could tell he got his brows waxed often.

"Pleased to meet you, Ms. LaRue. James White. I didn't mean it like that," he corrected her while unbuttoning his overcoat. "I just didn't expect someone so painfully beautiful."

Camille blushed a little and smiled bashfully. "Nice to meet you, Mr. White."

"Please...call me Bobby. Everyone does. Can we go someplace with a little more privacy?" he asked while briefly scanning the room.

"Would you like to grab a table?" she gestured with an extended hand towards the many empty table in the lounge.

"Sure."

She grabbed her coat, then led him to a secluded table near the exit. As soon as they were seated, he calmly placed the case on top of the table and clicked both locks open. "Would you like a drink, or something?" she asked.

Still looking through the case, he quickly replied, "This isn't going to take long," while removing a thick, white envelop and tossed it on the table directly in front of her.

She picked it up and looked inside. Pleasantly surprised, she looked at him. "This is way more than what was agreed upon?"

"Mr. Spurlock didn't make it. Our employer thought you should be entitled to his pay. After all, the two of you did work together."

She smiled. "Whoever he is, he's certainly very generous, but Spurlock wasn't my partner. People like Mr. Spurlock is precisely the reason I work alone." She tossed the envelope back on the table.

He smiled. "I know you usually work alone, Ms. LaRue. I also understand you're working with one of our people was a courtesy to our employer simply because you are an unknown. Take the money. He's a business man who likes doing business with you. Not to mention you came highly recommended by someone whose judgment he values," he smiled again and slid the envelope back across the table in front of her. "Keep the money. You earned it." He closed the brief case, locked it, then stood.

When she stood, his eyes pored over her entire body. From what her handler had told her about him, she knew he was the type of man who could never pass up a nice piece of ass. "Maybe you can thank our employer for me?"

"I'm sure he's well aware of your appreciation." He grabbed the case from the table, then said, "Now if you'll excuse me, I have one more appointment. Some greedy attorney, you know how lawyers are?"

"Of course."

"I'd like to get it over with so I can go home and get some sleep," he smiled again and was about to leave, but stopped as if he had forgotten something. "Can I drop you someplace?" he asked.

"Thank you," she replied. "But I think I'll hang around here. Besides, I have my car."

He smiled disappointingly and left as quickly as he had arrived.

It was at that moment Camille decided to follow him. While maintaining a safe distance, she made sure to keep within the speed limit. The last thing she wanted was to be pulled over by some over-zealous cop trying to make his quota on speeding tickets.

Twenty minutes later, he pulled up in front of a white, single family Victorian in Hoboken, New Jersey where she parked five cars in back from his.

Still sitting in her car, she watched through a riflescope as he got out of his car and entered the house. She waited a few minutes, then slipped out of her heels. Driven by a single impulse, she produced a .9MM and attached a suppresser before getting out of the car.

On stocking feet she cautiously crept up on the house in the dark and made her way to the side window. She could clearly see him with an elderly man she had assumed was the owner of the house. The two men stood in the foyer before stepping to the right into the living area. As they sat in a pair of vintage wood-framed chairs, their conversation had been briefly interrupted by an elderly Latino woman wearing a nurse's uniform. The moment the owner had finished with the Latino woman, the two men left the area.

Camille tried the window, but it was locked. She quickly moved around to the back of the house and tried another window, one that led to the pantry; it was unlocked.

Inside the house, she heard the two men talking. She slipped out of the pantry and eased down a short, dark hallway and stopped when she heard their voices coming from a closed door of what appeared to be the study. With her ear to the door, she overheard the two men going over the final details of what sounded like some kind of extraction. The target to be extracted appeared to be a woman. Something that had to do with a disk the elderly man was suppose to have already given Bobby White's employer.

Satisfied she had heard all she needed to hear, she decided to leave. Careful not to bump into anything while backing away, she took one step backwards before abruptly stopping when she over-heard the elderly man mention the name Crain. He was conveying his thanks to Johnathen Crain Junior for the generous finder's fee he had not received yet.

As the two men voices became closer, Camille knew they were approaching the door. Quietly she eased back into the shadow of the dark kitchen and continued listening.

Bobby White was pressing the greedy lawyer for more information about the female and her associates.

Apparently Johnathen Crain was concerned about copies of the disk being made. The attorney assured Bobby White that none were made and promised to look further into the matter.

Having heard all she needed to, Camille slipped back into the pantry and out the window.

After returning to the Hotel, she decided to have a night-cap before retiring. Not too long after she took a seat at the bar, she was surprised when she saw Bobby White entering the lounge. As he approached, the two of them locked eyes.

"You forget something?" she asked for a lack of anything else to say.

He smiled handsomely displaying a perfect set of teeth he obviously paid good money for. "Actually," he began, leaning on the bar beside her. "I came back looking for you."

"Is that so?" she asked exhibiting a hint of surprise.

"It was a long shot. I really didn't think you'd still be here, but I'm glad I was wrong."

"You have good instincts," she said with a flirtatious smile before continuing. "I guess we both have good instincts." "Oh? And why is that?" he asked as he leaned closer.

"I stayed a little longer with hopes you'd return."

He blushed and took a seat next to her. "Then I'd say it's *you* who has good instincts."

"Shall we go?"

"Your place or mine?" he asked.

"Your's. Something tells me your place will be much more interesting than mine."

He gave her a curious look, furrowing his brows and then laughed a little. "Presumptuous. I like that in a woman."

She leaned closer and whispered, "You'll like me even more later." She stood, grabbed her coat and clutch before casually strolling towards the exit. Bobby White followed.

Instead of accompanying him in his car, Camille followed him in hers to a New York City white-box loft apartment. Inside, he fixed the two of them a white wine before showing her around the apartment. The master bedroom was the last stop of the tour and he wasted no time making his intentions known.

Two hours later, the two of them lay side-by-side, spent. "You were something else," she stroked his ego. "I don't think I can remember the last time I've had so much fun."

"And you have exceeded all expectations," he replied before getting out of bed. He looked down at her. Her eyes were closed and he thought he heard her lightly snoring.

Just before entering the bathroom, he looked at her again. Her eyes were still closed as she lay comfortably on her back with her hands interlaced behind her head under the large, fluffy pillow. He smiled and grabbed a cell phone that had been sitting on top of the dresser.

Inside the huge bathroom, he sat on the edge of a spoon-shaped tub and made a phone call. "I have her here at my apartment," he whispered into the receiver. "How soon can you have someone here? Okay, okay, I heard you," he whispered before hanging up.

Still resting comfortably in the very same position he had left her in, he sat on the opposite side of the bed and removed a 12 rounds, semi-auto 9-millimeter from under the mattress. Then he stood at the foot of the bed in front of her. The moment he cocked a round into the chamber, her eyes opened.

"Sorry, baby. Our employer doesn't like leaving any loose ends," he said.

Still lying with her hands behind her head under the pillow, she seemed unshaken by the sudden change of events. "Somehow, you don't strike me as a killer," she pointed out.

"Actually, I'm not but please don't underestimate my ability to do what needs to be done for a certain price. And the price on your head is just too attractive to pass up."

"Whatever you're being paid, I'll triple it."

"And have Crain come after me for crossing him? I don't think so. I'm greedy, not stupid."

"Johnathen Crain, the developer?"

"Hardly. More like the son. And yes, your employer. Or should I say former employer."

"Why kill me? How could I possibly hurt the son of a man like Johnathen Crain?"

He looked at her strangely. "Because you, like everyone else in his world, are expendable. The Crain name is much too important for the likes of someone like you tarnishing it with unfounded innuendoes.

"I don't understand?"

"It's very simple, my dear. He used you to neutralize the target like he used Spurlock to take the target out." He smiled to himself, then continued. "Spurlock was supposed to take you out of the equation. I guess he wasn't as good as Junior thought. At any rate, you served your purpose and now it's time to clean up." He glanced at the small alarm clock sitting on a small table next to the bed.

"Expecting someone?"

"As a matter of fact, I am." Just then they heard someone down stairs ringing the buzzer. "Ah! Here they are now." He motioned for her to get out of the bed.

"What's the matter, can't stomach the murder game?"

"As I said earlier, don't underestimate me. Now let's go!"

When Camille removed her hands from underneath the pillow, she was clutching a semi auto .9MM. Bobby White's eyes grew with alarm when he saw the weapon aimed straight at his head. In a state of panic, he pulled the trigger, "Click!" A combination of confusion and terror covered his face as he looked at his weapon before pulling the trigger again, "ClickClick-Click!" He realized the gun was empty.

Hers, however, was not. "POP!"

When the two men heard the gun-shot, they pulled out their weapons and tried the doorknob. It was locked. "Stand back!" one of them said while kicking the door open. Both men rushed up the narrow stairwell with weapons drawn. The place was quiet as they cautiously looked around the apartment. When they checked the bedroom, all they found was the body of Bobby White. He had been shot in the head but was still breathing.

"You better call it in. I'll check the rest of the place out. She may still be here," said one of the men while the other used the phone next to the bed to make the call.

"Mr. Ross," he spoke into the phone. "Mr. White is down. He's still breathing, but he took a bad one to the head," he said staring at Bobby's head wound. There was brain-matter on the wall where White had been standing before he was shot. "I don't think he's gonna' be much good to anyone anymore. No sign of the target, but she's armed and on the move, Sir." he listened into the receiver before continuing. "I'm afraid not, Sir. Unfortunately the only people who actually know what she looks like are dead. Yes, of course. I understand, Sir. Yes. Mr. White briefed us. We'll meet you at the extraction sight tomorrow." He wiped the phone down before hanging up and both men left the apartment.

Back at the hotel, Camille went straight to her suite. Still thinking about the extraction tomorrow, she stripped down to her underwear, walked into the bathroom where she started a hot bath and brushed her teeth.

Once she finished, she left the bathroom, sat on the bed and began counting her contract fee.

After a while, she remembered her bath-water and quickly placed the bills back into the envelope and slid it underneath the mattress before rushing off into the bathroom.

"Just in time," she heard herself saying aloud while stepping over to the tub to turn off the water. As she sat on the edge of the tub, she ran her fingers through the water to check the temperature. The water was too hot for her taste, but it was what she needed at the moment. She removed her bra and thong and eased in.

Forty-five minutes later, she emerged from the bathroom as a completely different person. Wrapped in a full-length, white, terry-cloth robe drying her short, black hair with a large white towel, her physical appearance had completely changed into something attractive, yet totally opposite to what she looked like earlier.

Without the long extensions, light-brown contacts and make-up, she looked like a completely different person. Her real hair was four to five inches long, naturally straight and jet black. Her eyes were dark brown and the color of her skin was ambiguous — seemingly changing with each ethnic role she assumed. Standing at a modest 5'7", she had the body of an Olympic track and field star and the training of a C.I.A. operative. But Camille LaRue, if that was her real name, was something of a chameleon.

It was almost midnight. Even though she had a long day ahead of her tomorrow, she knew she would be unable to sleep. Instead of going straight to bed, she turned off all the lights and sat in a chair by the window of her fourth floor suite staring out on Market Street as the cars zoomed by. She wasn't watching anything in particular; it was just something she often did to help clear her mind of all the clutter.

While sitting in the dark, she recalled the conversation she over-heard between Bobby White and the lawyer. She thought about the disk her former employer was so concerned about falling into the wrong hands and couldn't help but wonder.

CHAPTER 24

It was Thanksgivings day. Because of the special relationship TooSweet had with the Lieutenant, he took her to his favorite place to for dinner.

MAMA'S PLACE was the neighborhood greasy-spoon that had been in business for over twenty-five years. A family business that specialized in 'southern soul foods' owned and ran by Mama Wilson herself. Over the years, rumors were told that MAMA'S PLACE had been fined by the Health Department on several different occasions — a charge generated by the growing competition in the area. It was also because of those rumors that Mama Wilson's clientele began to dwindle. There were, however, those who remain loyal over the years. Mostly old-school patrons who had been eating at MAMA'S PLACE since it first opened back in 1968. One such loyal patron was the Lieutenant Ralph Sheets.

While the Lieutenant and TooSweet patiently waited for their meal, TooSweet looked around with a hint of disapproval. The greasy spoon was hardly her choice of places to have dinner. But because it was the lieutenant's treat, she didn't want to spoil it for him. "Thanks again for dinner, but as I told you earlier, it really wasn't necessary."

The lieutenant smiled as he tucked a large handkerchief under the collar of his shirt. "Just my way of saying thanks for the tip on the house in Queens." He carefully spread the handkerchief across his chest before adding, "Besides, I honestly couldn't think of anyone better to share a nice turkey dinner with on such a historical day."

TooSweet smiled out of politeness. Being a health-nut, she made it a habit to avoid foods that specialized in the preparation of high cholesterol and unhealthy fats.

After waiting a few minutes, an old woman came with their meals. TooSweet couldn't help notice how slowly the woman tip-toed towards them as if the soles of her feet were on fire.

The old woman placed their meals in front of them and asked, "How 'bout a nice slice of Mama's home-made sweet-potato pie for desert?"

TooSweet politely declined by giving an excuse about trying to watch her weight, but the lieutenant agreed to have a small slice.

The old woman smiled and jotted down his second order on her small pad before leaving them to enjoy their meal.

"How old is she?" TooSweet whispered.

The lieutenant chuckled lightly. "Old enough to be my mother."

She laughed wondering if he was serious or just kidding with her.

While the lieutenant ate, TooSweet glanced down at the greasy turkey dinner in front of her, then looked up at him. Because he seemed to be enjoying his meal, she held her tongue and proceeded to move the food around on her plate with her fork.

Briefly glancing up at her, he said, "I know how you women enjoy watching your weight, but can't you live a little for just one day? I mean... it is Thanksgiving."

TooSweet frowned and wanted to give him a lesson in history but decided against it. Not because she thought he couldn't appreciate her point of view but because he was from another era — an era where blacks died on the front-line just to get white America to tolerate them. He and so many others like him never realized the only thing their Civil Rights movement achieved in the eyes of white America was assimilation. In her view, assimilation was the worst thing that could have ever happened to blacks subsequent to slavery. Because America had allowed people of color into her institutions, she was now in the position to mis-educate them. Something she saw as a blatant form of racism that is not only practiced in this country to this day, but institutionalized as well. She knew most blacks from his era were under the misconception that the Civil Rights Movement did away with racism and afforded blacks equal rights. What they couldn't, or refused to see was the fact that racism did not cease to exist; it's just practiced with a little more diplomacy nowadays.

The lieutenant, and those who thought like him, had been blinded by the crumbs given to a selective few to pacify the many with hope of achieving the same. For TooSweet, that so-call 'American Dream' few blacks managed to achieve with the greatest of ease. Seems to be nothing more than a show for the many.

Melvin Vincent was excited about his newly found friendship with young Crain, sole heir to his father's fortune. Crain Industries was one of the largest developing company on the east coast.

He had never actually met the man personally, but the moment he viewed the disk he had received by certified mail from his client, Tyrone Sharp. He realized there was enough incriminating evidence on the disk to bury Junior Crain under the jail for the next 400 years.

His father, Johnathen Crain Sr. was a powerful man. The last thing he wanted to do was create a scandal for him. Which was why, against his better judgment, he came up with a plan that would take care of his financial problems without jeopardizing the integrity of his profession in the process.

As Melvin took his time navigating his '92 Honda Accord to the specified location in the north east section of Manhattan, he smiled to himself while remembering the phone call he received from Tyrone Sharp the day before; a phone call that would ease the pain of his financial strain.

He had been sitting at home in his office going over some bills when his wife's nurse informed him that he had a phone call. He was about to tell her to take a message, but when she told him it was a Mr. Tyrone Sharp, he immediately took the call.

Tyrone Sharp was one of his biggest clients. Financially making it possible for him to finally leave the firm he had dedicated his services to for so many years, only to be down-sized by younger and cheaper talent. It was because of Mr. Sharp he was able to finally start a private practice that was doing very well. That is, until his wife suffered a massive stroke that left her partially paralyzed. Since then, Melvin had been struggling to keep his private practice afloat. Business was not bad, but the money he was making paled in comparison to his wife's medical bills. Not to mention her private nurse, physical therapy, and rehabilitation.

Married for forty-four years, Melvin and his wife were high school sweethearts who never had any children. Not because they didn't want any; the timing just never seemed to be right.

"Mr. Sharp, how are you?" he remembered taking the call.

Not being one for small talk Tyrone Sharp came straight to the point. "We think an associate of ours may have gotten herself into something with New York's finest."

"Has she been arrested yet? And if so, what are the charges?"

"She hasn't been arrested yet, but something tells us there will be charges forth coming, so listen very closely. You remember that certified package I sent to you?"

"Yes. I have the package here with me now. You instructed me not to open it, right?"

"Yeah. Right. I think now would be a good time to open it."

He reached down and opened the bottom left draw of his desk to retrieve the unopened package. "What's in it?" he asked while carefully opening it.

"A disk that contains enough damaging information I think the Federal government would be very interested in seeing."

"And you want me to do what?"

"We would like you to trade our associate for the disk. Whatever charges that are being fabricated against her must disappear."

Melvin Vincent began to lightly chuckle. "I think you've been watching too much television, Mr. Sharp."

"Don't patronize me, pussy! Just look at the disk and give me a call on my car phone," Tyrone hung up.

He still remembered the feeling he got after scanning the wealth of incriminating information each file contained, but it was the Crain's name on the disk that made it so valuable to him. An hour later, he was back on the phone with Tyrone Sharp fishing for more information. "Why should I, or the District Attorney's office, believe this disk is authentic?"

"Just make the trade. My associates and I are confident once the Feds see what's on it, they ain't gonna' have a problem granting our friend full immunity. We need this deal to happen like yesterday."

"I'm afraid it's not that simple, Mr. Sharp. I have to...."

"Make it happen!" Tyrone had cut him off before hanging up on him again.

He had already formulated an opinion concerning Tyrone's level of understanding of the situation and couldn't resist using it to his advantage.

Afterwards, Melvin Vincent managed to set up a meeting with Junior's representative at his home in Hoboken, New Jersey. Who, without so much as viewing the disk, wanted to know how he was able to obtain it.

"Don't you want to at least know what's on it?" asked Vincent.

"The disk belongs to an associate of ours who made the mistake of keeping an electronic journal. It was stupid of him, but fortunately he, his cousin and their wives are no longer with us. What exactly does your client want for the disks, Mr. Vincent?" asked Bobby White whose only interest was in what he had been retained to do — secure the disk and any copies that may have been made.

Vincent hesitated before speaking. He knew he had them by the balls. He also knew he was engaged in a very dangerous game trying to play both sides of the street. Unfortunately, he was too far in to turn back now. His plan was simple — proceed with extreme caution.

After Vincent suggested a reasonable finder's fee of one-hundred thousand large, he came up with an intricate strategy that would satisfy the two parties in question, Johnathen Crain Junior and his client, Tyrone Sharp.

Vincent watched while Bobby White made the call for confirmation. After hanging up, he looked at Vincent and smiled. "Looks like you have a deal."

"Good," said Vincent.

"Of course, we'll need a few hours to procure a binding Federal Material Witness Warrant." He then produced a pen and a small pad. "Now... what did you say your client's name was?"

"Audrey Strong. I'm not sure of the charges yet, but..."

"It doesn't matter. We'll tract down all the details and give you a location where to collect her. There's one more thing," Bobby White continued. "Who else know about the disk, and how do we know your client hasn't already made copies?"

"As far as I can tell, the only people who know about the disk are me and my clients, but I seriously doubt if they actually knew what they had?"

"Be that as it may, we'll need files on them; all of them. It would also help if you could find out how they came in possession of the disk."

"I'll have everything you need within an hour."

"Good," said Bobby White. "We'll get back with you." As he turned to leave, he stopped and said, "We'll need hard copies of those files."

"Not a problem," Vincent assured before concluding their meeting.

When he arrived at the specified location, Vincent noticed at least three identical light blue sedans parked there. He knew they were his contacts, but didn't see Bobby White in any of the cars. "What happen to Mr. White?" he yelled out his car window at a tall, slim man who was approaching his car.

"My name is Ross," said the man before walking up to the passenger side of Vincent's car and getting in. "Roger Ross."

"I was supposed to meet Mr. White?"

"Mr. White is no longer with us. You'll be dealing directly with me. Now... before we get started, where's my files?"

Vincent was getting a bad feeling about this, but it was too late to pull out now. There was something about Ross that just didn't sit right with him. Still, as part of the agreement, Vincent handed Ross the Intel-files on his clients and watched as Ross briefly scanned through them. Once he was satisfied everything was in order, he gave Vincent a briefcase containing his finder's fee of one hundred thousand dollars.

Vincent smiled nervously as he peeked inside the case. "What now?" he asked. Now that he had his money, he wanted to get this over with as soon as possible.

"We wait until we get word it's going down," Ross simple replied.

"Then what?"

"We collect your client and meet you back here," he said just before getting out of the car.

Apprehensive about waiting alone in such a neighborhood with so much money, Vincent began voicing his concerns; concerns that ultimately fell on deaf ears.

"Don't worry. It shouldn't take more the ten minutes," Ross assured. "After all," he went on to say, "we're only going two blocks down the street." He smiled coldly at Vincent before walking off towards one of the blue sedans.

As both parties waited in their perspective cars, Vincent glanced in his rear-view and saw Ross going over the Intel-file. Feeling guilty about the whole thing, he couldn't help wondering if he was making a terrible mistake. Mainly because he had betrayed his client's trust.

While the lieutenant was preoccupied eating his meal, TooSweet asked, "Whatever happened to that girl you were looking for?" without looking at him. When he didn't reply, she looked at him only to find him staring at her with a suspicious gaze. Fearing he was beginning to suspect something, she quickly changed the subject. "So when you suppose to be retiring?"

He wiped his mouth and pushed his plate to the side. "I plan to finish the rest of the year before turning in my badge." TooSweet noticed he had a little stuffing on his salt and pepper mustache. She brought this to his attention by scratching her own upper lip, indicating for him to do the same.

He quickly wiped his mouth and looked up to find the old woman arriving with his slice of pie.

She placed it in front of him and proceeded to clear the table.

After noticing TooSweet's plate had been barely touched. She looked at TooSweet and said, "Sugah, you sure you finish eating? You barely touched a thing on your plate?"

In an attempt to assure the old woman she was unable to eat another bite. TooSweet rubbed her stomach with a satisfying smile while conveying how much she had enjoyed what little she did eat. The woman smiled politely and said, "I guess trying to talk you into having a slice of that home-made pie is out of the question, huh?"

"Please, don't tempt me," TooSweet jokingly replied.

They both laughed.

Neither the lieutenant nor TooSweet noticed the dark skinned man with short, thick dread-locks when he walked into the small, family greasy-spoon. As obscure as a fly on the wall, his only interest, or so it would seem, was in a pack of cigarettes. As he stood at the register paying for his purchase, he inconspicuously looked around. After receiving his change from the cashier, he lingered at the counter for a moment, eyeing TooSweet while she chatted with the old woman who had waited on them. The moment he suspected they had finished eating, he left.

It wasn't long before the lieutenant wiped his mouth and tossed the napkin onto the empty desert plate. TooSweet looked at him and said, "You sure can put it away, can't you?"

The old woman chuckled some more before removing the lieutenant's small dessert plate. When she finally left their area, he told TooSweet he had something for her while removing the large handkerchief from his collar to wipe his hands.

"What?" she asked.

"You'll see." He reached into his coat pocket that hung over the arm of his chair and pulled out a half of cigar he had budded out earlier. He re-lit it, stood, grabbed his coat and walked over to the register to pay the bill.

Outside, across the street, the dark-skinned man continued to watch the couple through the window. He watched as the old man stood at the register paying the bill. He looked at the tall, dark-skinned female who was saying her good-byes to the old woman who had waited on them.

Once TooSweet and the lieutenant were sitting in his car, she inquired again about his plans after retiring?

"Let's put it this way," he began. "I'm too old to be running around and too young to just sit around doing nothing." He leaned over her lap looking through a stack of unorganized papers that had been stuffed into the glove-compartment. He finally found what he had been looking for and held it up.

"What's that?"

"The rolodex my men found at the scene of that shoot-out in front of J's Corner. It's also what I was talking about when I told you I had something for you." He was about to hand it to her, but then decided against it. "Before I give you this, I want you to be straight with me about something?"

"I thought that was evidence in your investigation surrounding the death of those two men? You could get in trouble for this, you know?" she stared at him a bit confused.

He smiled, "No one cares about the death of two four-time losers, Audrey. Our people wrote the report as drug related. That's, that. Now, about this Robin Hoods woman…"

She looked at him oddly. "Why the hell did he decide Robin was a she all of a sudden? Something ain't right," she thought. "I already told you I never heard of anyone by that name."

He chuckled a little as if he knew she was lying. "Then why did you ask, whatever happened to that girl I was looking for?"

Before TooSweet had a chance to respond, he blew the car-horn twice. Within seconds, four white, plain-clothes detectives approached the car.

"What the hell is going on?" she shouted.

A few cars ahead of them was a black, 1970 'cuda. Sitting behind the wheel of the 440 was the same man who had been previously watching them. As he watched from his car, he noticed a parked sky-blue Ford Sedan. It was the same car he saw following the couple when they arrived. Two Caucasian men wearing dark suits under their dark, single-breasted trench coats sat in the car observing the couple. As the inconspicuous stranger continued to watch both parties. He was about to light a cigarette when he saw a third party, four white, plain-clothes detectives surrounding the car occupied by the couple. Fearing his cover had been blown, he was about to bolt until he saw the old man emerge from the car, leaving his angry young companion still sitting in the front seat.

With two detectives on each side of the car, one of them opened the door to the passenger side and yelled, "Step out of the car!" The moment TooSweet was out, one of the two detectives thrust her up against the side of the car and twisted her hands behind her back. As several curious onlookers gathered to be nosy, she angrily shouted, "What the hell is going on?"

Instead of an explanation, one of the detectives pat-searched her while another informed her of her constitutional rights.

"Audrey Strong, you are under arrest for the murder of Benny Sylvester Wells and Richard Smith."

"What!" she shouted in protest as if she had found the accusations totally ridiculous.

"You have the right to remain silent. Anything you say, can and will be used against you in a court of law. You have a right to an attorney..."

While the detectives continued reading her rights to her, the inconspicuous stranger had managed to blend in with the on-lookers. Curious to what was really going on, he glanced at the old man and suddenly realized for the first time, he too was a cop. He had the same smirk on his face all cops wear after making an arrest. He looked at the female, who was angrily staring at the old man.

"... If you cannot afford one, one will be appointed to you. Do you understand these rights I have just read to you?"

She angrily replied, "Whatever!"

"Do you choose to give up these rights?"

She looked at the detective and yelled, "HELL NO!" before returning her attention to the lieutenant who stood silently watching as she was handcuffed and led to an unmarked police car.

She couldn't believe she had been foolish enough to think she could actually trust a cop. "Why?" she couldn't resist asking just before being placed into the back seat of one of the detective's car.

The lieutenant stepped over to the car where she was being detained and got in up front. "I'm a cop, Audrey.

"So you've been using me from the jump, right?"

"That's not true. We met by chance, remember? It was only recently I became aware that you were involved with those murders."

273

"Murders, huh?"

"What else would you call them?" Before giving her a chance to answer, he continued. "Look, Audrey, you're in serious trouble. I can help you if you level with me. All we want is the truth about that house in Queens? I don't give a shit about those two bodies. If you level with me, I'll make it all go away. Now... about the house in Queens? How did you know about it? Somebody had to tell you something?"

"I told you. I don't know shit."

"Don't play games with me, girl! Your ass is on the line. We want to know who tipped you off? You know we don't really need you. We'll find out, with or without your help. The question is, are you stupid enough to go down for those two bodies alone?"

"Like I said, I don't know shit. You have the wrong person. Now... if you don't mind. I think I'm entitled to one phone-call? If I'm not mistaken, my lawyer is probably expecting my call."

"Suit yourself!" he angrily said before storming out of the car.

The inconspicuous stranger was about to leave when he heard the old man say, "She's all yours."

Just as two of the arresting detectives were about to get into the car, two sky-blue Ford sedans pulled up out of nowhere and came to a screeching halt directly in front of the car TooSweet was being transported in. Five men wearing dark, single-breasted trench coats emerged from the two cars. Two of which approached the old man.

TooSweet identified the men driving the Sedans as federal agents. "Damn!" she thought out loud as she watched Lt. Sheets and the four detectives argued with the federal agents. She wasn't sure what they were arguing about. She did, however, have a pretty good idea. She never dreamt FOLD's activities would catch the attention of the Feds. Hell, she never thought her once trusted friend would eventually flip on her. After all, she practically made his career. Yet, that didn't stop him from crossing her. 'SunRise always said,' she thought aloud as she watched from the back seat of the unmarked car. 'Never trust a cop.'

The agent who seemed to be in charge was a tall, pale, middle-age Caucasian man with bad skin. The other was medium height, stocky built, and also Caucasian with a crew-cut and huge, imposing arms. "FBI," the fair-skin, tall man stated before continuing. "Special agents Ross and Hilton." Both men quickly whipped out their badges while the tall man with the receding hairline continued. "We have a federal material witness warrant signed by Judge Wyett Huge of the Federal District Court to place Ms. Audrey Strong in our custody. The D.A. believes she has pertinent information in an ongoing investigation."

Lieutenant snatched the document from the agent, removed a pair of reading glasses from the inside pocket of his wrinkled trench and placed them on his face. As he read, it became painfully obvious that the document was authentic. "You boys have to wait your turn," he said, forcing a smile while handing the court order back to the federal agent. "We have her for a double homicide. After she's booked, arraigned, indicted, tried and convicted. You're welcome to her."

"And you are?" asked special agent Ross.

"Lt. R. Sheets of the 81st precinct."

"Apparently, sir, you over looked the part about full immunity pertaining to any and all charges concerning the death of..." he opened the order and began scanning it. "...Oh, yeah. Here we go. A Benny Sylvester Wells and Richard Smith."

The old man's jaw dropped. "What? Let me see that." He snatched the order from the agent again and commenced in reading it a little more carefully.

"What's going on, Lt.?" one of the arresting detectives quickly asked the moment he saw the baffled look on Sheet's face.

Lieutenant Sheets slowly folded the order and hand it back to the agent.

TooSweet was still in the dark about what was going on. When three of the Federal agents walked over to the car and took possession of her, she was convinced she was facing federal charges. But when they forced Sheets and his men to remove the cuffs before escorting her to the back seat of one of the Sedans, she didn't know what to think.

As she sat quietly in the back seat between two poker-faced agents, she looked at Lieutenant Sheets who, along with the other four homicide detectives, stood angrily watching from the sidewalk. As both Sedans pulled off, she looked at one of the men sitting next to her and asked, "Can someone please tell me what's going on?"

The inconspicuous stranger pulled out and followed the sedans. When he drove past the Lieutenant and his four detectives, who were still standing at the curb watching, he locked eyes with the old man and smiled before accelerating.

When neither of the men in the car answered TooSweet's question, she became angry, shouting, "Look! I know my rights! And none of you muthafuckaz' read them to me yet? According to the constitution, not reading me my rights is in direct violation of the...."

"WE'RE HERE!" one of the agents yelled before TooSweet had a chance to finish her statement.

When both Sedans came to a complete stop, TooSweet looked around somewhat confused.

"Here where?" she asked. As far as she could tell, they had only driven a few blocks from where they had picked her up. "Somebody wanna' tell me what the hell is going on?"

"Get out of the car, Ms. Strong. You're free to go," said the driver. The agent who sat next to her got out of the car to allow her passage.

"What?"

TooSweet looked down the street in the direction the driver had indicated and spotted the car of FOLD'S New York branch attorney. Behind the wheel sat the man Tyrone Sharp personally retained as a criminal attorney for FOLD members. "Son-of-a-bitch!" she blurted while getting out of the Sedan. Words could not describe her relief as she quickly headed in the direction of her lawyer's car while wondering how SunRise knew she was about to be arrested or where to find her?

To be continued....

ABOUT THE AUTHOR

Tehuti Atum-Ra is a 52 year old native of Paterson in New Jersey who, as a youth, spent most of his time hanging in the school's bathroom getting high and gambling. By the time he was fifteen he dropped out of the tenth grade and enrolled himself into the mean streets throughout New Jersey and New York where he continued his informal education. Graduating with a degree in stupidity, fate finally caught up with him receiving a life sentence in New Jersey's super max, Trenton State Prison.

Tehuti attributes his love for writing to the time he spent on a Management Control Unit (MCU) at Trenton State Prison. It was during those years when he realized it was time to grow up by being accountable for his actions. While educating himself, he realized he had found a creative way to occupy his time by writing.

Still serving the life sentence he receives for his crime over thirty years ago, Tehuti is working on his third book, *Nemesis III: Summit Of The Murder Game*.

Tehuti's fiction is written to entertain. Any characters or events in this book are fictional. Any resemblance to actual person, living or deceased is purely coincidental.

Tehuti Atum-Ra's other book

Raped, beaten and betrayed. Vicki Lane left her quiet, middle-class home in Ocean City, Maryland to live with her sister in the mean streets of Paterson, New Jersey only to learn her sister had been murdered by the very same people who left her for dead. But as fate would have it, Vicki would not die so easily. Rescued by Londell Dixson, a young street thug who nurses her back to health and trains her to be the goddess she was meant to be: the goddess of divine retribution.

To order additional copies of this book, Nemesis II The FOLD, or copies of Tehuti Atum-Ra's first book, please send check or money order to:

Midnight Express Books
POBox 69
Berryville AR 72616

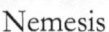

Nemesis   Nemesis II The FOLD

QTY ORDERED

_____   NEMESIS $14.95 $_____

_____   NEMESIS II The FOLD $14.95 $_____

Subtotal $_____

How many books are you ordering   _____ x $3.99 = $_____

TOTAL ENCLOSED $_____

Ship to:
NAME _____

ADDRESS _____

_____

www.ingramcontent.com/pod-product-compliance
Lightning Source LLC
Chambersburg PA
CBHW070314260626
47160CB00003B/837